# TWISTED TRUTHS

## HIDDEN: BOOK 4
## CLARE DAVIDSON

For all my readers. Thank you.

# ACKNOWLEDGEMENTS

Edited by Sarah Chorn and Charlotte L R Kane
Proofread by Sylvia Williment
Cover illustration by Bramasta Aji

Thank you to everyone who supported me while I was
writing 'Twisted Truths' and the rest of the 'Hidden' series.
It's been a long journey, but we've reached the end at last.

# CHAPTER ONE

I get dressed while AJ is having a shower and then head to Chris's room to find clothes that stand the slightest chance of fitting him. Matthew watches me from the bed as I root through drawers at the bottom of Chris's wardrobe.

"AJ is here," I say, although I'm sure Matthew knows.

Matthew nods once, the movement slow and alien. I turn away, gritting my teeth. It's only been a few hours since I encased him in the clay golem—a temporary solution to prevent his soul from fragmenting and save him from dying. He needs healing but he can't use his abilities, which means he can't contact the Shamari, or go home. The damage done by the Baneem who hijacked Phailin's body has magically crippled him. I ball my fists, digging my nails into my palms as though the brief burst of pain will help absolve my guilt. He went to the flat because of *me*. What happened to him is *my* fault. *I* should have known something wasn't right with Phailin, *I* should have faced her alone.

I slam the drawer shut with a resounding bang and tear open a bag containing clothes bought for my brother, Chris, last Christmas. They're too big for Chris, because grandma doesn't have a clue about what size he is. The bag rustles in my tight grip. How am I going to tell AJ what's happened to Matthew? My shoulders droop.

"I said everything would be okay." My voice is quiet and strangled. "I told AJ I'd stop Saul."

The springs in Chris's mattress creak, signalling Matthew has moved. Heavy clay footsteps trudge across the floor, causing the floorboards beneath the cream carpet to squeak.

"Don't make promises you can't keep," Matthew says. His voice has a deeper, coarse quality now that no longer pours over me like molten chocolate. Far more unnerving than comforting.

I shudder as he looms over me. Even without the power of Matthew's aura, the bulky form of the golem is intimidating. The pair of pale blue jeans I grab are too long for Chris, but might fit AJ. "I'll find a way."

"We know little about Saul."

The only information we have came from Phailin and Gage. Saul's magic destroys—the opposite of AJ's power to heal—and he wants to create a hidden army to attack the Shamari. A shiver snakes down my back at the memory of Phailin attacking Matthew. No, not Phailin. A Baneem soul hidden inside, controlling her body.

"AJ knows more about Saul." I pull a black t-shirt out of the bag, arching an eyebrow at its size. It'll be baggy on AJ, let alone Chris. It's no wonder Chris stuffed all these clothes in the bottom of his wardrobe and forgot about them.

"How is AJ?" Matthew asks.

Why wasn't that Matthew's first question? He probably doesn't care for AJ's wellbeing at all. He protected AJ because of me, a cold truth I must remember. Shrugging, I press my lips into a tight line.

"Hard to tell. He wanted to protect and heal me, but once he realised there was no immediate danger, he... crumpled."

A huge pine green hoodie is the next thing out of the bag. The colour won't suit AJ, but it's better than having him put his filthy clothes back on. I inhale, pushing away dark thoughts about the origins of the stains.

"Get him to talk," Matthew says. "So we can decide what to do when Saul comes looking for him."

I hug the clothes close, and stand and spin round to face Matthew, focussing my gaze on him. "I have to be careful."

Matthew's mouth twists into a grimace. "There's no time for caution."

I don't want to admit he's right, so I push past him and storm back to my room. With a growl, I toss the clothes onto the bed. I brush my fingertips through my hair, raking it back from my forehead as I let out a long sigh. I'm glad to be away from Matthew. What he's become is too much of a reminder of all the terrible things that have happened.

"Kim?"

I swing round, almost crashing into AJ. How did he get so close without me realising? He looks better for being clean. Beads of water still cling to the tips of his dark hair. He's wearing Mum's white towelling dressing gown.

"I'm fine," I say, in response to the unanswered question in his eyes. "Are you feeling any better?"

It's a stupid question. A shower can't wash away the things Saul did.

For the briefest of moments, the corner of his mouth hooks up a fraction. "A little."

I motion to the clothes on the bed and turn away. I should leave the room, but my feet won't move. Questions race through my mind, but I can't vocalise them. How do I tread the mine-field of AJ's emotions to get the information we need to stop Saul? I can't shake the memory of the profound sadness in his eyes, when he first walked through the front door. The way he'd looked shattered, tormented and lost. But I had also seen a glimmer of hope, albeit a fleeting one. He trusts me to find a way to stop Saul, so maybe he'll trust me enough to open up to me.

I rub my left arm just above the elbow, tilting my head to the same side. I don't want to force him to talk. Not yet. What I want to do is hold AJ and offer him silent comfort.

"I'm done. Thanks."

I don't move. I want AJ to come and slip his hand through mine, or trail his fingertips down my arm. But he doesn't. The silence expands into a gulf of awkwardness, which isn't bridged when I turn back round. The hoodie hangs on him like a thick, shapeless sack, but the jeans are a better fit.

I transfer my weight onto the balls of my feet, with every intention of moving closer, but something holds me back and I thud back onto my heels. Why is this so awkward? It's only been a week. Not a month. Not a year. One short week. Last time I saw AJ, we held hands, embraced and kissed.

I clear my throat. "Where's your mum?"

He sinks onto the bed, eyes unfocused and staring. "Dead." He almost whispers the word, making it a fragile, wavering sound that carries far too much weight.

His soft, sorrowful voice liberates me and I find I'm not pinned to that spot anymore, so I sit and throw my arms around him, hugging him tight, tears falling down my cheeks, whilst his eyes stay dry.

"I'm sorry." Useless words, but what else can I say? "What happened?"

A pained whimper escapes his throat. My tears fall faster as I'm forced to accept Phailin's death.

"It's okay to cry," I say, stroking his back. "It's all I did when Charley died."

He stiffens and pulls away, standing, forming a chasm between us. "This is different." He strides to the door. "What happened to Charley had nothing to do with you. There was nothing you could have done to protect her."

I press my quivering lips together. For a few seconds, the renewed pain of losing Charley eclipses my concern for AJ. He's wrong. Her death was partially my fault. I should have known Charley was keeping secrets, that she was dealing with things beyond the scope of my imagination. I swallow down my grief.

"Tell me about Saul." My voice commands him to stop before he can touch the door handle. "I promised I'd stop Saul, but I need more details."His expression remains guarded, his lips clamped shut.

"I know you're in pain and it will be hard, but you have to talk." I clench the quilt in my fist, as though it's strong enough to shackle me to the bed, forcing me to give him physical space, when all I want to do is hold him until his pain eases.

AJ stares at the floor. He won't meet my eyes and I feel the gulf between us keenly.

"Start by shouting, screaming, or crying, if it'll help."

"*Help*?" he growls, clenching his fists. "It won't erase what Saul did, or bring Mum back."

"No, but keeping the hurt inside won't help, either."

He glares at me.

I grit my teeth, take a deep breath to calm myself and try again. "You need to tell me why Saul wants you."

I don't think Saul knew AJ could heal when he abducted him. Was it curiosity that drove him to hunt AJ down initially, or did he do it to spite Phailin? The woman who had been strong enough to betray him and run away from him with AJ, his son. Whatever the reason, I'm sure it's AJ's ability to heal that makes him so valuable to Saul. When the Baneem inhabited Phailin the power of her soul burned her from within. But I can't imagine Saul caring if a human dies—he clearly didn't care whether Phailin lived or died—so who did he need AJ to heal?

"The soul swapping thing... does it damage the human host *and* the Baneem?"

AJ nods after a moment's hesitation. "Having your soul ripped out and stuffed back in again hurts like hell. It's like... like..." His eyes become distant, as he sags against the door.

My chin trembles. "He did it to you."

I can't stand to see his pain. I clutch the quilt tighter, fighting against the urge to hold him. It's obvious he doesn't want to be touched right now.

"Yes. Well... no... Saul can't manipulate souls."

"His magic only destroys?"

"Yes."

"There was someone else? An accomplice?"

"Adele."

Good. We're getting somewhere. I wish I could take the victory and leave it there, but Saul could come looking for AJ at any moment. When he does, this will be one of the first places he looks.

"Who else is working for him?" I imagine hundreds of Baneem flocking to Saul to take part in his sickening plan of butchering the Changed Shamari.

"There were five others present and Saul said Gage was working for him." His eyebrows pinch inwards at the mention of Gage's name.

I blink. So few? Gage had bragged that Saul was creating an army. Five people doesn't make an army.

"There was the girl who's soul..." The words stick in my throat. She almost destroyed Matthew, whilst I was powerless to defend him.

"Stole Mum's body?"

"Yes."

"Stella."

Having a name doesn't help. All I can remember are the torturous memories pouring into my head at her command. I saw Charley, dead, in excruciating high definition detail. Somehow, I fought free of the suffocating vision in time to prevent Stella from destroying Matthew.

"And the others?"

He shrugs. "There were a couple of guys I only saw once, or twice, plus Flame Guy and Ice Man. I saw them a lot."

"So... fire and ice magic?"

"Yes and no."

I allow my lips to tease up into the smallest of smiles, just enough to encourage him to explain his cryptic response.

"I didn't see Ice Man use magic, but needed to call him something, and he was..." His eyebrows drop to hood his eyes. "Cold." He stuffs his hands into the pockets of the borrowed jeans.

I take the action as a prompt to stand and move close enough to touch his arm. I doubt he can feel the faint pressure of my fingers beneath the heavy fabric of the hoodie.

"You're doing great," I say.

He shrinks away. "Don't patronise me."

"I didn't mean to..." But he's right, I did. *You're doing great* is something a teacher would say to a kid struggling with their classwork.

"Of course not," he spat, his voice full of caustic sarcasm.

I step back, hating the venom in his voice. "You're angry," I say, fighting to keep my voice calm. "I understand that." I don't want to argue with him.

"You have no idea."

"So tell me."

He paces to the window, turns and strides back to the door. "It's my fault."

"What is?"

"What happened to Mum." He doesn't stop moving, pacing to the bed and back again.

"No. It's Saul's fault."

"What happened to Matthew." He stops. "What happened to Matthew?"

"Stella attacked him, but he's okay now."

AJ's lips part. He doesn't believe me. "Stella said she'd poured enough magic into him, she was sure he would die."

I hug my arms around my waist. I must be careful. It's not the right time for AJ to discover the truth, but if I hold things back, he'll sense I'm telling half-truths and jump to the conclusion I'm lying.

"She attacked him with magic. A lot of magic. It damaged his soul, but Sophie and I managed to save him."

"How?"

I press my fingers into my sides so tightly, my stomach aches from the pressure. "By creating a golem to house his soul."

AJ gapes. "A golem? What? How?"

I wave my hand. "It's a long story. Let's just say I had to learn more about the pictograms Matthew uses."

"And now he's okay?"

I bite my lower lip. "It's... not ideal, but it'll do. For now."

AJ wipes his hands over his face. "It's my fault."

"No..."

"It is! You weren't there. You don't understand." His voice rises in pitch, getting more desperate with each statement.

I clutch his hands, even though he tries to pull them away. "It's not your fault." I bite my lower lip and squeeze my eyes shut against a fresh onslaught of tears. I can't let him blame, or hate, himself. "It's *my* fault."

"How?"

I drag in a deep breath. "Taylor figured out that Matthew couldn't tell you were Baneem."

He presses his lips together, his mouth twisting into a faint grimace.

"And instead of saying something, I let you believe you were safe here, even though you weren't. I hid the truth because I wanted you to stay. I'm sorry."

He rips free from my grasp, turns and yanks the door open. It thuds against the wall, the handle cracking the plaster. We both stare at the thin lines, which have spread out from the centre of the damage. It looks like ice cracking. AJ looks frantic, like he's drowning, trapped beneath ice that has formed above his head so fast, he can't break free. I want to smash through it to save him, but I'm afraid he'll let himself sink, rather than allow me to pull him free of the freezing water. But I have to try.

"I'm sorry." The desperation in my voice needs to be enough to stop him. "AJ, please. We need to talk."

"No," he snarls, without a backwards glance. "I'm done talking."

He bolts down the stairs and through the front door before I can catch up. By the time I've stepped out onto the garden path, he's out of sight, leaving me standing in the small front garden alone, sobbing.

# CHAPTER TWO

Kim's words burn in my mind as I stride through the once familiar city. Now, I'm even jumpier than before. I search every face, wondering if I'm walking past a Baneem sent by my father to retrieve me. Any second, someone could make a grab for me. Even in the throng of rush hour, I don't feel safe. I doubt I'll ever feel safe again.

Except Kim promised I wouldn't have to run again. I cough out a laugh at the irony. Right now, it's her I'm running away from. I couldn't face her, or acknowledge her admission of guilt, without turning the mirror back on myself. It would be easy to allow her to take the blame. It would be even easier to use her as the scapegoat for my anger, but what happened to Matthew and Mum is *my* fault. Kim can't absolve me of my mistakes, no matter how much she wants to. It's why I stormed out on her and acted like the world's biggest jerk. She was trying to help, to soothe my pain and console me, but I didn't want her to.

I don't want to stop hurting. Right now, pain is all I have. The rest of my life is in tatters. Even before Saul appeared, everything was unravelling. Mum lost her job. School found out we'd lied about my exam grades. Despite everything, Kim's promise that I wouldn't have to run again shone through like a beacon and for a split second, gave me hope. But how can I hold onto the lifeline of hope Kim is trying to throw me, when everything else has slipped through my fingers like precious grains of sand?

I stop in my tracks, causing a man in a smart navy blue business suit to crash into me.

He looks me up and down as he pushes past, his mouth curling into a semi-snarl. "Watch yourself."

I mutter an apology without looking him in the eyes. I'm nothing to him. A stranger in the street who got in the way. Everyone around me is a stranger. It's the busiest time of day, but I'm utterly alone. I walked out on the only person in my life who actually gives a crap about me.

I carry on, slower now. My feet feel heavy as I trudge along the streets, through the city centre and out the other side, until I'm moving against the flow of people. Soon, it's quieter and I'm pretty much alone, except for the occasional dog walker or runner. I lift my head, more alert, scanning the road ahead and glancing back over my shoulder so often my paranoia is obvious.

The block of flats rises in front of me. I'm still a couple of streets away, but stop anyway. I shouldn't have come here, but I did. I want to go into my flat and gather up the small handful of things that meant something to Mum. I need to feel closer to her, but I know I can't go any nearer to the flats. Going there would be asking to get caught by Saul again. If he's going to send people anywhere to look for me, it's the flat. I grimace. He'll probably send people to Kim's, too. I clench my fists, my palms prickling with sweat. If he hurts her, or Sophie, or Matthew...

I swing round, ready to run all the way back to Kim's, but find that my feet refuse to move. Going back there is as stupid as heading to the flat. If I can't retrieve Mum's stuff and I can't go back and make sure Kim is okay, what can I do? Run? I'm tired of running and too worn down to fight. Saul is smarter than Gage and Taylor, with bigger plans and people to do his dirty work for him.

I trudge on towards a mirror block of flats on the opposite side of the road. The only person around on the ground floor is a young woman pushing a pram. She looks tired and her baby is crying. She jabs her finger against the lift, cooing to her baby and rocking the pram back and forth as she waits. The lift doesn't come. She slams her hand against the button, cursing. It would be easy to ignore her and walk away, but a dose of normality is exactly what I need right now.

"Need a hand?"

She stares as though I'm speaking gibberish.

"Is the lift broken?"

"It's always bloody broken and when it is working, it stinks of piss. I wish I didn't live in this shit hole. It's no place to bring up a baby, is it?"

"Do you need help? I can bump the pram up the stairs for you."

She raises her eyebrows. "I'm on the fifth floor."

I shrug. "I don't mind."

She purses her lips, before relaxing them and allowing a tentative smile to appear. "Help would be great, thanks." She unbuckles her baby, who is wearing a pastel pink snowsuit, and lifts her out of the pram, bouncing her against her chest. I take hold of the pram and begin to manoeuvre it up the stairs. The pram is sturdy and heavier than I expected it to be. I can't lift it, so I have to bump it up each step.The baby cries until we're on the first landing and then closes her eyes and sleeps. For the next two flights, the only sound is the rhythmic thump of hard pram wheels against concrete.

"Do you always help damsels in distress?"

I jump at the sound of her voice, my voice catching in my throat as I struggle to think of a response to the glib question.

"Most people who live here would have ignored me. It's nice to think not everyone is selfish. What floor do you live on? Have you moved in recently? I don't think I've seen you around before." She only pauses briefly between each question, not really giving me enough time to speak, let alone think of a reply.

I'm not sure why she's asking so many questions. Maybe because I'm helping her she thinks she has a right to intrude on my life.

"I'm visiting someone."

She fishes a set of keys out of her pocket. "This is my floor. Thanks for helping."

I return the pram to her, watching as she pushes it with one hand, to the final door. Once she's safely inside, I turn my gaze over the balcony and stare at the block of flats I used to call home. Two more floors. I turn and start climbing them, my feet are so weighed down by dread that it makes my pace slower than when I was manhandling the heavy pram. For some reason my thoughts flit back to the young woman. She's the sort of person the Baneem target—tired, desperate for change and willing to accept any offer of help.

I stand on the balcony of the seventh floor, gazing across at my old front door. It's been boarded shut and has police tape all over it. Crime scene. Do not enter. My entire life is behind that door: Mum's things, clothes, school books, my hat. Everything is so close and yet beyond reach, probably forever. My chest tightens. This is worse than packing everything up and catching a train or coach to another city. At least then I wasn't alone. I was with Mum and we took everything that mattered: clothes, school textbooks, silly presents we'd bought one another over the years and a small collection of photos. And my hat, of course. Not only is Mum gone, but every physical memory I had of her is beyond my reach.

I tap my fingertips against the guard rail, creating a ringing sound as my nails strike the hollow metal tube. Being here isn't helping. It's not giving me any clarity, it's only making my mind hazier and my thoughts angrier. I should go.

I lean back onto my heels and pause. There's movement on the stairs. I retreat as far back as I can, into the shadows of the stairwell and watch as two men wander towards my flat door. They're not wearing police uniforms and their clothes are too scruffy for them to be plain clothes cops. My blood seems to freeze as one of the men turns round and stares over the edge of the balcony. Ice Man. Despite the distance between us, I know it's him. His bulky form and pale hair are etched into my mind. My instincts beg me to run, but I linger. He can't see me. I'm safe here, hidden in the shadows. I find myself shaking my head that Ice Man is here at all. It didn't take Saul long to get a human to open up a gateway. If Ice Man is here, maybe Flame Guy is, or Stella or Saul. My body convulses with a violent shudder. Even the thought of Saul being close by terrifies me.

The two Baneem exchange words and then move to the next door along, knocking until its opened. I watch their brief conversation, which ends in a slammed door. They move along again, repeating the process. They must be asking about me. I clench my hands. I can't see a way out of this nightmare and I don't know whether that's because my mind is too bogged down by fear and grief, or because running is all I've ever known. I don't know what to do, think or feel. All I know, right now, in this moment, is that I can't stay here.

I flee, taking the steps two, sometimes three at a time. I don't stop sprinting until I'm several streets away, my chest growing tighter the further I go. Finally, I come to a halt in an underpass beneath the main road out of the town centre. I lean against the graffiti covered wall and rest my hands on my knees and gulp in air. Slowly, I'm able to breathe more easily and my thoughts come clearly. With them, comes the sickening realisation that Saul won't stop looking for me. I can't run forever and I can't protect everyone he would hurt to get to me. I have to stop him, but I can't do it alone.

# CHAPTER THREE

"I've screwed everything up." I cradle a mug of hot chocolate, allowing its warmth to permeate my skin.

Sophie sits opposite me at the small kitchen table, staring, eyebrows raised in a reprimanding manner. "I doubt it."

"If I hadn't, AJ wouldn't have stormed off. He must hate me."

I stare at the steaming dark brown hot chocolate, inhaling. I wrinkle my nose and put the mug down. It's too sweet. Sophie pulls her feet up onto the chair, resting a mug on her knees.

"He needs some space, but doesn't hate you." She blows across the top of the mug. "Did AJ tell you what happened?"

"Not much."

She takes a sip, watching me. I've said very little since AJ stormed out. Our raised voices summoned Sophie, who guided me to the kitchen and made us hot drinks.

"Phailin is dead."

Sophie draws in a breath so sharp it makes her squeak. "Oh, God."

"I'm sorry." Matthew's gravelly voice makes me jump and twist towards the doorway where he's standing, leaning against the frame.

I narrow my eyes. "*Sorry*?" The word hisses off the tip of my tongue. "*Sorry*? You told me to get AJ to talk. Well I *tried* and now he's *gone*."

I slam my fist on the table, making the mug wobble. The hot chocolate splashes over the side, leaving dark trails on the white ceramic, before pooling on the wooden surface of the table. Sophie puts her mug down, stands and fetches kitchen towel to mop up the mess. I continue to stare at Matthew, waiting for him to speak.

"Where would he have gone?"

"How would I know? I can't call him, because he left his phone at the flat the night he—." I stare at my fists. "Saul will be looking for AJ. What if he's found him?"

"It hasn't been very long since he left," Sophie says. "I'm sure he's fine and will come back when he's calmer." She drops the stained and soggy kitchen towel in the bin and sits. "Fretting won't help. We need a plan."

I sit in silence, absorbing Sophie's all too sensible words. I don't know how she can hold herself together, let alone me, when she's only known about magic for a couple of days.

"Saul *will* send people to find AJ. There's two places I'd look: the flat and here," Sophie continues.

"We can't stay here." A weight settles in my stomach, making me feel sick. "We can't go to your house, either. Or Dad's." So where can we go? I drum my fingers on the table, hoping the monotonous action will help free up my paralysed mind.

"AJ can't stay here," Sophie says. "But we should. We have to act as normally as possible. Not only to throw Saul and his lackeys off the scent, but to protect our families, too."

The doorbell rings before I can open my mouth to argue. Sophie and I exchange nervous glances.

"Maybe it's AJ." Sophie says.

I shake my head and stand. As much as I want it to be him, I know he needs more time alone to process everything we discussed. The visitor hammers at the door, demanding I answer. Goosebumps erupt across my skin and it feels like an army of ants is dancing in my stomach. It's still early. I can't think of anyone who would visit at this time, let alone be so vigorous about getting my attention.

"They're impatient," Sophie says.

"Stay here." I head to the doorway, pausing next to Matthew. "Hide. No one can see you."

Without a word, he leaves via the back door. I take a deep breath before opening the door.

A woman in a black skirt suit stands on the doorstep, smiling as she flips open a black wallet. I catch a glimpse of a police badge, but can't make out her name or photograph before she puts it away. Was it even real?

"I'm looking for Aran Jao. I've reason to believe he's here." She cranes her neck to peer inside, looking up the stairs and then to the left, towards the closed sitting room door.

My forehead crumples into a deep frown. "Aran? Why would he be here? I haven't seen him in days. I thought he'd left town." It can't be a coincidence that she's here now, a few hours after AJ came back to me. I fix a smile on my face to hide my nervousness.

The woman watches me for a moment, her lips blanching as she presses them together into a flat line. "Can I come in?"

I open my mouth to object, but she pushes past into the hall. I step in front of her before she can open the sitting room door.

"Don't you need a search warrant or something?" I press my clammy palms against my jeans. "My parents are out."

"You're over sixteen. Your parents aren't needed." She smiles. "Do you have something to hide, Miss Welles?"

Only a not-angel trapped inside a golem. This isn't a coincidence. Saul must have sent her. At least she's human. If she were Baneem, she wouldn't keep up the pretence of being a police officer now we're inside the house. I return her too sweet smile, even though I want to make her leave so I can slam and lock the door.

"No." I open the sitting room door and stand aside.

She saunters in, pursing her lips as she glances around the room.

"We both know Aran and his mother didn't leave town," she says, wandering into the kitchen diner."Hello." Sophie says, before taking a sip of hot chocolate.

The police woman doesn't acknowledge her. A scowl crosses Sophie's face. I share her irritation at the woman's rudeness, but there's not much I can do. Besides, I want her out of my house as soon as possible.

"Aran hasn't been in school," I say.

"Or answering calls," Sophie says. "He moves around a lot."

The police woman comes back into the hallway and pauses, staring at me. "So you weren't at his flat two nights ago?"

"No."

She snorts and makes her way upstairs. Dry mouthed, I follow, even though my feet are like lead as I walk up the steps.

She opens the bathroom door. It's empty and warm, the mirror still misted from where AJ took a shower. She turns and lifts a strand of my dry hair. She must have noticed that Sophie's hair was dry, too.

"Shower cap," I say.

She frowns and slips past, opening each bedroom door. Every room is empty, every window shut.

"Aran isn' t here," I repeat.

"Apparently not," the woman says in a dry tone.

"The door is downstairs." I purposefully clip my words, leaving no doubt I want her gone.

She narrows her eyes. I expect her to hand over a business card, so I can call her if AJ gets in touch. Instead she leaves without closing the door, allowing me to watch as she gets into a dark blue car. She buckles in and pulls out a phone, staring at the house—at me—as she makes a brief call. I can't work out what she's saying, but she doesn't seem happy as she puts the phone away and drives out of the street.

I hurry down the stairs and shut the door, turning and pressing my back against it. My legs are weak, as though I've been spinning on a round-a-bout for several minutes.

We can't sit around talking. AJ is in danger. But how can I protect him if I don't know where he is?

*

"What's the plan?" Sophie asks as Matthew and I enter the kitchen.

I run my hands over my face. There isn't one, only problems and hastily spoken promises. I need to focus on one thing at a time. Small chunks and baby steps. What's the easiest problem to overcome and check off the list?

"None of us can stay here, so what about a bed-and-breakfast? There are several along the seafront that'll be empty. Who wants to come to a dismal beach in winter? We can keep in touch with our parents. They'll assume we're still here, studying."

Sophie raises her eyebrows. "More lies?"

I cross my arms. "Do you have any better suggestions?" I blow a breath out. "I didn't mean to snap, but staying here is a bad idea."

"If we don't carry on as normal, we might as well put out a memo that tells Saul we're with AJ," Sophie says.

"She's right," Matthew interjects.

Great, now they're ganging up on me.

"I won't leave him alone." I stare at Sophie, resolute. "You can stay here, or go home, but I will stay with AJ."

Sophie sighs and turns her palms up in a submissive gesture.

What's next? Only big sweeping things that are too over-whelming: finding AJ, stopping Saul, fixing Matthew. Where should I start? I lean my elbows on my thighs and drop my head into my hands, taking two deep breaths to calm myself. It would be easy to let everything overwhelm and bury me and give in before I've begun. I can't do that.

"We must stop Saul." I lift my head and count things off on my fingers. "His magic is destructive, he's working with others to create a hidden army to destroy the Changed Shamari." I pause, glancing at Matthew, but the golem shows no outward trace of emotion. "But why? Besides, he's probably still in Uralahnd, safe." My hand to flops against my thigh.

"We can guess," Matthew says.

I shake my head. "No guessing games."

"AJ might know why," Sophie says.

I nod, wishing AJ was here and willing to chip into this conversation. I turn to Matthew. "Will the Shamari come looking for you?"

He shrugs. "Perhaps."

"You don't sound worried."

"To my knowledge, none of the Changed have ever vanished. However, I am sure they will notice my absence."

"You haven't vanished."

His mouth curls into an awkward smile. "I have. I'm not dead, but I am cut off from the other Shamari. I cannot communicate with them, nor can they with me."

"So when they try to communicate with you, they'll worry and come looking?" Sophie says, hope filling her voice.

"I suppose so," Matthew says. "But it won't happen soon. It isn't as if we..." he pauses, searching for the right word, then points at the telephone sitting on the kitchen counter. "... call regularly."

"So it'll take a few days."

"Longer, Kim. Time is abstract for immortals."

"Maybe your soul will heal itself," Sophie says, her tone hopeful.

"No. I have to return home for healing."

"Could AJ help?" she says.

"I doubt it. AJ's magic heals the body, not the soul." He stares at his clay hands. "Nor can he heal this vessel, as the golem is clay, not flesh, blood and bone."

I stand and wander to the window, but resist opening the curtain to peer at the street. I imagine people going about their daily lives, oblivious to magic, Baneem and not-angels. My neighbours will be at work, or school—where Sophie, AJ and I should be. It's almost the end of term. From past experience, normal lessons will have been disbanded in favour of silly quizzes, or watching Christmas movies. The comforting mundanity would help us forget magic exists. Except forgetting isn't possible. Our lives changed forever because I wouldn't accept Charley' s had committed suicide. I don't regret my actions. Gage and Taylor would have hurt more people if I hadn't stopped them, including Sophie's family.

I fold my arms and face Sophie and Matthew, dipping my eyebrows in a silent apology to him.

"There's nothing we can do except wait for the Shamari to worry about you. But we can do something about Saul. Sophie, earlier you said AJ would come back when he's calmer. You're right, but we should be ready when he does. Will you get some clothes for us? And look in the bottom of Chris's wardrobe for more clothes that'll fit AJ. Christmas presents," I add, when she cocks an eyebrow at me.

"It's a bad idea for the two of us to hide," Sophie says, heading upstairs without further argument.

"Matthew, keep trying to reach the Shamari. There's a chance Sophie is right—now your soul can't degrade anymore it might heal itself."

"I'll try," he says, his voice lacking in confidence.

"I'll look for somewhere to stay." I pull my phone out and use a web browser to search for available bed-and-breakfast rooms close by. It doesn't take long to find half a dozen possibilities. I select the first one and press on the linked number, which automatically calls it for me.

Five minutes later I've booked two rooms, which was the only way to get enough beds for four people. After hanging up, I see several missed calls from an unfamiliar number. Frowning, my finger hovers over the green dial button. Before I can press it, the phone rings again.

"Hello?"

"You are receiving a reverse charges call, will you accept the charges?"

"Umm... yes."

"Putting you through."

My fingertips quiver with anticipation at the sound of a loud beep.

"Kim?"

"AJ." Relief makes my knees weak. I sit, perching on the edge of the chair, whilst my legs jog up and down. "Are you okay? Where are you?"

"I'm fine. We need to talk."

"Saul sent someone here. A human woman."

He hisses in a breath. "There were Baneem at the flat, too."

I gasp. "Why did you go back there?"

"I didn't." He sighs. "Is there somewhere I can meet you?"

I give him the name and address of the bed-and-breakfast. "I've booked two rooms. We'll be there as soon as we can."

"Okay."

"AJ..."

"Yeah?"

"I'm glad you called. I... I was scared..." I can't express myself. There are too many words fighting to get out, but I'm afraid if I let them, I won't be able to stop speaking and I'll scare him away.

"I'm sorry. I'll see you soon?" His voice is soft, calming my tumultuous thoughts and reassuring me.

"Yes."

The line goes dead and I hug the phone to my chest. We'll be together again and then we can figure a way to stop Saul.

# CHAPTER FOUR

AJ is waiting when we arrive at the bed-and-breakfast. His eyebrows lift in an apology as his eyes meet mine. For a second, nothing else matters but the fact that AJ came back. I'm sure my shoulders lift visibly as the fear and worry I've been carrying around dissipates. I want to throw my arms around him, hold him and kiss him, but I don't let myself. Instead I dip my chin to my chest to hide the warmth spreading across my cheeks.

"We can talk once we're checked in," I say.

Matthew keeps his head lowered and his hood raised as we jog up the steps of the converted Victorian era house. The hallway used to be wider and grander, but a new stud wall creates an office. A neat woman with blonde hair peers from behind a desk, her lips pinched. I pause for a moment to re-member the name she gave when I spoke to her earlier on the phone. At least, I presume it's the same woman I spoke to earlier. Simone, I'm sure that was her name.

"Hi, Simone?" I say. "I booked two rooms by phone."

She tidies a folder away before joining us in the hall. "You didn't mention you were kids."

"I'm seventeen."

Simone's gaze drifts to the others, lingering the longest on Matthew. "Shouldn't you all be in school?"

"Training day," I say. "Nice way to start the Christmas holidays."

Her nostrils flare. "I'm sorry, you must leave."

My eyes widen. "Why? We can pay up front."

She shakes her head. "What kind of establishment do you think I'm running? I can't let four kids stay here unsupervised."

I open my mouth to object, but she cuts me off with a raised hand.

"Couldn't wait until prom night?" She tuts. "If you can't do it at home, you can't do it here. Off you go."

"But—"

AJ grabs my hand and tugs me out into the winter sunshine. I stare over my shoulder as we traipse down the stairs. Simone is watching us the whole way.

"She meant well," Sophie says, once we're across the road and on the deserted strip of imported beach. "She assumed we were going to—"

"Have sex," I say, my tone miserable. "Now what?"

"We could try another bed-and-breakfast," Sophie says. "Not everyone will care. Or you could listen to my advice and go home."

I roll my eyes. "We've been through this, it's not safe."

AJ squeezes my hand. I realise he hadn't let go. I smile, both surprised and happy at his touch. It's the longest contact we've had since he escaped Saul.

"Sophie's right. I'm the only one who needs to hide," he says in a quiet voice. "Besides, if you vanish, how will your parents react?"

Sophie lifts her chin. "Maybe you'll listen to AJ."

"You're both being naïve." I stroke my thumb over the back of AJ's hand. "I don't want to leave you alone. You're not Okay."

His eyes dance with moisture as he stares at me. He looks fragile, as though he could crumple at any moment. Saul must have put him through hell, plus he's coping with his mum's death, which is enough to make anyone fall apart.

"I'm fine." His voice is hoarse. "I..." He lets out a heavy sigh and stares up at the blue sky. In the harsh winter sunlight, his face is gaunt. "You can't run away."

I study him, trying to work out what he couldn't say. Part of me agrees with them. Running away would be a clear indicator we know where AJ is. And it would hurt Mum. She's been through enough. I clench my free hand. "Saul had no reason to send Gage after me, but he did."

AJ dips his chin to his chest. "Matthew." He clears his throat. "It was to keep Matthew around."

Matthew folds his arms. I wish I could see his face, but it's hidden by the shadow of his hood. He probably hasn't forced any emotion into the golem's features anyway. Beside me, AJ hunches his shoulders. His fingers twitch in mine, so I squeeze tight to convince him not to let go. I tell myself it's to comfort and support him, but the truth is, I need the contact as much as he does. AJ's touch has always made me feel safe.

"Let's say we vanish," Sophie says. "Who will Saul target?"

"Our parents." I hang my head.

"Who know *nothing* about magic. At least we're aware and prepared. Our parents would be easy prey."

"Okay." I lift my head to stare at AJ. "You still need somewhere to go, until I've stopped Saul."

"Until *we* stop Saul," he says, fierce determination burning in his eyes. "There are derelict warehouses along the river, near the railway bridge."

I wrinkle my nose. "It's the middle of winter, AJ."

"We've got camping gear," Sophie offers. "Mum and Dad had to get arctic weight sleeping bags when they went husky sledding one year. We've got a camping stove, too."

There isn't a better solution, I throw my hands up. "Fine. Matthew, will you go with Sophie? We'll meet at the warehouse later."

*

Rotten pieces of wood cover the entrance to the abandoned warehouse. The bottom two planks are buckled and splintered, kicked out from the inside. After checking to make sure no one is watching, we crawl through. Light filters in through dozens of grimy windows. Empty packing crates, covered in a thick layer of dust and bird droppings, stand in one corner. I rub my arms to ward off the bitter cold. Pigeons coo in the rafters. Something squeaks and scratches close by, making me shudder.

"You can't stay here."

"Is there a choice?"

"I can book a room somewhere?"

AJ shakes his head. "Even if a landlord let me stay, I'd never be able to pay you back."

"AJ—"

He turns away, moving further into the vast space, leaving me with no choice but to follow. I watch where I'm treading, trying to avoid standing in fresh bird droppings, but it's an impossible task.

"I'm sorry," AJ says. "I was a jerk. I shouldn't have shouted, or walked out. You didn't deserve it."

He turns and holds the tops of my arms. I try to ward off the excited shiver that snakes down my body, but fail. If he notices, he doesn't show it. I'm glad he's holding me, even if his touch is tentative and his stare is dipped, avoiding mine.

"Nothing is your fault," he says.

"But..."

His small smile silences me as he lifts his gaze to meet mine. "I'm not an idiot. Taylor watched me heal you. He had to have realised Matthew thought I was human. It was only a matter of time before he told someone." He sighs. "I put two and two together and made five, so I could fool myself into believing everything would be okay, because I *wanted* to stay."

"I thought you were good at maths," I mutter.

I'm relieved when he chuckles. "Sometimes I'm not smart."

"Please tell me what happened?"

He drops his arms to his side and wanders to the windows and slouches against the wall, the energy draining from his body. "I can't."

I stand, unsure what to say. I fold my arms, unfold them, interlock my fingers behind my back, then twist my fingers together in front of my stomach. My motions are unnatural and forced as I try, and fail, to find the right words.

"We need more information about Saul and his plans, so we can work out how to stop him."

AJ stares out the windows.

I follow his gaze, stifling a gasp with my hand as I recognise the curve of the river the warehouse overlooks. I was there last night. Saving Matthew. Killing Gage. Feeling sick, I focus on AJ again and edge closer, placing my hand on his shoulder. Such a useless action. I can't make the hurt better with a touch, any more than I could ease Phailin's suffering when she was falling apart over losing AJ to Saul. It seems like a lifetime ago. My throat constricts at the thought that we'll never see Phailin again.

"You can't keep it all locked up," I say.

His eyebrows drop to cast his chestnut eyes in shadow.

"When Charley died, I was lost and empty. But worse, I was alone, because there was no one to talk to. Everyone believed Charley had killed herself, even Sophie. And when things got weird with not-angels and magic, I became more isolated. I'd have done *anything* to have someone to turn to. Someone to talk to, who could've held me and said everything would be okay. It's not the same for you. You have me. I love you, AJ. Whatever you're feeling right now... whatever Saul did... you don't have to cope alone," the words tumble out of me. It's a huge relief to be able to release them, but I also choke on them, wondering if I'm saying too much and pushing too hard. I don't want to push AJ away. I want to bring him closer to me.

He stiffens, and raises his chin.

"Say something."

But he doesn't. Despite being grimy, the window captures his reflection—a translucent apparition of grief and guilt.

"Please," I whisper. "Don't shut me out."

Nothing. Only silence.

I wrap my arms around him, linking my hands over his stomach as I press my cheek against his back. I will not let him a build a wall between us. The tension in his muscles slips away, and he curves into my embrace, resting his hand over mine. Together, we create a silent statue. The minutes slip by until Sophie's voice calls my name. AJ wriggles out of my grasp.

I clear my throat. "In here."Sophie crawls through the small entrance, pulling a carrier bag and a rucksack with her. "We should have agreed *which* of these buildings you'd hide out in. There's quite a few."

Matthew's bulky form snaps another plank of wood as he struggles to fit through the half-barricaded doorway. He reaches through the gap and grabs two more bulging bags, which he sets down in front of him. He pushes the hood down, revealing the chiselled features of the golem.

When AJ sees him, he inhales and staggers back into the windows, his jaw slack.

"It's temporary," Matthew says. "Didn't you tell him?"

"I did." Not that my words could have prepared AJ to face the golem. I can't get used to it and I trapped Matthew's soul within it.

"Right, hopefully I've got enough to keep you going for a few days, AJ," Sophie says in a bright tone, cutting through the tension in the room. She tugs the rucksack off and puts the bags down, pulling a foam mat and sleeping bag out of them. "There's also a small camping stove, three spare can-isters of gas, a pan, plate and a set of travel cutlery, plus I grabbed food. Tins of beans and soup. Easy things to cook. Oh, and a tin opener and bottled water. Good thing I had Matthew with me to help carry everything." She stands up, beaming at AJ.

AJ runs his tongue over his lower lip as he tears his gaze away from Matthew. "Thank you."

Sophie shrugs. "No problem. You won't have to stay here long. Oh, I almost forgot." She pulls a box out of one bag and wanders over to AJ, holding it out. "A new phone. It's got a pay-as-you-go sim. I put credit on it and there's a charging block in there. I didn't think there would be any live plug sockets here." She frowns when AJ doesn't take the box. "We need to contact each other."

His shoulders droop, but he relents and accepts it. "Thanks."

"I've made a note of the number," Sophie says, glancing at me.

AJ takes the phone out of its packaging and slips it into the back pocket of his jeans, before retrieving the sleeping bag and mat. He carries them to the edge of the room and begins to unroll them.I take a few, faltering steps towards him. "You shouldn't have to be alone."

"I'll stay," Matthew says.

AJ freezes, tension making his body shiver.

"Matthew—" I begin, but he silences me with a stare.

"I can't use my abilities, but this vessel is strong. Besides, I draw too much attention."

"It's true," Sophie says. "He had to wait outside the shops as they don't like people going inside with helmets on or hoods up, but it's not like he can take it down, either. He got a lot of odd stares too, while he was waiting for me. People must have thought he was up to no good, lurking outside shops with his hood up and head down."

"AJ?" I say.

He nods as he smooths out the sleeping bag though he doesn't look at any of us. I draw Matthew to the opposite side of the room, out of earshot of AJ and Sophie. She is starting to organise the cooking provisions she bought, setting them up a short distance away from where AJ is placing the sleeping bag.

"Don't hassle him," I say.

Matthew's face is expressionless as he stares at me.

"He's not ready to talk."

"And in the meantime, Saul will gather more allies to help him find AJ," Matthew says.

"Do you think AJ doesn't know?" I sigh and pinch the bridge of my nose. I only continue to speak once I'm sure my voice will sound less irritable. "He needs more time. I'll talk to him again tomorrow, but please, until then, leave him alone," I plead, not wanting to continue with the conversation.

Matthew tips his head to the side. "All right."

Relief tugs the corners of my mouth upwards. "Thank you."

Matthew moves across to the windows where he stands, arms folded, staring out at the river. I watch as Sophie shows AJ how to work the camping stove and how to connect a new gas canister. Her relaxed, animated actions are an odd juxtaposition to AJ's dull ones. I'm glad she's here. We need her optimism, plus her presence gives me comfort.

"We should go," she says once she's finished. She gestures to the door. "I'll wait over here."

AJ stands as I approach.

"I don't want to leave you." I'm a broken record. "But you'll be safe here, with Matthew. He'll keep watch." Knowing Matthew will be here makes it a little easier to let AJ go. I don't want to think of him being stuck here, alone with his grief.

AJ's gaze flickers across to Matthew as he nods. "It's my fault. I did that to him."

"You need to stop apologising for something Saul did. Besides, you heard him," I say through a forced smile. "It's temporary." I scuff the toe of my trainers against the filthy floor. "So is you being here."

I try to hug him, but he pulls away and draws his hand across his eyes. "I'm sorry I can't face things right now."

"I'm here."

"I know."

There's nothing more to say, not that AJ would let me say anything else. Holding each other felt good, a silent promise there's still a connection between us, and a strong one at that. It's just disrupted at the moment, like a phone line corrupted by a violent storm. Tomorrow I'll push him harder, because we can't hide from Saul forever.

# CHAPTER FIVE

The front door is ajar. I freeze on the footpath, unable to make myself move toward my home. The last time I arrived home to an unlatched front door, I found Charley, dead. But this is a different door. A different house. There's no loud music thumping through my head, drawing me inside. Knowing that doesn't stop my heart from thudding, or my mouth from going dry. Sophie squeezes my hand and steps in front of me, smiling.

"Wait here," she says. "I'll take a look."

Clutching her hand, I hold her back, not wanting her to go inside. I'm sure I locked the door. Someone must have broken in. What if they're still inside? Sophie prises her hand from my grasp.

"Hello?" she calls out as she slips inside the house.

I thread my fingers together and press my knuckles against my lips. I can't move, so I'm thankful for Sophie being braver than me. My heart hasn't slowed down. Every time I blink I see Charley, her blonde hair spread out over her pillow, her beautiful blue eyes wide and staring. The blood dripping from her wrists. Tears prickle my eyes and a lump forms in my throat. Why is it taking Sophie so long? I worry something might have happened to her, but then she appears, biting her lower lip.

"We should call the police," she says.

"Why?"

"Someone has trashed the place." She dips her chin to her chest. "I'm so sorry, Kim."

My legs work again and I stumble forward. Sophie grabs my shoulders, stopping me from entering the house.

"You shouldn't go inside. Call the police and your parents. Wait for them."

I shake my head, I don't want to wait for anyone. I push past her, entering the house. She's right. Someone has violated my home. The kitchen drawers are all open. Broken plates and dishes litter the floor. The sitting room is an equal picture of devastation: the sofa and chairs lay upended, the TV is smashed on the carpet. Tears run down my cheeks. I go upstairs, only to find a similar scene of destruction. Clothes are strewn over every bedroom floor. They even ransacked the bathroom. Heaps of towels, toothbrushes and bottles of shampoo lay on the floor. The laundry basket is on its side, the clothes all pulled out. I press my hand to my gaping mouth and then drop to my knees, sorting through the clothes. Whoever did this, took AJ's clothes.

"It was the Baneem." I say as I feel Sophie's presence behind me. "I'm sure of it."

Saul sent them to my house in search of AJ. We have to stop him. We have to stop all the Baneem. I'm sick of them trying to hurt and destroy everything and everyone around me.

Sophie curls her hand around my shoulder. "We should call the police."

That's one thing I don't want to happen. I shake my head and stagger to my feet. "What good are the police against magic? Saul sent a police officer this morning. He could have more working for him."

"At least call your parents," Sophie says.

"No." I can't. Mum is fragile enough as it is and Dad would insist I went to stay with him.

I pick things up off the floor, putting them back in their rightful places in the hope I can make it look like nothing has happened at all. "Will you help me?"

Sophie stares at me for a moment, a look of worry evident on her face. Her shoulders sag as she sighs. "All right."

Neither of us talk as we tidy. I feel if I try to speak, I'll end up sobbing. Not everything is salvageable. I end up having to get a bin bag and newspaper to clear up the remnants of the shattered porcelain ornaments that had stood on a shelf in Mum's room. At least one of them was from Charley and now it's gone, destroyed by the Baneem for no good reason. It's obvious they were looking for AJ, or proof he'd been here. They didn't need to turn the whole house over, or destroy my family's memories, like Gage destroyed Charley. It's all a game to them, one in which humans are their toys, their playthings. I'm tired of it all.

"We could stay at mine," Sophie suggests, as we trudge down the stairs to start work on the sitting room.

"No."

"Dad knows."

Even though I can't tell Sophie why, I can't stay under the same roof as her father. Manipulated by a Baneem, he shot me. If AJ hadn't been there to save me, I would have died. Sophie can't find out what happened. It would destroy her. The Baneem have ripped apart enough lives, without adding hers to the list.

"I'd rather stay here." My voice wobbles. "I know it sounds crazy."

"It doesn't," she says, but I'm sure she's lying.

"You don't need to stay with me. I'll understand if you want to go home."

She flashes me a grin. "What kind of best friend would I be if I left you alone? I might insist on barricading the doors shut though." She rubs my upper arm. "Come on. Let's clear up down here, then I'll cook for us both. Okay?"

I press my lips together so hard, I make my chin wobble. "Okay." I don't know what I'd do without her.

*

"We're fine, Mum." The lie trips off my tongue, even though we've barricaded the doors and I can't relax.

Sophie pauses from cooking to half turn and grin at me. It's the fourth time I've given Mum the same reply and we've only been on the phone for a few minutes. She's trying to cheer me up and set me at ease, but it isn't working.

"And you're taking care of yourselves?" Mum asks.

"Yes. Sophie's cooking."

"Spaghetti Bolognese," Sophie calls. "Hi, Mrs Welles." She goes back to stirring.

A wonderful aroma fills the kitchen which helps to settle my nerves. I can't name the herbs she's used, but the scent floods my nostrils, making my mouth water. Since Mum and Dad divorced, we've lived off ready meals and take away, apart from a few days after Charley died, when Mum tried to make an effort. The downside is, I can't cook either, so I'm glad Sophie enjoys it.

"Are you doing lots of revision?" Mum asks. "It's unfair your mock exams are after Christmas."

I hesitate before replying. Even though I've done plenty of it, I hate lying to her. "Yes. We're working hard. Try not to worry."

Mum sighs. "I always will."

I trace circles across on the table top with my forefinger. "Are you taking care of yourself? Is being at aunt Sarah's helping?" I wait the pause out, my chest tightening.

"Yes. I'm sorry I'm not at home, Kim. Will you reconsider going to stay with your Dad and Chris?"

"I can concentrate better here."

She sucks in a breath. When she releases it, there's an obvious wobble to the sound. "Okay. If you're sure."

"I am."

"Food's ready," Sophie says, before grabbing a colander to drain the spaghetti.

"Mum, I've got to go."

"All right. Call me tomorrow?"

"I will. Mum... I love you." I don't say it enough.

"I love you too," she says, a smile clear in her voice.

I put the phone down after she's hung up.

"You okay?" Sophie asks as she sets a steaming bowl in front of me.

I rest my chin in my hand. "I wish this were over."

"Me too," Sophie says.

"We're wasting time."

"Eating is never wasting time," Sophie says. "What good are you to anyone if you faint through hunger or exhaustion?"

I cough out a laugh. "That's not what I meant."

"You mean you don't want to discuss what we're going to do without Matthew and AJ's input. They can't be here, but we have to be, to keep up appearances."

"Yes. It's frustrating."

"We can chat," Sophie says. "And try to relax. You haven't forgotten how to loosen up, have you?"

I inhale. "No, I haven't. But we can't afford to relax." The Baneem coming here and ransacking my house is proof of that. She glances around and lowers her voice. "We're taking care of ourselves."

I curl my mouth into a smirk. "Do you think someone has bugged the house?"

She shrugs. "You never know." She pops a fork full of Spaghetti Bolognese into her mouth, leaning back in her chair as she chews. Once she's done, she reaches across and puts her hand over mine, preventing me from drumming my fingers. "You won't be any good to anyone if you exhaust yourself worrying. You're trying to be strong for everyone and come up with all the answers, but we're in this together, Okay? We'll stop Saul *and* fix Matthew."

I twist my hand round so I'm holding hers and squeeze it. "Thank you."

"For what?"

"Being you. Being ace."

She beams. "I can't help it."

We both laugh although the sound coming out of my mouth sounds hollow and forced. Sophie frees her hand and goes back to her food. "You don't need to do everything on your own, Kim."

For so long it felt like I did. When Matthew left, I had no one to talk to. I only dragged Sophie into this mess because I had no choice. Matthew's soul was unravelling before my eyes and I didn't know what to do. I've put her in danger. I shouldn't have called her. But I did and she's here, standing by my side, helping me and comforting me, even though I pushed her away and almost destroyed our friendship. I know she'll do everything she can to help me.

"I know." Tears prickle my eyes. I need her to change the subject onto something frivolous. Instead, she falls silent. I pick at the food. It was a good idea when Sophie suggested it, but now it's in front of me my appetite has fled.

"*Eat*," Sophie says. "Don't make me come and feed you."

I snort, but do as I'm told. She's right, I need to take care of myself or I'll be useless to everyone, including AJ. The food becomes tasteless in my mouth as I imagine him sitting in the cold and dark, eating beans straight from a pan. I open a text message to *grandma*. Paranoia stopped me from putting AJ's new number into my phone under *his* name. I consider calling him to tell what happened, but there's too high a risk he'll bolt. No, I need to tell him face-to-face. We need to figure out our next move together. Instead I type *I love you*. My finger hovers over the send button.

"Send it," Sophie says. "He'll want to hear from you."

I nod and hit send, staring at the screen as I eat until a reply comes. It takes longer than I expected and isn't the response I wanted. A lonely word stares at me—*thanks*. I turn the phone over, hiding the offending response, and try to concentrate on eating, but my twisting stomach objects to every bite.

We clean up the bowls and pans, double check I've locked and jammed shut the doors and then traipse upstairs, our movements lagging from the long day we've had. Last night's lack of sleep, combined with the break-in today has left my mind dull and my body tired. AJ coming back has sapped me of emotional energy. Too much has happened.

"Sophie..."

She pauses in the doorway to Mum's room, where she's been sleeping.

"Can I stay with you tonight?"

She grins. "Sure."

I slip into my room, change into my pyjamas and then stop by the bathroom to brush my teeth before joining Sophie in Mum's room. Even though Mum and Dad are divorced, she still has a double bed. Sophie has claimed the left-hand side. I slip beneath the covers and turn off the light using the wall switch. An amber glow from the street light outside slips through gaps in the curtains, casting eerie shadows that seem to move about the room. Shuddering, I switch the light back on.

"Everything will be okay," Sophie says, holding my hand.

I close my eyes, wishing I shared her confidence, and try to allow myself to drift off to sleep. It comes easier than I expected.

# CHAPTER SIX

*Mum's eyes open, they are the only undamaged things on her scorched face. She's shivering, her teeth chattering together so loud they eclipse the sound of my own laboured breathing.*

*"Don't," she whispers.*

*I ignore her, inciting my magic to carry on saving her. I can't let her die. I chose her over Matthew.*

*"Don't."*

*She drags her hand free of mine.*

*"I won't let you die," I say desperately.*

*I attempt to reach her, but the harder I try, the further away she is. A heavy weight presses against my chest. Saul's laughter floods my ears but I focus on touching Mum so I can save her.*

*I'm almost close enough. Our fingertips millimetres apart. Her eyes drift shut as her arm drops against the side of the altar. Her chest falls still. The tremor in her body subsides.*

*No.*

"No. No!"

I sit upright, gasping for air. I wipe my cheeks dry with my sleeve.

"Bad dream?" Matthew's voice echoes through the darkness. He spoke in a soft tone, but there was a harsh quality to it.

"It was nothing."

I calm my breathing and wait for my eyes to adjust. Moonlight seeps into the warehouse, tempered by dirt, allowing me to locate Matthew. He's standing by the windows, arms folded and face turned towards me.

"What was it about?"

I ignore his question. I lay down and pull the sleeping bag around me as I tell myself it's the cold making me shiver, instead of the clear and painful memory of watching Mum die. I squeeze my eyes shut, only to see her burnt body. A sharp hiss escapes my lips and I twist onto my side, staring at Matthew once more.

When Kim told me she'd put his soul into a golem to save him, I didn't know what to expect. Matthew looked normal enough, until the moment he'd pushed the hood down. At a glance, someone might be able to believe it was human, but it only took a few seconds to take in the blocky nature of his features and the unnatural pallor of his skin. The way the moonlight creates highlights and shadows on his face, combined with the lack of any outward emotion, is unsettling.

"What's it like?" I'm not sure why the question tumbles off my lips.

He tilts his head to the side, his eyebrows slowly sliding up into a questioning gesture.

"Inside the golem?" My voice grates out of my throat. Part of me hopes it was too weak to travel to him.

"Heavy." He drops his arms to his sides and takes a step towards me. "Confining." He strides forward, marking each pace with his words. "Suffocating. Difficult. Cumbersome. It's a prison. A tomb."

I push the sleeping bag aside and get to my feet, standing tall. It's not enough. He's taller, looming over me the closer he gets. I tilt my chin up, meeting his dark gaze, holding my expression rigid so it doesn't betray the thoughts churning in my head. It's my fault. I fell for Saul's lies and did this to him.

"You said it was temporary."

He answers with a shrug. "In theory. I need healing from the Shamari."

"Could I heal you?"

"Your magic heals the body, not the soul." Disgust pollutes his voice.

I clench my jaw. "Will you let me try?" I need to do something, especially as it's my fault he's in this position at all.

His eyes narrow. Every action he makes is slow and forced. His attempts at normality make the golem appear even more alien.

"No. Magic did this. Why would I allow you to make it worse?"

I gape at him for a second before gritting my teeth hard to get a grip of my annoyance. "Make it worse? I want to help."

"You are Baneem. You cannot help me."

"I'm half human." It doesn't matter to him, it never has. He tolerates my existence because of Kim. We're barely on speaking terms, let alone anywhere near the top of each other's Christmas card list. "You'd cling to your pride, rather than accept a chance at being healed?"

His head jerks back. "You can't heal me." He speaks in a guttural snarl.

"Arrogant jerk." I square up to Matthew, gesturing towards him. "You won't accept my magic, because I'm Baneem, but you'll let Kim use magic to animate a lump of clay?"

"The power of my soul animates the golem, *not* magic."

"Uh-huh."

He moves closer, so his chest is almost touching mine. If he was human, I'd be able to feel his breath on my face. Even without the power of his aura to make me senseless, he's still intimidating. I hold myself rigid, not letting myself show fear.

"Saul won't stop looking for you." He rests his hand against the wall beside my head. "If he finds you, he'll destroy my people. In the meantime, he'll hurt Kim to get to you."

The abrupt change of subject leaves me reeling. Are his veiled threats a way of denying the things I've said? Things he doesn't want to hear? I clench my fists, digging my nails into my palms. Although his face is expressionless, his eyes burn as his gaze bores into me. From the corner of my vision, I see his fingers twitch, as his hand raises towards me. My pulse quickens as I anticipate the hit. I twist away into the centre of the room to put distance between us.

Matthew turns. "You need to tell us everything you know about Saul, his plan and how we can stop him. Kim won't push you because she's worried."

"And you?"

"I care about my people and Kim. Not you. Your silence puts them all in danger." He crosses to the windows and stares at the river again.

It's impossible to read the golem. Whatever Matthew's intentions, his words have left me shaking. I go to the sleeping bag and lay down, but can't close my eyes. I keep my gaze fixed on Matthew. He's forbidden from hurting humans or Baneem. I don't know what price he'd pay for breaking those rules and I'm not sure he cares. If he has to choose between destroying me to save the Changed and Kim, I'm certain he won't think twice.

# CHAPTER SEVEN

As soon as it's a decent enough time to call morning, I send AJ a text: *Hope you're OK*. His reply is swifter than last night: *Tired, but fine*. I can't remember how many times I told everyone I was fine after Charley died, when I wasn't. I doubt AJ is, either. At least Saul's cronies haven't found him. That was one fear that kept me awake most of the night.

Sophie and I take a round-a-bout route to the warehouse, doubling back on ourselves several times to make sure we aren't being followed. Paranoid? Maybe.

When we arrive, Sophie and I make ourselves as comfortable as possible by sitting on our coats on the filthy floor. AJ sits opposite us on the camping mat, his back pressed against the wall, his knees drawn up to his chest. Matthew stands apart from us, beside the windows. We break the news of the break-in to them both. Matthew's face is expressionless, whilst AJ curls in on himself, dipping his chin to his knees.

"You were lucky you weren't there when the Baneem came," Matthew says. "They could have—" He lets out a growl, clenches his fists and turns away. The light from the windows makes the unnatural contours of his face abstract in a chilling way.

"Whoever broke into Kim's house found AJ's clothes," Sophie says. "They know he's in the city, or at least that he was. They won't stop looking."

"We need to take control," I say, firmly and positively. "From the moment Charley died, all I've done... all any of us have done, is react. Even you, Matthew. You find the Baneem after they've used their magic to screw with humans, not before."

Matthew folds his arms.

"AJ, all you've ever done is run away." He opens his mouth, but I cut him off. "And I'm not saying that's wrong. Between staying away from Saul and hiding from the Shamari, you didn't have any other choice." I take a breath, clenching my shaking hands. I can't let any of them see how scared and unsure I am. "I'm sick of standing back whilst the Baneem hurt everyone around me."

"What do you suggest we do?" Matthew says. "*Kill* Saul?" His dark gaze burns into mine.

I should have an instant answer to give him. I wish I did.

"The Shamari are dealing with the Baneem," Matthew says, turning to face us. "The Changed hunt them down and take them to purgatory."

I cough. "Really? I'm not sure they're doing a great job. Look at Gage. He murdered Charley and Amy and destroyed Tia before you tracked him down. Even when you took him to purgatory, he was there for less than a year before they released him to wreak havoc on my family again. Besides, the Shamari think *you're*... policing this area, but you're not are you? You've already said you have no idea how long it will take them to realise there's a problem."

Matthew's mouth pinches at the corners, his eyes narrowing. Maybe I went too far. Matthew is trapped and dying, he doesn't need me highlighting his failings or those of the Shamari.

"I trust you," I say. "You've always done your best, I know that."

"But it's not good enough?"

I gesture towards him. "Right now? No. You're too weak to hunt Baneem down."

Sophie touches my arm. "If killing or imprisoning Saul aren't good options, what can we do?"

I still haven't figured that out. Matthew doesn't give me time to think. He glares at AJ and takes two long strides forward to close the gap between them. "Why does Saul want to kill the Changed?"

AJ squirms under his gaze.

"We need to know," Matthew says, his voice cold and detached.

AJ glances at me and then sighs and pulls at each of his fingers. "He has some crazed idea that if he kills all the Changed, he can live here like a god, lording his magic over the humans." The words rush out of him in a subdued mutter.

I press my lips together. Saul has a god complex. It doesn't surprise me. But knowing the reasons behind his crazy plan doesn't get me any closer to working out how to stop him and the rest of the Baneem.

"And he intends to do that by hiding Baneem souls in human bodies?" Matthew asks. "Like he did to your mother."

AJ stares at the floor through shimmering eyes, blinking. I glare at Matthew, willing him to shut up.

"She was burning from the inside out." Matthew carries on like a bulldozer destroying a house. "I doubt a Baneem soul can stay within a human body for long, can it?"

The colour drains out of AJ's face. "A matter of hours."

I move onto my knees and crawl toward AJ. "AJ, what happens if the human host dies whilst the Baneem soul is still inside it?" I rest my hand on his knee.

"They both die." His voice is strained, cracked.

"Is that what happened to your mum?" I ask.

"No." He squeezes his eyes shut.

I move my hand in slow, calming circles over his knee. Although I want to know what happened to Phailin, now isn't the time to ask AJ to relive it. Gage told me Saul was going to strip AJ's magic. Now I understand why. When he healed my gunshot wound, he took all the damage onto himself, rendering himself unconscious whilst he healed. It took days for him to recover, so there's no way he could heal more than one or two people at a time. Let alone the hidden army Gage referred to. But I'm guessing Saul believes that AJ's magic could be used to heal more people, if it's outside the physical constraints of his body.

To protect AJ, the Changed Shamari and everyone else, I have to come up with a plan. Soon.

"Does it matter what Saul's plan is?" Matthew asks, taking another step forward. "Without AJ, he has no plan."

AJ shivers beneath my touch and hunches his shoulders, his gaze fixed on the strip of floor between us.

"How do we keep AJ safe from magic?" Sophie asks, looking to Matthew. "Do they have the magical equivalent of sniffer dogs? Is that why they took AJ's clothes?"

Matthew shrugs. "There are as many magical abilities as there are Baneem. It's possible one of the Baneem could use magic to track him, at which point, there's nowhere he can run and no way we can protect him."

"Enough," I say. The way Matthew is talking is creeping me out. "It's not just about Saul, or AJ."

Matthew pinches his eyebrows as he shifts his stare from AJ to me.

"Saul is a massive problem, yes, but he's not the only Baneem who wants to mess with humans and destroy lives. We can't kill Saul. We can't kill any of them. I won't sink to their level. The Baneem don't place any value on human lives. I'm not even sure they place much value on each other's lives." I glance at AJ, hoping he'll say something to confirm or deny my words, but he doesn't. "I won't be like them."

"What are you saying?" Matthew says. "That we ignore Saul? Ignore that if he finds AJ and takes his magic, he could potentially kill all the Changed?"

"I'm saying to protect everyone—AJ, our families, every human *and* the Changed—it's not only Saul we have to stop."

Matthew shakes his head, his upper lip curling.

"I get it," AJ says, looking up to lock gazes with me. "It's bigger than me and Matthew. It's bigger than all of us. Even if we stop Saul now, sooner or later, another Baneem will get the same ideas of grandeur and try something crazed. In the meantime, individual Baneem are hurting people over and over again."

Sophie sucks in a breath. "So... what *do* we do?"

I glance at each of them. "We stop gateways being opened between our two worlds. Permanently."

Matthew shakes his head, the movement slow and deliberate. "Do you have any idea how insane that sounds?"

I stare at him, unsure why he would be so dismissive. Out of everyone, I would have thought he would have understood. He's spent four hundred years hunting down the Baneem. Shouldn't he want to find a permanent solution?

"Don't you think we would have stopped travel between the worlds if we could have?" He looms over me, his gaze intense. "If the power of the Shamari cannot stop the Baneem from coming to earth, what makes you think you can?"

I scramble to my feet, fold my arms and glare up at him. How dare he try to intimidate and frighten me? "Oh, I don't know, maybe the same way I created a golem to save *your* life."

Matthew lets out an indignant cough. "You tapped into the power of my soul to create the golem. Humans have no power or magic of their own."

AJ drags himself to his feet, pulling a piece of dirty, crumpled paper from his back pocket. He holds it out to me. "Would this help?"

Our fingertips brush and his gaze burrows into mine, his chestnut eyes churning with hurt and hope. I unfold the paper, trying not to think too hard about whose blood is staining the surface. I gasp as I see the diagram before me: a circle, divided into twelve segments, each one containing a glyph. Even though I'm not familiar with every pictogram, I recognise their source instantly: ancient Hebrew. The same symbols Matthew uses. The symbols I used to fuse Matthew's soul with the golem.

"What is this?" I ask, my voice shaking.

"It's a gateway diagram," AJ says. "It's how I escaped."

"The Baneem cannot open gateways." Matthew says, pacing like a caged animal.

AJ's eyes narrow. "I'm half human," he spits through gritted teeth.

"Thank you." I cup his cheek in my free hand, hoping the action, combined with a soft smile, will temper the anger he must be feeling. "Matthew, do you have any idea why the gateway spell created by humans would use the same glyphs you do?"

He shakes his head, his relentless pacing becoming faster, his footsteps heavier.

"Is it possible the Shamari taught humans magic?"

"No." He stands still, clenching his fists until they shake. "The Shamari don't use magic. Perhaps humans saw us channeling the power of our souls through the glyphs and sought to do the same. Perhaps it was the Baneem who helped them pervert the glyphs as a channel for magic."

I twist a strand of my hair around my fingertip. "Matthew... the Baneem can't open gateways," I say, echoing his words. I try to keep my voice gentle, so it acts as a balm to his anger. "They don't... *can't*... use the glyphs. I thought... maybe if the Shamari taught glyph magic to humans, we could ask them how to communicate with the Baneem."

Matthew backs away, holding his hands up, palms facing me in defiance of my words. He turns his hands back toward himself, curling his lip as he stares at them, as though realising for the first time it was magic that saved him. He must have known before, or perhaps, afraid of his soul fragmenting to the point of destruction, he refused to acknowledge it so he could live.

"Kim, do you know what all the symbols mean?" Sophie asks.

I force myself to look away from Matthew as he turns his back on us all. "No, but I know someone who's an expert in ancient Hebrew, remember?"

"Professor West," Sophie nods. "He helped you work out how to animate the golem. Except the university term ended yesterday. How are you going to get in touch with him?"

"I don't know, but I'll figure it out."

"A phone book?" AJ suggests.

Sophie snorts. "I don't know anyone who has a physical phone book anymore. I'll use the internet on my phone and see if there's some sort of online phonebook." She stands and heads towards the door.

She doesn't need to leave to use her phone, but I'm not surprised she wants to escape the stifling tension in the room.

"I'll go with you," Matthew says.

Sophie opens her mouth and then snaps it shut. "Sure. I wasn't going to go far, but yeah, okay."

I move to block Matthew. I understand the conversation left him uncomfortable, but in the same way he wants me to push AJ for information, I need to get more out of him. "Have you tried to contact the Shamari?"

"Yes, but it didn't work."

I didn't expect it to, but I needed to know he was trying. "Are you sure the Shamari wouldn't have taught magic to the humans, so they could protect themselves?"

"From what?" Matthew says. "There was nothing to protect them from until they opened a gateway to Uralahnd and allowed Baneem to come through. I've told you all this, Kim. The Shamari were created to stop the Baneem."

I shrug. "It must be a coincidence both the Shamari and humans use the same glyphs."

From the corners of my eyes, I see AJ raise his hand to rub his neck. I wonder how much of an effort it is for him to hold his tongue, as Matthew refuses to entertain any possibility except his own rigid truth.

"Or the God... the *Creator*—whatever you want to call it— gave both humans and Shamari the same means of working magic," I suggest. "I guess we'll never know the truth."

"No." Matthew's voice is tight. "What I... what the Shamari do... it's *not* magic."

I force myself to smile. "No, you're right. I'm sorry for suggesting it." Right now I think he's the only one still in denial of the obvious truth.

"You should think carefully before speaking to Professor West again," Matthew says. "You shouldn't take using magic lightly. The Baneem use magic to corrupt humans, remember?"

"We don't have any other options, Matthew. To fight magic, we need magic. It's the only way to save ourselves from the Baneem forever."

Like encasing Matthew's soul in the golem was the only way to save him.

Why can't he see not all magic is bad? Or am I fooling myself into believing that using it is okay if my intentions are honourable? I twist my fingers together behind my back. Are my intentions pure?

"We have to stop the Baneem from coming here. It's the only way to protect everyone from them. If the Shamari can't help, we have to figure it out ourselves. Magic is the only tool we have and Professor West is the only person I know who can tell us more about the pictograms."

Matthew snarls and shakes his head.

I rake my fingertips through my hair. We're getting nowhere. I have to resign myself to the fact I'll never be able to convince Matthew I'm right. All I can hope is that, when it comes down to it, he'll help us and not work against us.

"I'm going to go," Sophie says, breaking the stalemate between me and Matthew. "Are you coming?"

She glances from me to AJ and back again in a purposeful way. She doesn't need to speak for me to understand Matthew's prodding has left AJ raw and hurting. With both her and Matthew gone, maybe I'll be able to offer him some comfort.

Matthew glares at me a moment longer and then nods. He follows Sophie to the door and then pauses, staring back at me. "I'll keep trying to communicate with the Shamari. I want rid of this shell. I want to be whole again."

I blink as realisation hits me. It's not just AJ who's hurting. Matthew is too. He's wearing his pain on his face for all of us to see. As much as his expression stabs at my heart, seeing how trapped and afraid he feels is better than staring at a blank clay face.

"You will be. I promise," I say. I mean it. I won't rest until he is.

"Don't make promises you don't have the power to keep," he growls. "There's nothing you can do to reunite me with the Shamari. I'm not your priority. Stopping Saul is." He shifts his expression to one of anger, his upper lip curled, his eyes narrowed.

"Matthew..." Why doesn't he want me to try to help him?

"You can't fix everything, Kim. This grand idea of yours to stop the Baneem... you need to realise it's beyond your grasp. Just like saving me, is."

It's obvious he'd rather I didn't try to help him at all, than try and fail. I blink back tears and stare at the floor. He's wrong. There has to be a way I can fix him. If it wasn't for me, he wouldn't be half-way to dead. Before I can rouse myself to give him words of reassurance, he's gone. I stare at the half-covered doorway, the fear I've lost his support and friendship driving an ice pick through my heart.

*

With Matthew gone, it's as though the vast interior of the factory has released the breath it's been holding. AJ trudges back to the camping mat and sinks down, wrapping his arms around his knees. He seems more broken than when I left him yesterday, more fragile.

"You said you were tired, I guess you didn't sleep well?"

He shakes his head, his gaze flicking to the door before settling on me.

"Matthew." I clench my fists. "Did he try to pressure you into talking?"

AJ's mouth twists into a grimace, but he corrects his pained expression, setting his lips into a straight line of resignation. "No. He suggested I should. He's worried about you, Kim. About what Saul might do to you in order to get to me." He sighs. "So am I."

I shake my head. "I've told Matthew before that I'm sick of his big brother act. I can take care of myself."

AJ smiles. "I know." His face promptly droops into a sombre expression. "But Saul is dangerous."

"*All* the Baneem I've encountered have been dangerous. That's why we need to stop them being able to come here."

"I know." Frustration twists his voice into a growl.

"*Is* there anything you can tell us that would help?"

He stares straight at me, his expression intense. "Uralahnd... it's as beautiful or as ugly as the Baneem want to make it."

I frown, not understanding.

"It's like a blank slate. It reacts to the magic of the Baneem. To make it flourish, the Baneem have to *want* it to. If they don't, it withers and dies." He taps his finger against his knee. "From what I saw... they've stopped caring about it. Almost everything I could see from the place Saul had me was desert with withered plants. I glimpsed a couple of pockets of beauty, but the rest was barren."

"Why wouldn't the Baneem want it to be beautiful?"

He stares at the floor. "Saul said it was too easy to make Uralahnd flourish. There was no challenge in making it look beautiful."

I jerk my head back. "So they grew tired of their own world and decided to screw over ours instead?"

"I guess." His mouth and chin tremble. "I don't get it." Tears sparkle in his eyes.

I stand still, waiting. As much as I want to go to him, I'm afraid if I'm too clingy he'll pull away. I have to take his lead, follow his clues.

"Why did he force me to choose between Mum and Matthew? Force me to use my magic to help him. He didn't need to do any of it." He drops his head as his shoulders begin to shudder violently. "Uralahnd could be an amazing place. It *should* be."

I can't hold myself back any longer. I move to him, kneel behind him and drape myself over his back, wrapping my arms around him. His body trembles and shivers in my arms, as he lets his tears flow freely.

"Why did he have to kill her?" Tension coils within him, manifesting in his shaking clenched fists.

"I don't know," I whisper. There's nothing I can do to ease his pain, no answer I can give to any of his questions, and no explanation to justify what happened to him and his mum.

"To hurt me? To show me how powerful he was? To break me?"

"I don't know," I say again. My voice is fragile, like a stream of bubbles that will break as soon as they reach the surface of his pain. Words, meant well, but ultimately meaningless.

I wish I did know what had been going through Saul's head. How could one man be so cruel to anyone, let alone to his own son and the woman he claimed to have once loved? I doubt he ever cared about Phailin at all, any more than Gage had cared about Charley, or Tia. Or me. I shiver, remembering how I almost fell for his charms. How I let him touch me. I feel sick. I straighten and release AJ in time to smother a gag in my hands.

AJ twists round and cradles my face in his hand. "Are you okay?"

I can't help but smile at his reaction. I'm supposed to be comforting him, but here he is worried about me, despite everything that's happened and everything he's going through. Without thinking, I lean forward and kiss him. It's a quick kiss, so light our lips barely touch.

"I'm sorry," I mutter, turning my face away.

"For what?"

I rub my upper arm. "For being selfish." I brush my hands over my face in an effort to compose myself. "I don't know why Saul hurt you, or your mum. Probably for all the reasons you mentioned. Possibly just because he could." I reach out to stroke his face, a mirror of the way he's caressing mine. "It's what the Baneem do to us. Manipulate us. Twist us. Hurt us." I clench my free hand into a fist. "It has to stop."

AJ places his hand over mine, gently easing away the tension in my fist, until my fingers fall limply against my knee. He turns my hand, then, threading his fingers through mine and applies slight pressure to his grasp. I'm not sure what's happening. Are we reconnecting? I can't make myself relax into the moment. I'm worried he'll pull away, like he's done so many times before. He's got even more reason to now, after everything that's happened to him.

"You can tell me anything, you know that, don't you?" I say.

He rakes his teeth over his lower lip, before jerking his chin down in a slight nod.

"Whatever Saul did to you..." I allow my voice to trail off, unsure how to phrase what I'm trying to say.

I want to tell him it doesn't matter, but the truth is it does. Just like the things Gage did to me will always leave an imprint on my mind, so will the things Saul did to AJ. Just like I'll always carry the grief of losing Charley, like a noose around my neck, AJ will always have the grief of losing Phailin with him. Soft words can't take away pain like that. Tender kisses or skin softly stroked can't remove the unseen scars caused by violence and manipulation.

"I'll help you come to terms with it," I say. "If you'll let me."

"I'm not ready to tell you everything."

I trace the contour of his jaw with my fingertips. "I know."

"I don't know when, or if I will ever be."

"That's okay."

It really is. That he's told me anything at all is a sign he's not completely broken inside. Saul hasn't destroyed him. The AJ I fell in love with is still there, even if he is shrouded in guilt and grief.

I brush the back of my hand over his cheek, glad when he leans against my touch. He lifts his head, softly stroking my temple with his thumb. "I agree the Baneem need to be stopped, but it's not up to you to do it."

"Who else will? The Shamari?" I choke out a laugh. "They're shackled by ridiculous rules. Like I said, they just react. They've had hundreds of years to do something proactive to stop the Baneem, but they haven't."

He presses his fingertip against my lips. "You don't have to do it alone." He takes a deep breath. "I might be scared and broken right now, but I'm not useless. I'll do what I can to help you. Saul can't be allowed to go through with his plan of destroying the Changed, nor can we continue to let the Baneem run wild here. We can't." Fresh tears shine in his eyes.

"We won't." My voice is muffled against the barrier of his finger, which I kiss.

He lowers his hand from my face, freeing my lips.

"We'll talk to Professor West. We'll figure out the pictograms so we can use them to do more than open gateways or create a golem." My voice is full of confidence, even though I don't really feel it.

Not only is it such an overwhelming task, but I don't even know if we're going to be able to find a way to contact Dan West. Waiting until the university returns from the Christmas holidays isn't an option. But I have to be confident, so I can act as a life buoy for AJ, holding him above water, even though it would be easy to slip beneath the surface with him, both drowning together in our doubt and fear.

"I don't think I've ever known anyone as brave as you," AJ whispers.

It's my turn to cry. I smile through a sob, blinking back tears. "I'm not brave."

His eyes widen. "How many times have you faced the Baneem?"

I shiver. Too many. More than I care to think about.

"You never give in," he says. "You keep fighting. Why?"

I shrug. "It's the right thing to do? I can't shut my eyes to the Baneem, or magic and not-angels now that I know they exist. I can't stand by and do nothing when people around me are being hurt, or killed. First Charley, Amy and Tia, then Sophie's family and now you and your mum. I've already lost too much to the Baneem. I won't lose anyone else. I won't lose you." I'm crying freely now, the words hiccupping out of me in a fierce staccato rhythm. AJ thinks I'm strong, but my composure is crumbling before his eyes. That's all my so-called strength is, a facade.

He pushes himself a little more upright, leans forward and kisses the tears from my face. His lips, gentle as a falling leaf against my cheeks, send shivers of delight racing up and down my spine. Then his lips find mine, the contact no longer tentative but confident and sure. He wants the connection as much as I do. His hands wrap around me, his thumbs tracing small circles on my back through my t-shirt. I return his embrace, holding him tighter, pulling our bodies together.

"I missed you so much," I whisper, as our lips part. "I'm so sorry we couldn't get to you. We tried. *I* tried."

"I know."

"I'm sorry about your mum. I'm sorry for every—"

He kisses me again, silencing me. Tears roll down both our cheeks, intermingling into a pair of salty rivers that wind their way to our lips, making our kisses bitter, even though the taste of him is sweet.

We pull away at the same time, gazing into each other's eyes. A moment of silent understanding passes between us. I tuck a strand of auburn hair behind my ear and stand, hugging myself as I move towards the centre of the warehouse. Even though I want to be close to him, this isn't the time or the place.

"Sophie and Matthew will be back soon," I say, rubbing my arms. "She'll have found a way to get in touch with Professor West."

AJ shuffles back against the wall. "Thank you."

"For what?"

"Being here. For understanding."

I smile. "I love you. Where else would I be?"

"Do you remember after I healed you, when you came to visit me at the flat?"

I nod, although I'm not sure which moment specifically he's referring to.

"We laid together. Holding each other. You made me feel safe and grounded."

I smile. "And your touch kept me from thinking about what Gage had done to me."

He pats the camping mat beside him. "Can we do that now? Just be together?"

I nod and sit beside him, leaning my back against the wall. He wraps an arm around me, coaxing me to lean my head against his shoulder. I snuggle against him, looping my arm over his stomach. He begins to stroke my hair. I close my eyes, relaxing and allowing all the anxiety to ebb away from me. Even though we're surrounded by filth and dirt and everything is so uncertain, the moment couldn't be more perfect.

# CHAPTER EIGHT

I'm not sure what I will say to Dan West as I stand on his doorstep, finger poised to ring the bell. "This was a bad idea."

I attempt to turn around, but AJ is behind me. He grips my shoulders and sets me back in front of the door. It was hard enough persuading him to leave the safety of the warehouse to come with him, I can't be the one to act the coward now. I doubt Dan will be pleased to see me, though. Finding his address and visiting during the Christmas holiday must count as stalker behaviour. But we need to talk to him.

I press the doorbell and then push myself onto my tiptoes and back onto the soles of my feet over and over until the door opens. A pretty brunette opens the door. She's shorter than me, with curves that look amazing in the chevron patterned dress she's wearing.

"Hello?" Her chin dimples as she stares at us

"Is Professor West in?" My voice is little more than a squeak.

"Who is it, Leanne?" Dan's voice calls from somewhere in the house.

The woman, Leanne, stands aside. "There are two kids here to see you."

Dan appears in the hallway a moment later. He's holding a tea-towel and a still wet bowl in his hands. When he sees me, his eyes narrow.

"I'll handle it," he says, handing the tea-towel and bowl over to Leanne.

She gives AJ and I a nervous smile before walking off into the room Dan came out of.

Dan rests his hand on the door handle, ready to shut it in our faces. "What are you doing here, Miss Welles? How did you get my address?"

I jerk my head back a little, affronted by his tight tone. When I met him at the university, he had been fun and casual. I guess he was in safe territory there. Now I've discovered where he lives and I've invaded his home. I'm in the wrong, not him.

"I... we need your help," I say.

Dan shakes his head, but pauses as he catches AJ's stare. I'm not sure what he sees there. I'm too afraid to turn and look myself, but his resolve to turn us away drains out of his face. His shoulders slump and his hand drops away from the door handle.

"Fine. I'll give you five minutes. Come in."

He leads us through his cream hallway, into a small downstairs study. A cluttered desk takes up one wall. Photographs, maps and diagrams cover every available inch of wall space and even on the back of the door. There's diagrams of ancient scripts, photographs of hieroglyphs and ruined cities in vast deserts. The maps all have flags stuck in them and several post-it notes with scribbles on them. Above the desk three rows of shelves are filled with reference and note books.

Dan sits down in the office chair at the desk. There are no other seats, leaving AJ and I standing.

"What's this about?" Dan says.

I nudge AJ, who pulls the blood-stained gateway diagram out of his pocket.

"We need to understand what this means and how it works," I say, as Dan takes it and opens it, splaying it on his desk.

His eyes widen at the sight of the blood rather than at the pictographs set within the wheel.

"Why?" He asks, as he lays the diagram down on his desk and smooths it out.

I glance at AJ. We haven't talked about what we should or shouldn't tell Dan. I wonder if we should tell him the truth—all of it—, but even if we did, we can't prove any of it.

"It opens a gateway to another world," AJ says, taking the decision out of my hands. "Just like the glyphs you helped Kim with before enabled her to animate a golem."

I expect Dan to laugh, but AJ's voice is so solemn that all he does is stare at us.

"We need to know more about the glyphs—how and *why* they work," AJ carries on.

Dan inhales. "Is this a joke?"

"No," AJ and I say in unison.

"Other worlds? Gateways? You expect me to believe any of this?"

"No," AJ says. "But we won't lie to you." He jerks his head towards the diagram. "Does it matter if you believe us? Can you tell us what the pictographs mean?"

Dan twists his chair round. "Yes, but I'm not sure I should." He purses his lips. "Either this is a joke, or you two are high on something." His fingertip hovers over one of the larger bloodstains.

"It's mine," AJ says. "I don't take drugs." He tucks his chin against his chest. "They wouldn't work, even if I did," he mutters, so only I can hear him.

He turns away and pretends to study the photographs, but I can see moisture glistening in his eyes. I can see the veins protruding in his neck, where he's holding his body tense and rigid. When his gaze alights on a photograph of a ziggurat, his hands curl into tight fists and he closes his eyes.

"Please help us," I say. "I know what we're saying sounds crazy."

"You bet it does," Dan says. "First golems and now this? What's the connection?"

"Ancient Hebrew," I say, with a shrug.

It's easier than explaining the pictographs might have been an angelic language, which humans somehow learned and adopted as their own.

The books, leaflets and maps on Dan's desk rustle as he shoves them aside, rooting around until he's located a small pad of paper and a pen. He drops the pad next to the gateway diagram and taps the top of the pen against it. I can't tell if he's looking at the symbols to translate them for us, or if he's deciding whether he should help us.

I step forward. "I'm surprised you haven't thrown us out already."

He snorts. "I'm thinking about it, trust me."

"You're the only person I know who can translate this for us. If we could have gone to someone else, we would have. We wouldn't be here if it wasn't important."

"I can tell it's important," he says. "But I'd like it if you told me the truth."

"I did," AJ says in a quiet tone, which makes me grimace.

Dan wrinkles his nose, but says nothing. He leans on the desk, shoulders hunched and twists the gateway drawing around a few times.

"I don't suppose you know what the start point is?" he says.

I move over to the small window, to let AJ stand in the space I was occupying. He stabs his finger so hard against the diagram there's a thud as he connects with the desk beneath.

"You read Hebrew from right to left," Dan says.

"So... counter-clockwise around the wheel?" I say.

He nods. "Pictograms are literally that. They represent concepts rather than individual words. So, this one," he points at the symbol AJ indicated, which is a circle with a wiggly tail, kind of like a tadpole. "This is *tsade* The pictogram itself represents a man, lying on his side. But it's meaning is desire, or having a need for something."

He jots his translation down on the pad.

"The next one looks like a five-year-old's attempt to draw a bull," I say, peering over Dan's shoulder.

He chuckles, the sound the most relaxed I've heard him since we showed up on his doorstep.

"It's the *aleph*," he says. "Which represents an ox and therefore strength. They were used as ploughing animals."

"Desire, and strength," I say, frowning.

Dan makes another note on the pad and carries on to the third symbol—the eye. "*Ayin*," he says. "I doubt you need my help to guess it's meaning.

"To see?" I say.

He nods and moves his fingertip around the wheel to the fourth symbol, which is a circle with a line extending horizontally through its centre.

"*Qof*. The pictogram symbolises the sun on the horizon, but it's meaning is, 'behind'."

I tug at my lower lip, not understanding the connection at all. I don't need to, I only need to trust Dan is right.

The fifth symbol looks similar to the Roman numeral for three, only with the vertical lines more spaced out.

"*Chet*," Dan says. "It's literally a wall, or a separation between two things."

The sixth is also familiar. It's the symbol Matthew drew so he could take Gage, and later Taylor, away. Two horizontal lines, with an l and a j curled around the bottom. Or at least, that's how my mind sees it.

"*Kaf*. The pictogram represents an open palm. It means, to open. Next is *Dalet*."

I peer at it. For a second I think I'm looking at a top hat, which would be impossible. But I realise I'm looking at it upside down.

"It means pathway," Dan says. "But the pictogram is of a tent door, so you could take it to be either."

"The next one looks like a man," I say."

"A man worshiping, or beholding Yaweh, yes," Dan agrees.

"And the last one?" I say, gesturing to the pointed waves that cut across the centre of the wheel. "What does that mean?"

"Chaos," Dan says, leaning back in his chair. He picks up his pad of paper and frowns. "So, what you have is: desire, strength, see, behind, separate, open, door, behold and chaos."

I squint at the words he's written on the pad of paper, trying to imagine what they would be with articles, such as 'the', to connect the words. AJ beats me to it.

"I desire the strength to see behind the separation and open the door to behold chaos," he says in a distant tone, his eyes half-closed, as though he's remembering something. He shudders. "Chaos? I don't get it. Chaos is random."

"Or whatever you want it to be," Dan says. "Look, let's pretend I believe this can open a gateway between two worlds. You'd need to direct the gateway somehow, right? Otherwise you could end up hundreds of thousands of miles away from where you wanted to be."

I watch AJ's reaction to Dan's words. His eyes widen a little and he takes a half step back.

"So perhaps having *mem* as the final pictogram, is a way of directing where the gateway will lead to. Almost as though you are imposing your will upon the destination." He scratches his chin. "Thinking about it that way, the *aleph* might refer to strength of mind, rather than physical strength."

I nod, as I allow his words to absorb into my mind. It all makes sense. I reach out and graze my fingertips over the back of AJ's hand, reminding him I'm here, because the tension has returned to his body.

"That's what they mean, but how does it work?" I ask, even though I know I'm pushing Dan too far.

He was animated while he was translating the pictograms, excited almost. Right now we need his enthusiasm for knowledge and understanding.

"It's a group of pictograms in a circle," Dan says. "There's nothing magical about it. There's no way to imbue it with power."

I scrunch my mouth up. He can't be right, because AJ opened a gateway to get home. The woman Saul killed opened a gateway so he could take AJ to Uralahnd. The gateways are real, just as magic, the Baneem and Shamari are real. But I can't prove it to him.

"Humour us."

"I've humoured the pair of you enough," Dan says, his voice tight. "I agreed to give you five minutes, it's been more like half an hour. You should leave now."

I can't let him throw us out of his house. We still need his help.

"What harm will it do to help us?" I say. "If, as you believe, magic doesn't exist, then all you'd be doing is helping us put another group of pictograms together. That's it."

He stands and gestures to the door. "It's time you both left." His tone is sharp, his words clipped. He's done with humouring us.

AJ leans round him and grabs a letter opener from the desk. Before I've had time to realise what he's going to do, he scratches the point over the palm of his hand, drawing blood.

"What the—" Dan begins.

The wound closes, the jagged skin knitting back together as both Dan and I watch.

"Magic *is* real," AJ hisses. "Will you help us?"

Dan slumps into his chair, still staring at AJ's palm. There's still a trail of blood, but AJ wipes it away with his sleeve, revealing unflawed skin. Dan grabs his hand and turns it over and then back again. He runs his finger over where the wound had been and then yanks the letter opener from AJ's other hand. He tests the point, which scratches his fingertip even though his pressure was light. His hand opens and the letter opener clatters to the floor. I retrieve it, setting it back on the desk.

"Now do you believe us?" I ask.

"It has to be a trick," he says shaking his head.

His refusal to believe what his eyes are showing him makes me grit my teeth, but at the same time I understand—we're asking him to rethink everything he believes. I had a hard time doing it, too.

"It's not a trick," I say."

"Do you need another demonstration?" AJ asks. "You could go fetch a different knife, if it makes all this easier to accept."

Dan pales and his mouth becomes slack. "No. Don't do that again." He wipes both hands over his face, before letting out a big sigh. "What do you need?"

I'm not sure if his offer of help is because he really believes, or if it's because he knows it's the only way he'll get rid of us.

I don't really care which it is, either. "How many more pictograms are there?" I ask.

He twists the chair round and runs his thumb along the spines of the closest books. He selects one and pulls it out, handing it to me. "This book lists all the pictograms, their meanings and how they've evolved into modern Hebrew. I can assure you, there's nothing about using them for magic."

I grimace as I take the book. "I didn't think there would be."

"I'm not sure what else I can do for you," Dan says. "*If* those pictograms can open a gateway to another world, I don't know how. There's no magic in symbols. Belief and faith, maybe, but no magic." He taps his fingertips against his chin and stares at AJ. "How..." He shakes his head, as though telling himself not to believe what he saw with his own eyes.

AJ curls his hand into a fist. "It's my curse," he says in a quiet voice. "Thank you."

Dan folds the gateway diagram up and gives it back to AJ. "Is there anything else I can do for you?"

I shake my head and then step aside, so Dan can see us to the front door. He lets us out with nothing more than a slight wave. I tangle my fingertips through AJ's as we hurry away. "When you used the gateway, what were you thinking about?"

He lowers his head, fixing his glare on the pavement. "I was scared Gage was going to kill you."

A small smile flickers at the edge of my lips. I already knew it was me he was thinking of, but hearing him say it ignites a spark of warmth inside my gut.

"Where did you end up?"

"The warehouse I suggested hiding out in." He sighs. "I passed out as soon as I was through. I was in a bad way. I wanted to get to you sooner, but couldn't. Maybe if I had, you wouldn't have had to..."

Kill Gage, I finish mentally. He doesn't need to say the words for me to know what he was going to say.

I jerk him to a halt and use my hands to coax his body round to face me, making a soft hushing noise in my throat at the same time. He was close to me when Sophie, Matthew and I were at the river. He was close when Gage attacked me and I didn't know.

"We're going to make things right," I say. "We'll figure out how to prevent any more gateways being opened. And by doing that, we'll free you." I thread my fingers through his, feeling a genuine shred of confidence for the first time.

"I didn't see any clues in the meaning of the gateway glyphs, that might help us figure out how to stop them being opened," AJ says.

His words are like a pin, popping my fragile balloon of optimism.

"We'll figure it out, together. All we need is time."

"We don't know how close Saul and his people are to finding us." He glances around, as though expecting Baneem to be standing on the street corner, or hiding behind a garden fence. "I shouldn't have come here. I should have stayed hidden."

"I needed you." I squeeze his hand. "You convinced Professor West to help us. I couldn't have done it without you."

"What if Saul goes after your family again, or Sophie's?"

I stare ahead, not focusing on anything, relying on AJ to keep me from stumbling or bumping into anyone.

"You should warn your parents," AJ says.

"I can't."

"Kim..."

"You saw how Professor West reacted to our story. He thought we were mad."

"But he still helped us."

"Only because you used your magic."

AJ shakes his head. "No. He helped us before I did that. They're your parents, Kim. They'll listen to you."

We pause at a crossing, waiting for the green man to signal it's safe to cross the busy road.

"Telling them the truth will only make things worse." I roll my head back, focusing on the crisp blue sky as AJ continues to guide me, his grip firm in mine. "No. I... we have to focus on our goal: preventing gateways being opened. The faster we do that, the faster everyone we know will be safe."

AJ sighs, his shoulders slumping as he relaxes his grip to pull away from me. I try to stop him, but realise there's no point. He's given up on the argument, but releasing my hand is his way of showing he thinks I'm wrong. Maybe I am. But trying to tell my parents the truth is too much of a distraction right now. I have to focus on what's ahead of us. It's all I can do.

# CHAPTER NINE

Silence creates a heavy distance between Kim and I as we walk the rest of the way to the warehouse. Part of me doesn't understand why she's being so pig-headed about talking to her parents, but I have to admit it was different for me. Mum had known about the Baneem and magic long before I was born. She'd been sucked in and manipulated by Saul. Would she have ever broken free of him if I hadn't existed? I shudder, as I try to push the alternate reality out of my mind.

Sophie's anxious expression gives way to a broad grin as we crawl into the warehouse.

"Professor West explained what each of the glyphs in the gateway diagram mean," Kim explains to Sophie and Matthew. She waves the book in the air. "This has explanations of all the Ancient Hebrew pictograms. Hopefully we'll be able to figure out a way to use them to do more than open a gateway."

"Hopefully?" Matthew asks, snorting. "We don't even know *why* the gateway works, or why humans can use the pictograms to create magic and Baneem can't."

Kim's shoulders sag. She hugs the book to her chest, her chin trembling as she stares at the floor. I hate the way Matthew is making her feel right now. He must be angry. He's trapped in the golem and Kim used magic to put him there, but it doesn't give him the right to weigh her down with negativity. Kim might not think it's our first priority, but we need to find a way to heal him. Fast.

"It doesn't make sense," I say.

"What doesn't?" Sophie asks.

"Matthew's right, the Baneem *can't* open gateways. Which means they can't have taught humans how to."

"What are you saying?" Matthew asks in a low voice.

I stare at him. "Maybe all the facts you're working on aren't true? Or maybe Kim's theory was right and the Shamari *did* teach humans about the glyphs."

"We *did not* teach humans how to use magic," he mutters defensively.

I sigh. "Maybe humans figured it out themselves, using the language of the angels. All throughout history there's talk of people trying to make magic work. Given that we know magic is real, it's not a big leap to assume someone succeeded."

Kim frowns and shakes her head. "But why do the Shamari need to channel their magic through the glyphs at all?"

"Because they were human once?" I say.

"Only the Changed were humans once," Matthew says.

I pinch my lips together. "Have you ever met a True Shamari?"

I expect him to nod, but he doesn't, he looks away from me, shying away from my question. I narrow my eyes, peering at him. I understand why the True Shamari don't want to risk coming into direct conflict with the Baneem—I'm not sure I'd want to risk my soul being annihilated, having it dragged out of my body was bad enough—but why would they hide from the Changed? Their own creation?

"If humans did work out the gateway on their own, it means we can work out how to use the pictograms to do other things," Sophie says, her voice brimming with confidence. "Maybe Kim's crazy plan isn't so crazy at all."

"Thanks—I think," Kim mutters.

"The Baneem whispered to humans, to seduce them into finding a way to cross between the worlds." Matthew says.

"All of them? Or one of them?" I ask. "It would only have taken one Baneem with the magic of communication to do it. It would allow them to talk to as many humans as possible.

They would promise them unlimited magic and set them to work on opening a gateway to let Baneem through. Power, strength, magic, however you want to package it, is one of the biggest driving forces of humanity. It always has been." I rub the bridge of my nose. "Saul gave me a history lesson while I was with him. His version of events didn't match up with yours, Matthew."

"I didn't lie to Kim," Matthew says.

I shake my head, tired of his antagonism. "I didn't say you had. I don't think Saul was lying to me, either. Look at all the different beliefs humans have. Even different sects of Christians can't agree with one another on everything."

"History is written by the winners," Kim muses. She gives me a sheepish smile when I stare at her. "I heard it somewhere. Or read it somewhere. I can't remember. I also read somewhere that American school history books give a different rendition of the Second World War than ours do. I'd guess if you looked at books in a Japanese school, or a German school, you'd find the same. History is open to interpretation. Belief and faith even more so and time twists things even further."

We all fall silent, staring into the empty space between us. All we've really figured out is that the *truth* is something we'll never know. It doesn't put us any closer to making Kim's idea to stop gateways being opened into our world a reality, or to figuring out a way to heal Matthew. One thing's for sure, he won't let us use magic to help him a second time. Not directly, anyway.

"The central symbol on the gateway means chaos," I say, thinking out loud rather than talking to anyone in particular. Even so, everyone's attention snaps to me. I fidget under the weight of Matthew's dark stare. "In theory, the gateway can take you anywhere you want to go." I meet his stare. "*Anywhere.* Including your home."

Matthew turns his face away. "I doubt it."

"Why wouldn't it work?" I rub at my ear, not really sure if I should go any further. "Because you don't use magic?"

Matthew juts his chin into the air. "I don't use magic. The Shamari don't use magic."

I open and close my mouth a few times. How can he stand there and deny it? The symbols he uses and those that open the gateway are the same. If the gateway uses magic, so must his *abilities*.

Kim turns to me. "Are you saying you think you could send Matthew home, so he can get healed?"

I nod. "In theory, yes. If the gateway will open to anywhere you want to go, all I'd have to do is concentrate on sending Matthew home. Any of us could do it." I bob my head from side to side. "Of course, it would help if we knew *where* Matthew comes from."

Matthew snorts. I didn't think he was going to offer that information.

"You're the only one who's used the gateway," Kim said. "If you think you could do it, maybe you should try."

I dig my teeth into my lower lip as I consider her response. Not the words, but her tone of voice and the way she dipped her face away from me when she spoke. She knows as well as I do any human can open a gateway, but she doesn't want to. It's the only assumption I can leap to.

"It won't work," Matthew says.

I let out an annoyed growl. "You're not willing to try? Even if it means giving up on a chance to go home and get healed?"

"If it means using magic, no, I'm not."

Kim tilts her face to the ceiling and plants her hands on her hips. She presses her lips together, but remains quiet. I can't help but wonder what words she's holding back.

She might be feeling diplomatic, but I'm not. Now isn't the time to pander to Matthew's stubbornness. "But you're going to sit there while we try to figure out how to use the pictograms to stop anyone from travelling between here and Uralahnd?"

Matthew glares down at his hands. "I cannot stop you from using magic and, right now, I'm not in a position to offer any alternatives."

Sophie whistles. "Talk about double standards."

"Would you rather I stopped you?" Matthew snaps.

"No," Sophie replies. "But it doesn't stop you being an idiot. You think all magic is evil, but it's not." She puffs her cheeks out in a thoughtful manner. "Magic saved you, didn't it?"

Matthew hunches his shoulders. "I was wrong to allow you and Kim to create the golem."

Kim suppresses a gasp behind her hand. She turns away, bowing her head. I watch as a tear slips down her cheek. I can't begin to imagine how much Matthew's attitude is hurting her. She used magic to save his life and he's as good as throwing it back in her face.

"But you *did* let us save you," Sophie carries on. "And I don't remember you arguing much about it then. The way I see it, magic is like guns."

I stiffen. A quick sidewards glance shows Kim has had a similar reaction. Of all the analogies for Sophie to pick, why did it have to be one that reminds Kim of what Sophie's father did? Kim can't have told her what happened.

"Neither are intrinsically evil," Sophie says, seemingly oblivious to our reactions. "They're tools. It's the people who use them that decide whether they're going to be used for good or bad."

"I've never known a Baneem to use their magic for good," Matthew says.

Sophie points at me. "Hello? AJ?"

"All right, I've only ever known *one* Baneem to use their magic for anything even remotely good," Matthew concedes.

"Half-Baneem," I say, unable to stop the words twisting into an annoyed snarl. The distinction might not be important to Matthew, but it is to me.

"Enough," Kim says. "Arguing amongst ourselves isn't getting us anywhere. AJ... will you look at the pictograms with me? Help me work out what concepts or words we need to put together to stop gateways being opened?" Fear swirls in her wide eyes as she stares at me. It's the final piece of the puzzle I've been trying to put together—she doesn't want to use magic herself. "I don't know enough about magic to do this on my own."

"Of course." I file the knowledge away, making a note to talk to her about it the next time we're alone. It could be because Matthew has been nothing but hateful to her for saving him, but the churning in my gut tells me it's something else. Something deeper.

*

Kim and I spend the rest of the afternoon sitting by the grimy windows, reading through the book Dan West gave to us. Sophie supplies us with paper, pens and pencils before leaving to check in with her parents, allowing me to make a cheat sheet of the pictograms and their rough meanings. It should help, but it doesn't. Nor does the translation we have of the gateway spell. Neither of us know where to start and Matthew's looming presence doesn't help. He's not standing over us, or even near us, but he hasn't stopped watching us. At one point, I turned my back on him, but I could still sense him staring at me.

The light begins to fail outside and the sky turns to a muted shade of mauve. I grab the camping light and bring it over, but it doesn't help much.

Kim growls and rubs her hands over her face. "It would help if we knew *why* the pictograms work." She stares at me. "Humans don't have magic and I can't think of any reason why it *should* work."

"Can you think of any reason it shouldn't?" I ask.

She raises an eyebrow. "Oh, I don't know. The laws of Physics, maybe?"

"Then my magic shouldn't work either."

"That's different."

"Is it?" I tug the book away from her and lay it down on the floor, before scooting closer so our knees are touching and I can hold her hands. "Not everything in the world has a scientific explanation... yet. Science is founded on experimentation and repeatable results. If we can see the evidence of those results, then it must be possible, even if we don't know why."

She scrunches her lips up, her chin tilted up a fraction.

"Newton didn't publish his theories on gravity until 1687, but it had always existed. Before then, people didn't randomly float off the face of the earth, did they?"

She laughs and shakes her head. "You're such a nerd."

"Me? Why?"

"1687? I'm not sure I could have even gotten the century right."

As heat flushes my cheeks, I almost let go of her hands, but force myself to keep hold, running my thumbs over her skin. "I... had a lot of time to read."

"I'm sorry."

"Don't be."

Kim glances towards Matthew, who turns his back on us and moves further away, out of earshot. "Can you talk to me AJ? Can you tell me a little of what happened?"

I shake my head.

"One of the hardest things about losing Charley and knowing why, was not being able to talk to anyone about it. Matthew vanished and no one else knew the truth." She pulls her hand away from mine and presses it against her chest. "I had to keep everything inside and it hurt so much. But you do have someone you can talk to. You don't have to keep everything inside."

She slips her hand back into mine, but her words have made me too numb to close my fingers around hers.

"I know Saul made you choose between Matthew and your mum. You obviously chose her and he killed her anyway."

I bow my head.

"What do you feel guiltier for? What happened to Matthew or her death? Because I don't think you could have prevented either. Not really. What if you had called Saul's bluff and chosen to save Matthew? What if you had refused to use your healing magic to help his plan. What then?"

I don't know the answers. Even if I did, I'm not sure my voice would work right now. My throat feels hoarse from the effort of holding back tears.

Kim takes a deep breath. "AJ, Gage told me that Saul was planning on taking your magic away from you."

I gasp, my eyes widening as I take in the implication of what she said.

"He must have known you wouldn't cooperate with him in the long run. It was all a game to him. Hurting you. Manipulating you. I'm sure he got a kick out of it. It made him feel powerful. That's what he wants, remember? To come here and live like a god? He wants to be worshipped and feared by humans. There's nothing for you to feel guilty for. As hard as it might be to accept, he was never going to let your mum go. There was nothing you could have done to save her. If anything, by playing his games long enough to escape, you saved the Changed. Because of your actions, Saul doesn't have your magic. He can't create his hidden army. You should be proud of yourself, not beating yourself up for things he did."

It doesn't make me feel any better. Nothing will. Mum is still gone. Matthew is still a breath away from being destroyed.

"This is what he wants," Kim says, her voice soothing. "He wants you to doubt and blame yourself. He wants you to give up. So you can't, because if you do, he'll win. I know you don't want him to win."

"I don't want any of them to win." I grip her hands and raise them to my bent forehead. Her knuckles are cold against my skin, but it helps to ground me.

"Stop beating yourself up, AJ. Please?"

I lift my head, a smile twisting my lips. "Easier said than done."

"I know. If I could wave a magic wand and take your guilt away, I would." She frowns. "No, forget that, I probably wouldn't."

I lay her hands in her lap and then slips my fingertip beneath her chin, raising her face so she's looking directly into my eyes. "Why don't you want to use magic?"

She scowls at me, pressing her lips together until the colour drains from them.

"Something has made you afraid of using magic."

"I hate how you can read me so easily. Also, you're changing the subject away from yourself."

I smile. "I know I don't have any right to ask what I'm about to..."

"But...?"

"It's to do with Gage, isn't it?"

She nods. "How do you know?"

"Two plus two equals four. I'm good at maths, remember?"

She swats her hand across my chest and then sighs. "When he attacked me at the river, I asked him to tell me who opened gateways for him. He didn't, obviously. But he told me that, by wanting to use magic, I wasn't any better than him. And here I am... turning to magic, because I can't think of a better plan."

I move my hands to her upper arms and squeeze them. "You know it isn't true, don't you?"

She nods and then shakes her head.

"You are *nothing* like Gage. Since the moment I met you, all you've ever wanted to do is help people."

"Ditto," she mutters.

"You wanted to know how to use a gateway to get to me. We're trying to use magic now to stop the Baneem from hurting humans. How can any of that make you bad, or make you anything like Gage?"

She shrugs. "It can't."

I lean forward and kiss her forehead. "I'm not the only one who needs to believe in myself again. Am I?"

"No. We're both a mess, aren't we?"

I tip my head from side to side. "A bit."

"But we'll get through it, won't we?"

I kiss her softly on the lips. "Yes." I realise I mean it, both what I said and the kiss. Especially the kiss. I missed Kim so much, but fear and self-hatred were keeping me from her. I kiss her again, deeper and longer than before.

She angles her head back a little, putting distance between us, although I can still feel the warmth of her breath on my face.

"I should go home and get some sleep," she murmurs.

"You should."

She places her hand on the back of my neck, inviting me to kiss her again, to hold her close. We raise up onto our knees, our bodies pressing together. I slide one hand to the small of her back and rest the other against her cheek. I've missed this intense closeness and the sensation of her lips against mine.

"I love you," Kim whispers, her voice tentative and maybe a little scared.

"I love you too." I don't hesitate to say the words, even though I did before. I do love her, more than anything. What Saul did to me is still an open wound, but with her help, it'll heal.

The kiss ends and I nuzzle her nose with mine.

"You should go home," I say, glancing down at the ground. In the light of the lantern, the dust and filth is even more obvious and Matthew is still close, even though he's hidden by the darkness. "Be careful?"

She nods, stands, and makes an attempt to brush the dirt off her jeans. All she manages to do is cover her palms in dust.

"You won't have to stay here much longer," she says with a grimace. "We'll figure out how to stop the Baneem together." She smiles and then turns to leave, but the ring of her phone makes her stop. She pulls it out of her pocket and answers it. "Mum?" Her smile fades and the colour drains out of her face.

I scrabble to my feet and wrap my arms around her, holding her as tears flood her eyes.

# CHAPTER TEN

"Mum?"

"Kim, you need to come to the hospital, now." The wobble in her voice gives way to sobs.

I blink as tears pool in my eyes. AJ is by my side in a heartbeat, wrapping his arms around me.

"What's happened?" I manage to force out.

"There's been a fire... at your father's house."

Fire? Oh God. I pull the phone away from my ear as my stomach twists itself into painful knots of fear. I wish I could give the phone to AJ and let him get answers, whilst I curl up and cry, but I can't. Everyone thinks he left town. I take two deep breaths and then raise the phone again.

"Is Dad okay? Is Chris okay?"

"I don't know. I haven't been allowed to see them yet. The police called me. They said they'd gone to our house first, but no one was home. Where are you Kim? You were meant to be home with Sophie, studying."

I can't think. Dad and Chris have to be okay, they *have* to be.

"Kim, I need you at the hospital."

I start shaking my head. What if Saul has people watching the hospital, ready to follow me all the way back to AJ? I can't go, but I need to.

"Kim?"

I don't know what to say. "Is aunt Sarah with you?"

"Of course, but..."

"Go," AJ mouths. He must be close enough to hear Mum.

I shake my head and mouth back, "What about Saul?"

He leans closer, so he can whisper into my other ear. "We went all the way to and from Dan West's house without any sign of Saul or his lackeys."

I lower the phone and press my hand over it. "We were careful," I whisper. "But what if Saul did this? What if he had something to do with the fire?"

"You have to go."

He's right, but my stomach still churns with fear. "I'm on my way. They'll be okay, Mum."

"I hope so."

I hang the phone up and hug it to my chest, sobbing. AJ holds me tighter still. I glance up at him. He's trying to be brave faced, but I can feel him trembling as more guilt is shovelled onto the already immense pile within him. But by keeping my family in the dark, I left them vulnerable. This is my fault, not AJ's. I should have listened to him. I should have warned them.

"If Saul did this, it was to get to me," AJ says.

I pull away from him and begin to pace. "Don't even suggest handing yourself over to him. Because he won't stop. You know that, don't you? He'll keep hurting me and my family to spite you. It wouldn't solve anything. It would only make things worse. If he has you, he'll be able to strip your magic and destroy the Changed."

"I know."

Of course he does. Except Saul played his hand when he murdered Phailin. He showed how twisted and cruel he really was. I doubt AJ will allow himself to get duped again.

"I have to tell them the truth," I say. "I have to get them to leave." Assuming Dad and Chris are okay and fit enough to leave the hospital. "The only way they'll be safe is if Saul can't find them."

"And Sophie's family?"

"Yes, except that's easier, because Sophie's dad already knows more than she does."

AJ moves to intercept my manic pacing, placing his hands firmly on my shoulders to stop me. "You need to calm down first."

I place my hand on my forehead. "I can't tell them the truth." I squeeze my eyes shut. "I hate crying."

He pulls me into a firm hug. "You just said you were going to tell them everything."

"I can't. There has to be another way to convince them to leave. There has to be."

"I don't think there is. Kim... they're your parents. You can't keep this secret from them any longer. Call Sophie, get her to meet you at the hospital. She can help you convince them."

I nod, although I'm not sure I believe him. I'm even less sure I can bring myself to tell either of my parents the truth. It'll mean opening up the wound of Charley's death again. It'll mean risking them thinking I'm insane. But surely it's worth it, if it can help keep them safe?

*

Sophie isn't waiting for me when I arrive at the entrance to the accident and emergency department. Instead, her dad is. I've avoided him as much as possible since he tried to shoot me, except when I needed his help to get Matthew from AJ's flat to my house. I know what happened wasn't his fault. He was manipulated by Taylor. He was scared and trying to protect his family. But knowing it doesn't make me feel any less uneasy around him, even though I'm sure he'd never do anything to hurt me again. He loves Sophie too much to betray her like that.

Despite it being Saturday, it looks like he's dressed for work in smart black trousers, polished shoes and a mid-thigh length black woollen coat. Or maybe he's dressed for a funeral. I hesitate instead of approaching him, hoping he's not waiting with bad news.

"Kim, we need to talk."

My skin goes cold.

"I haven't been inside yet," he says.

I exhale and shuffle closer. "How much has Sophie told you?"

"Not everything, but enough." He gestures towards the carpark. "Can we talk before you go inside?"

I nod and follow him across the road to find his car and slip into the passenger seat. I can't relax. It isn't that long ago he forced AJ and I into the car at gunpoint.

Simon Jenkins sighs and grips the wheel with his hands. He isn't looking at me, which seems odd.

"You can't tell your parents the truth."

I gape at him. "You think I should keep lying to them?" I shake my head. "If I don't tell them, how am I going to convince them they have to leave until I've stopped the Baneem?"

He stares straight ahead. "And if you do tell them, do you really think they'll leave?"

"Yes." I ball my hands into fists and press them hard against my thighs. "They have to."

"We're parents, Kim. Our first instinct is to protect our children. Whether your parents believe you or not, they aren't going to run away and leave you to face this alone. *If* they let you face it at all." He sighs and shifts position, so he can face me without twisting his neck. "All I want to do is protect Sophie. But I know I can't." He shakes his head. "I couldn't even stand up to Taylor. You had to do it for me. As much as I want to step in and make all this go away, I know you and Matthew have the best chance of doing that."

I can't speak. No words form in my mind. I hadn't realised he had so much confidence in me. It's strange to have a grown man—a judge—tell me I'm stronger than him when it comes to the Baneem. Sophie can't have told him about AJ. It's for the best, but how does she feel about keeping secrets from her dad?

"Do you think the fire was something to do with Saul?" he asks.

I shrug. "I don't know what happened yet." I need to go to Mum. Every moment I spend in this car with Simon, she's alone, worrying about Dad and Chris. "It might be."

"I'll ask some questions," he says. "See if I can find anything out from the fire investigators."

"Thank you."

"Mr Jenkins... As long as Dad and Chris are okay, I need them all to get away from here. I need to know they're safe. If I don't tell them what's going on, how can I get them to go?"

"Let me make the suggestion."

I widen my eyes. "You'd do that?"

He laughs. "If it means I'm helping you make a stand against the Baneem, it's the least I can do." He stares at me, his expression solemn. "Kim, if there's anything else I can do, let me know."

"I will, thank you."

We leave the car and head inside the accident and emergency department. After speaking to the receptionist, a nurse shows us through to a cubicle, where Mum is sitting beside Chris, nursing a Styrofoam cup of coffee. It's not steaming anymore, but it doesn't look like she's drunk any of it. Chris is asleep. There are remnants of black around his nostrils and mouth, but otherwise I can't see any sign of injuries. When Mum sees us, she puts it down on the floor so she can hug me. Her grip is so tight I can barely breathe.

"You can let go, Mum."

"No, I can't."

I wriggle out of her grip. "How is he? How's Dad?"

She glances over her shoulder at Chris. "He'll be fine. The doctor wanted to keep him in overnight for observation. We're waiting for a bed on the children's ward. Although at least while he's here, I can stay with him."

"Smoke inhalation?" Mr Jenkins asks.

Mum nods.

"And Dad?" I say.

"The same and he burnt his hands while getting Chris out of the house." She chokes back tears. "He saved my baby's life."

"Do you know what started the fire?" Mr Jenkins asks.

Mum shakes her head and then sinks back down into the chair. "Why?" she mutters. "Haven't we been through enough as a family since..."

Since Charley died. She begins to sob. I kneel down and wrap my arms around her.

"How bad are Dad's burns?" I ask.

"Second degree. The doctor said he was lucky. With the right treatment, they should heal in a few weeks. He doesn't even need skin grafts." She leans forward on her knees, sinking her head into her hands. "They could have died."

"But they didn't," I say, stroking her knee. "They're both going to be okay."

She takes my hand and clings onto it. "I don't know what I'd do if I lost Chris. Or you."

"Or Dad?"

She stares at me through tear drenched eyes for a moment and then nods in agreement. "We might be divorced, but I still care for him."

But she doesn't love him. This is old ground I'm not prepared to tread right now.

"Do you know how long Dave has to stay in hospital for?" Mr Jenkins asks.

She shakes her head. "They are cleaning and dressing the burns now. He'll need help keeping them clean and changing the dressings each day." She purses her lips and turns back to me. "I was thinking of asking him to come home until he's better."

I raise my eyebrows. "Really?"

"He saved Chris's life. The least I can do is help him. Besides, he can't go home until the damage is repaired."

"It sounds like you all need a break," Mr Jenkins says.

Mum glances at him. "A break?"

He nods. "You've been through a lot. Maybe you should go away. Think of it as a retreat. Spend time together as a family."

Mum squeezes my hand. "What do you think, Kim?"

"I... have mock exams," I manage to stutter.

"After Christmas," Mum says.

"There's still another week before the holiday starts."

Mum's lips droop. "You're right. It was a lovely idea, Simon, but Kim needs to be in school."

Simon grins. "How about this then—Diane really wanted to go away this Christmas, but I have work commitments, so can't go. Why don't you, Chris and Dave go somewhere with Diane and Sophie and Kim can stay with me. I'll make sure they get on with their revision."

"What about Christmas?"

"The three of us can come and meet you on Christmas Eve."

I twist my head to stare at Mr Jenkins. It's not a promise I would have made, but I understand why he has. He smiles at me, though it does little to reassure me. Even though I know it's the best thing, I don't want my parents to go away. Besides, I need them. I want them to hug me and tell me everything is going to be okay. I want them to be able to make the world feel less crazy, like they did when I was small. But that would mean telling them what's really going on and I can't do that. I won't do that.

Mum starts to shake her head. "I don't know..."

"It's a perfect idea, Mum," I say. "At least think about it?"

She nods once, though she looks far from convinced.

We're distracted as a nurse enters the small cubicle. "We have a bed for Chris," she says in a cheerful voice. "Would you like to go up with him, Mrs Welles?"

Mum nods and then wrings her hands. "What about Dave?"

"We'll wait here," Mr Jenkins says. "That way Kim can see her father."

"All right."

"You'll need to go back to the waiting room," the nurse says. "But someone will come and get you shortly."

I give Mum a final hug. We hang back, waiting until Chris's bed is wheeled away, with Mum walking by his side down the corridor. I hate seeing him so fragile and Mum so lost. Mum was right. They've both been through far too much. We all have.

*

"Miss Welles?" a nurse says, disturbing me from my doze. Beside me, Mr Jenkins stirs.

"Is Dad okay?" I ask.

The nurse smiles. "A little groggy from the painkillers, but otherwise okay. Would you like to see him before he's moved up to a ward?"

Mr Jenkins stands when I do, but I motion for him to sit down. He raises his eyebrows in a questioning fashion.

"Do you mind if I go alone?"

"Of course not. Are you sure you'll be all right?"

Is he asking if I'm going to pour my heart out to Dad? "I'll be fine."

He grabs a broadsheet newspaper from a low table and sits down again. The pages rustle as he flicks it open.

"Just a few minutes, okay?" the nurse says, once she's shown me to Dad's cubicle.

I nod, tears stinging my eyes.

Dad is laying on his back, hooked up to a drip, eyes closed. His hands lay on top of the sheet and cellular blanket, fingers bent and tense. They're covered in what looks like cling-film, with open weave gauze dressings laid over the top, allowing me to see the angry burns beneath. Heat flushes through me, then, as I approach the bed, my skin feels deathly cold. My stomach churns and my legs wobble, forcing me to hold onto the safety rail with shaking hands. Was this how Mum and Dad felt when they saw me laying in a hospital bed after Charley died?

I bow my head. "I'm sorry, Dad. I'm so, so, sorry."

This is all my fault. I put my entire family in danger by standing up to the Baneem. Unable to hold Dad's hand, I rest mine on his arm and stand in silence, staring at him. Dad has always seemed so big and strong. When I was a kid, I worshipped him like a superhero. Now he looks fragile. His weak state takes my breath away. Seeing him like this is completely wrong, it's like he's Superman afflicted by kryptonite.

Thoughts race through my head. What if the fire had been set when he and Chris were asleep? What if... I squeeze my eyes shut and take deep breaths. He's here. Alive. He'll be fine.

"Hey, Kimmie." Dad's voice is cracked and faint.

His voice forces me to open my eyes. He clears his throat and coughs. I pour him some water from a jug on his side table and help him to drink. As much as I hate his nickname for me, it feels so good to hear him say it.

"Mum tells me you're a hero," I say, forcing a smile to my lips.

He coughs again and then groans, his eyes flickering. "Hardly. I did what any parent would do."

"Do you know what happened?"

"No. We were watching a movie together and then I heard an odd noise from the hallway." He winces. "I was stupid and opened the door without checking. The hall was full of flames."

I squeeze his arm. "You weren't to know. How could you have known?"

He shrugs and then hisses in pain. "It's how I burned my hands. We escaped through the window." His eyes become distant and watery. "Is Chris okay?"

"He's fine. Sleeping off the smoke inhalation. He'll be able to go home tomorrow."

Dad smiles. "Thank God."

"Like I said, you're his hero." I grin at him, hoping it will make him feel a little better.

The nurse pulls the curtain back. "I'm sorry, but we're going to move you now, Mr Welles."

"Dave, please," he says. "Come visit tomorrow, Kimmie?"

I nod, even though I'm not ready to leave. I lean down and kiss his forehead. "I love you, Dad. Get well soon, okay?"

"I'll do my best."

*

Mr Jenkins waits outside in the car, while I nip inside to throw some clothes in a bag. We didn't really talk about where I would spend the night, it was more an unspoken agreement that it would be best if I stayed at Sophie's. As I jog down the stairs, a bang catches my attention. I freeze, one foot still on the bottom step. Cutlery clanks as a drawer is shut hard. The kettle bubbles as it boils. *Not again.* I can't move. Mum can't be here. She would have stayed with Chris.

It could be aunt Sarah, but the goosebumps prickling my skin tell me otherwise.

I should leave. Run out the door and into Mr Jenkins's car. But I'm done with letting myself be scared. I take a deep breath and open the door to the kitchen. The strong scent of coffee hits me first. I stand and stare at the burly man who is sitting at the breakfast bar, sipping from a white mug like he's got every right to be there.

"Hello, Kim. It is *Kim*, isn't it?"

"Who are you?"

He smiles and stretches one hand out, palm up. Flames burst into existence a fraction above his skin, leaping and crackling for a couple of seconds until he balls his fist, dismissing the magic. Flame Guy. I grit my teeth.

"You started the fire at Dad's house, didn't you?" I stalk forward, arms folded, glaring at him. "You could have killed him and my brother."

"But I didn't." He sips at the coffee again.

"If you're here to gloat, don't bother."

He chuckles. "I'm here to give you a message from Saul."

I tilt my head to the side. "Too chicken to come himself, is he? Afraid of a seventeen-year-old human?"

The humour in Flame Guy's face drains away, his lips drawing out into a thin, serious line. "Believe me, Kim, you don't want Saul to come here."

He's right, but I lift my chin, hoping it adds to my visage of false confidence. "What's the message?"

"He wants Aran back."

"He's not here."

"We both know he *was*," Flame Guy says. "Whether he's still around, or done a runner is another matter. Not that Saul cares. As far as he's concerned, you either know where Aran is, or how to get hold of him." He puts the mug down and rubs at his neck. "Do yourself and your family a favour, and tell me where he is."

"Even if I did know, I'd never betray him."

Flame Guy sighs. "I figured you'd say that." He stands up and looks down at me.

He's a lot taller than me, broad and muscly. Even without his magic, I wouldn't want to get on his bad side.

"Well, I've given you the message and fair warning that things will get worse for you. What you do next is up to you. But, if you change your mind, tell Aran to go to his flat." He turns towards the back door.

"If you hate Saul, why are you working for him?"

Flame Guy pauses and glances at me over his shoulder. "What makes you think I hate him?" He asks quizzically.

"The look of regret in your eyes. You made sure Dad and Chris could escape, relatively unharmed, didn't you?"

His jaw twitches. "Let's say I don't have any choice but to work for Saul."

"But you don't agree with what he's doing."

He shakes his head. "I don't have to agree with it."

I step towards him. "You must realise he's a dangerous lunatic. Wanting to swap souls between bodies? How can you let him do it?"

He stuffs his hands into his pockets and bows his head. "Do you know what it's like, being hunted by the Shamari?"

"No. But they wouldn't hunt you if you stayed in Uralahnd, would they?"

He lets out a sharp laugh. "No, that's true."

"Why? Why take the risk at all? Is it worth it? Coming here and screwing with humans? Do you get a kick out of it? Does it make you feel powerful?"

I doubt he'll explain anything to me. AJ said Uralahnd could be beautiful. How could earth be better than a potential paradise?

"Look, you're brought up to say please and thank you and to respect your elders, right?"

I nod, wondering what his point is.

"Well imagine growing up, having *everyone* around you tell you how much better earth is and how humans don't deserve it. How you're destroying it with wars. How the advancements you've made because of your lack of magic are literally killing this planet. Why did the Creator give *you* a readymade world, whilst ours is only beautiful when we're all working together to make it blossom?"

Is he telling me all this to justify the things he's done? "You stopped working together because you were jealous?" I ask. Whatever the reason for his chatty mood, I'm happy to use it to my advantage.

He nods. "Pretty much. Uralahnd fell to ruin long before I was born. There are beautiful pockets of it, don't get me wrong. Not everyone has given up on it. But too many Baneem have."

"Why don't you join those Baneem?"

He tips his head back as his shoulders shake in a silent laugh. "Because Saul would hunt me down and kill me. You don't cross someone like Saul."

He makes Saul sound like a Mafia or gang boss. Then again, it's probably a good comparison.

"Saul won't stop looking for AJ," Flame Guy says. "He can't execute his plan without AJ's healing magic."

"Why not?"

Flame Guy's shoulders tense.

"What difference does it make if you tell me? What can I do to stand up to Saul? I'm just a human."

He stares at me warily.

"I couldn't even find a way to rescue AJ," I remind him. "I couldn't do anything to protect my Shamari friend when he was attacked. I just stood there, helpless, whilst the Baneem inside AJ's mum was destroying him." It's not exactly the truth, but he doesn't need to know that. "Why does Saul need AJ so badly?"

Flame Guy clamps his lips together.

I fold my arms and stare down at me. "Okay, so you don't want to talk. Fine. I don't blame you. I'm a kid and you're scared of Saul. Let me tell you why I think Saul needs AJ and his magic. I saw what was happening to Phalin whilst she was posessed. Her body was burning from the outside in. She would have needed healing. I also bet it hurts like hell to have your soul ripped out of your body, stuffed into someone else's and then put back into your own. It must cause some serious damage. Maybe even potentially fatal damage. So without AJ's magic, Saul would be asking Baneem to sacrifice themselves for *his* gain. Am I close?"

Flame Guy's skin has paled to a sickly shade.

"How long do you think he's going to keep searching for AJ? Don't you think he's going to get bored and just get on with his plan anyway? He's crazy enough."

Flame Guy pinches his lips. "No."

We stare at each other, panic flitting through Flame Guy's eyes.

"I've delivered my message," he says hurriedly. "Saul has someone watching Aran's flat all the time. Tell him to hand himself over."

This time, I don't stop him leaving.

# CHAPTER ELEVEN

Knowing Kim's dad and brother will be okay doesn't stop my desire to figure out how to use the pictograms. It's all I can do whilst Kim is visiting them. Sheets of paper are strewn all over the floor of the warehouse, all scribbled on with pencil, most crossed out with angry slashes. They've become dust stained already, grey flecks tarnishing the white weave of the paper.

Matthew watches in silence as I work, like a prison guard making sure I don't do anything illegal. I expected him to turn on me last night and blame me for what happened to Kim's family. I half wish he'd get any outburst over with. As it is, I'm tense with the memory of his thinly veiled threats, which doesn't help my concentration.

I stare at my latest concept, with no hope it would work. I've been trying to work within the constraints of twenty-two pictograms, forcing them to fit the effect I want, with little success, even though the all have multiple meanings. I've learnt from the book that each pictogram represents a sound, so together, they form words and sentences. But that isn't how the gateway used the pictograms. That spell relied on their individual concepts. I tear the sheet off and cast it aside, allowing it to drift to the ground in the breeze coming through the half-broken door behind me.

I grab Dan West's book and stand, scanning over the pictograms and their meanings again as I walk round the perimeter of the vast room, stretching my legs and easing away the pins and needles plaguing them. Then I stop, staring at the seventh pictogram in the list. It's a moment where I almost want to slap myself in the face and curse my own stupidity.

I turn back and scoop up the blunt pencil, but leave the pad of paper where it is. I'm done playing around with ideas. I go to the door and raise the pencil to the wood to draw a circle, then hesitate. The gateway diagram is formed around a wheel. There's no other way to describe the divided circle. But a wheel represents motion and momentum, which is the opposite of what I—what *Kim*—wants to achieve. I tap the pencil against my chin and stare at the door.

Perhaps I can use tet as both a pictogram and the visual image of the spell. I draw a large circle, with a cross inside, dividing it into four. Moving right to left, I place a pictogram in each space: *tsade, aleph, dalet* and *zayin*, which I'd ignored over and over again. I draw the final pictogram, a second iteration of dalet, over the centre of the cross. Holding my palm an inch away from the diagram, I stare at the glyphs and run through the meaning in my mind: *I desire the strength to surround the door and cut off the pathway.* I struck my palm across *mem* to activate the gateway, but I haven't used it this time. I take a deep breath and press my palm against *dalet*, not really expecting anything to happen.

A sharp light bursts out from the diagram, forcing me to stagger back. It surrounds the door and the hole at the bottom that we've been using for access, hugging it for a second before seeping into the wood and disappearing.

"What have you done?" Matthew asks, striding closer.

Ignoring him, I crouch and try to slip through the gap. An invisible force bars my path. A stupid grin spreads across my face.

"I did it."

My eyes narrow and I focus on the pencil marks. They are becoming fainter and misshapen, as though an invisible wind is pushing them away from their rightful places. My stomach drops. Once I'm no longer able to tell what it was

I'd drawn, I attempt to put my hand through the gap. It passes through with no resistance. I lean forward, hunching my shoulders.

I shudder. The gateway I opened to escape Uralahnd didn't stay open for long, either, which means blood is an easy thing for the magic to erode as well.

I push back and twist, so I'm leaning against the wall beside the door. My gaze falls on the camping equipment Sophie brought me. There's a knife amongst the collection of things.

"If we etched the symbols in, it would last longer."

"We?" Matthew asks.

I shake my head. "You know what I mean." I sigh. "Not that it matters."

Matthew raises his eyebrows.

I gesture towards the door. "The entrance exists and will be there as long as the building stands, whether there's a door or not. But the entrance to Uralahnd isn't a fixed point. It's a hole that's torn through both the fabric of our world and the Baneem's." I tip my head back against the bricks. "We can't forbid everyone, everywhere from opening a gateway."

I toss the book and pencil aside and then use the wall for support to push myself onto my feet. "We need help, Matthew."

He stares at me, his eyebrows tugging down to hood his eyes.

"We need the Shamari."

He begins to shake his head.

"I know I can send you home."

"No."

"You can get healed and ask for help."

"No," Matthew says, his tone low and dangerous. "We've been through this already. I will not allow you to use magic on my behalf."

"Why are you being so damned stubborn and selfish?" I demand, stalking over to him. "A Baneem killed you."

"I know that."

"You've spent four hundred years trying to stop them doing more harm. Now you have a chance to stop the Baneem for good and you're running away from it because you're afraid of using a bit of magic? Coward."

Matthew narrows his eyes. "I'm not a coward. I am telling you it won't work. Do not try to turn me into the villain here."

"I'm not."

"Yes, you are. You can't deflect your guilt onto me."

I glare at Matthew. "That's not what I'm doing."

"Isn't it?" Matthew demands. "If I thought human magic could reach the Shamari, I would allow you to use it. But it can't. From everything we've discerned, it's clear a few power hungry, greedy humans managed to use our glyphs to develop a form of ritual magic, so they could help the Baneem cross over to earth. But despite that, I've spent centuries trying to stop the Baneem. Humanity doesn't deserve to suffer at their hands, because of the arrogance of a handful of people. Humans have no innate magic and those few who developed the ritual magic should have left well alone. Meddling in things beyond your scope of understanding is never a good idea and always ends in tragedy."

"How can you say that?" I demand. "Did you understand what you were going to become, when you were transformed into a Shamari? All magic can be used for good. You use it for good."

"I don not use magic," Matthew growls. "What I do is nothing like Baneem magic or human ritual magic. *Nothing*." He bows his head. "What I could do. I direct the power of my soul through individual glyphs. That is *not* magic."

"So that's it? You say no and we're supposed to accept that?"

"Yes."

I shake my head and jab my finger against his chest, anger battling against caution within me. "You said my silence was putting Kim in danger. But so are you. We... *Kim* needs you to be whole again. She needs your strength and your... *abilities* and we need the counsel of the Shamari."

"Not through magic."

"There is no other way," I yell. "I'm sorry about what happened to you, both when you died and when Saul had you attacked. I'm sorry. But you can help us stop the Baneem forever."

Matthew turns his back on me. "Do you think shouting at me is going to change my mind?"

I shake my head, not caring that he can't see me. "I've tried reasoning with you. So has Kim."

"The only reason Kim and her family are in danger is because of Saul," Matthew says.

"That's not true and you know it. Whilst the Baneem can continue to come to earth, she's never going to turn a blind eye to what they're doing. Stopping them will consume her whole life and one day it'll..."

"Kill her?"

"Yes."

Matthew crosses his arms. I can't see his face, but I doubt the golem is showing any expression. Could I overpower him? Knock him out, open a gateway and haul him through? As appealing as the idea is, I'm no match for him physically. He might not have his abilities, but the golem still has the strength of a dozen body builders. I will have to find another way to get him home, no matter how much he ends up hating me.

I retrieve the book, pencil and drawing pad. "I'm going to keep trying. There has to be a way to stop gateways being opened. I won't rest until I've figured it out."

I sit on the camping mat, prop the drawing pad on my knees and try to focus, despite Matthew's cold gaze upon me.

# CHAPTER TWELVE

The sun is barely peaking above the horizon when I make my way to the warehouse. I couldn't sleep, even though Dad and Chris are both out of hospital. They're staying with Mum at aunt Sarah's. It's cramped, but it should only be temporary.

The weak, early morning sun is only just able to penetrate the layer of dirt on the warehouse windows, giving barely enough light to see the interior in muted shades of grey. Matthew nods to me as I crawl inside. He's standing amidst a sea of sheets of paper, all covered in varying chains of pictograms.

AJ is curled up on the camping mat, the sleeping bag pulled up to his cheeks. As I creep closer, I can see his brow is furrowed, his eyes darting from side to side beneath his eyelids. I kneel and press one hand against his cheek, using the other to shake his shoulder, rousing him from his dream. His eyes flick wide open and his breathing quickens. But as he focuses on me, he relaxes and sighs, pressing his palm against my hand on his cheek.

"Thank you."

I pull my hand away from him and gesture to the paper. "You've been busy."

AJ props himself up on his elbows and casts his gaze around the room, his mouth downturned. "I've not had much success." He glances at the windows. "What time is it?"

I check my phone. "A little past eight."

He strokes a strand of hair away from my face. "Couldn't sleep?"

I shake my head.

"How are your dad and Chris?"

"Home." I grimace. "Not home, but out of hospital. They stayed at my aunt's last night. Sophie's dad managed to persuade everyone it was a good idea to go away until after Christmas, for some rest and relaxation. They're setting off later today."

AJ frowns. "You didn't tell them?"

I fumble with the zip of my coat. "I couldn't. They'd never have gone away without me if I had." I don't expect him to understand. His mum knew about the Baneem. He never had to keep secrets from her, whereas I have to lie to my parents every day. Even though I know it's for the best, I still feel like a terrible daughter every time a lie trips off my tongue.

"I get it," AJ says.

"Do you?" I search his gaze in an attempt to work out if he's telling the truth, or seeking to make me feel better. "Tell me about all this."

He grimaces and pushes himself upright. "I figured out how to stop people going through a doorway."

I grin. "That's great!" My grin fades and I shake my head. He said *doorway* not *gateway*. "That's not great?"

"A doorway is a fixed thing. It exists in one place, all the time."

"But the gateways don't."

"Kim... how did you make the golem permanent?"

I stare at him. "Sorry?"

"I was using pencil to create the barrier spell. When it was activated, the magic blurred and distorted the pencil marks. Once they were no longer legible, the spell failed."

I nod, thinking back to when I used charcoal to write a pictogram on Matthew's feather to contact him. I only had seconds to try to reach out to him, before both the charcoal and the feather were gone. The woman who used the charcoal to open the gateway for Saul also used charcoal. It can't be a coincidence. I glance at Matthew. He's not moved from where he was standing but he is watching us. It's a safe bet that he's also listening to us.

I take a deep breath. "I guess we know why charcoal was used to open the gateways."

"Why?" Matthew asks, his voice laced with genuine curiosity. He moves closer, as though he's willing to participate in the conversation.

I doubt he will be once I've continued. "It would get blurred quickly, so a gateway wouldn't stay open long. I guess whoever came up with the ritual in the first place was worried they might be letting demons through. If the gateway closed quickly, not much could come through."

"They may as well have been summoning demons," Matthew says. He turns to walk away again.

"Matthew..." My voice stops him. "You told me I had to use charcoal to contact you. Remember?"

"I remember." His voice is taut.

"So maybe... maybe humans *did* learn about ritual magic from the Shamari."

"The creator made the True Shamari in order to stop the Baneem hurting humans," Matthew says, but it sounds more like he's speaking by rote than with passion or conviction.

"Matthew..."

He hunches his shoulders and stalks away, into the early morning gloom on the other side of the warehouse.

AJ touches my hand. "Kim... the golem. How did you make it permanent?"

I shrug. "I'm not sure. Professor West showed me how to make a *shem*, but that was just Hebrew script on paper. I used charcoal." I bite my lip. "But it didn't work." I widen my eyes, excitement bubbling up inside. "I wrote *emet* on the forehead of the golem in the clay itself. It vanished when Matthew's soul was fused with the golem and it looked more human... well, less like clay, anyway—"

AJ grips my shoulders. "Slow down. *Emet*?"

I shake my head. "It means *truth*."

"Truth? How could truth animate a golem?"

"I think it's something to do with God," I say with a shrug. "Maybe I should have asked more questions, so I could understand *what* I was doing, but Matthew was dying. I didn't have time for a lesson in Hebrew philosophy." Although I feel fairly stupid for not asking those questions, because maybe that knowledge might have been able to help us now.

"It worked," AJ says. "That's what matters." Truth," he muses. *Aleph*, *mem* and *tav*? Eh—m—t? Uh, the other way around, anyway. I can't get used to the whole right to left thing."

I nod. "Professor West said that by removing the Hebrew letter for *eh* from the head of the golem, truth turns into *met*, which means death. Supposedly doing that stops the golem from being *alive*." I screw my face up. "I believed it could work because I've seen too much magic to be skeptical. Besides, it *had* to work, to save Matthew's life."

AJ nods. "It was the same when I used the gateway. It was my only chance of escaping Saul." His gaze becomes distant. "I've been trying to think of a different way to stop the gateways from opening, or being used, but..." He waves his hand towards the mess of paper and then lets it flop into his lap. "But now I know we can use the pictograms to create words. We don't have to trap ourselves by only using their concepts."

I smile, glad of the breakthrough. "And from there, we'll figure it out together."

"I was hoping I could solve it myself, so you didn't have to. So you could concentrate on your family. I wanted to take *one* burden away from you."

I gather his hand up and kiss it. "You don't have to," I whisper. "You've got enough troubles of your own, without trying to lift weight from my shoulders. But I love that you wanted to." I lean forward and kiss him softly. "I love you."

The right side of his mouth hooks up into a lopsided smile, which makes butterflies flutter in my stomach. "I love you, too."

"Okay, so we can't stop the gateways being opened. Maybe we could find a way to close them faster when they are opened."

AJ frowns. "Surely we'd have the same problem? We can't cast a permanent, world-wide spell that can seek out gateways."

"What if we're thinking about this all wrong?"

He pinches his eyebrows together and stares at me. I pick up the remains of the drawing pad and the pencil AJ has been using, but instead of trying to draw any of the pictograms, I draw two worlds. At least, I try to. They end up looking like a pair of uneven circles, fairly close to one another.

"Sophie's the one who can draw," I saw, as I write E in one and U in the other. "Where is Uralahnd? It can't be one of the planets in our solar system, so *where* is it?"

AJ shrugs. "I don't know. A parallel universe?"

I can't tell if he's serious or not. I know physicists have hypothesised parallel universes do exist. It's no more crazy an idea than believing magic and not-angels exist. I draw two more circles, beside the first two, except this time they are touching one another.

"Is there something between them? Or are they right next to each other, touching?"

AJ rakes his teeth over his lower lip. "I don't think they're touching. When I escaped through the gateway... it wasn't like walking through a door." He closes his eyes, his features becoming pinched and troubled. "I don't remember much. I was falling unconscious. But I had to pull myself through. There was definitely *something* in between, but it felt like *nothingness*. Like a void I could tumble into and lose myself in."

"But you didn't," I say, stroking the back of his hand. "What if we could work a spell in the space between our two worlds?"

He stares at me, blinking at me with shimmering eyes.

"If it truly is a void, then there can be nothing there, right?"

He nods.

"So we could put some kind of destructive spell there. One that destroys anything that appears in the void.

"Like a gateway."

I nod. "Gateways would still open, on this side at least, but then it would be destroyed before anyone could go through."

"And it would never get as far as opening in Uralahnd, because it would be destroyed too quickly." He picks up Professor West's book, leafs through the pages and then taps one of the pictograms. *Shin*. Destroy.

"Another way might be to put destructive magic there."

He hisses in a sharp breath. "Saul's magic?"

I nod.

"We don't know how to strip magic. Or what happens to a Baneem when you do." He shakes his head. "It might kill him, Kim. I *know* he's a monster. I *know* he's done terrible things. But killing him? I don't think I could do that."

Nor do I. "You're right, it's a stupid idea."

"No, it's not. Putting a spell in the void, though? That's an amazing idea." His eyes sparkle. "I think we could figure that out, but..." He glances in the direction Matthew went, but there still isn't enough light for us to make out the other side of the warehouse. "What if the Shamari also have to travel through the void to get to... wherever home is for them?"

My shoulders slump. "It would stop them from coming and going, too."

AJ nods. "Which might not be a bad thing, in the long run. If the Baneem can't get here, then the Shamari won't be needed to protect us anymore. But, it will also stop Matthew being able to get home."

"He'd be trapped on earth, in the golem, forever." I squeeze my eyes shut. We can't force that fate upon him. "We have to send him home first."

"But how?" AJ asks. "He won't let us open a gateway for him."

I ball my hand into a loose fist. "I'm done pandering to Matthew. I think it's time we... *I*... made him see sense."

"Is that a good idea? He seems volatile at the moment."

I shrug. "What choice do we have? We can't trap him here. If he won't listen to sense, then we'll have to take him home against his will."

AJ's eyes widen. "Wait... you want to go to..." he presses his lips together.

"Heaven?" I offer.

He responds with a nervous laugh. "How do we even know *we* can go to wherever home is for Matthew? He's a walking talking soul, remember? We don't even know if *home* is physical."

"It must be. The Shamari imprison the Baneem there."

"There's also the small problem of me being Baneem."

"Half Baneem," I say with a smile. "And the magical quality of your soul is hidden, remember?"

He nods, but his frown betrays his uncertainty.

"Where else are we going to be safer from Saul, while we figure out how to put a spell in the void, than in a place he can't get to?" I stand.

"Where are you going?"

"To talk to Matthew." I force a confident smile to my lips. "I'm sure I can make him see sense."

I leave AJ to ponder the pictograms and our new idea, whilst I make my way across the warehouse floor. It feels more cavernous in the dark. I'd hate to have to spend the night here, I'm not sure how AJ can stand it, let alone sleep.

Matthew is sitting in the furthest corner, his knees drawn up and the palms of his hands pressed against the ground.

"Were you listening?" I ask.

He shakes his head. "My hearing isn't that good."

"AJ and I have a plan, but we need to send you home first."

"Not this again."

I crouch down in front of him. "If our plan works, you might be trapped here forever."

He narrows his eyes. "Why?"

"We're going to put a destructive spell in the void between the worlds. The void the Baneem have to pass through to get here. I'm betting you and the other Changed have to pass through it to get to heaven, too."

I wait for Matthew to say something, but he remains silent.

"Let us open a gateway to send you home."

"No. Using magic goes against everything I believe."

I let out a growl. "I don't want to hear it, Matthew. I've listened to all your objections and they all boil down to one thing: fear. You're afraid."

He turns his face away, his upper lip curling into a snarl.

"You're afraid that you're going to find out that everything you've believed is a lie. Maybe you will, but do you really think running from it is the answer?" I edge round so I can stare into his dark eyes. "When I discovered magic existed, it would have been easy for me to bury my head in the sand and refuse to believe any of it. But I didn't. I faced it."

Matthew stands and turns his back on me, shaking his head. For some reason, his action doesn't fill me with despair. I feel calm, as though I've quelled the storm of doubt that's been raging within me since I made my promise to AJ. I know what we have to do. I believe we can do it. Our biggest obstacle is Matthew's stubbornness.

"I'm done putting your ego above everything else. We need to stop gateways being used. It's the best way of stopping Saul and the rest of the Baneem. We don't need your help. We sure as hell don't need your approval. And if you really, truly want to spend the rest of your existence here, trapped in clay, then fine. We'll stop trying to help you. But I will not feel guilty for the idiotic choice you have made."

I walk away, back towards AJ. Either Matthew will come around, or he won't and we'll have to get him home by force. Despite my words, I can't stop worrying about him. He's helped me too many times to forsake him now, just because he's being an arrogant jerk. But I also need to focus on our tentative new plan. The faster AJ and I can figure out the destruction spell and how to get it into the void, the sooner Saul will no longer be a threat to any of us.

*

"Are you sure you don't want to come?" Mum asks, as she gives me yet another hug.

It feels like we've been standing outside Sophie's house for an hour, saying goodbye and hugging over and over. Not that

Mrs Jenkins seems to mind, as she waits in the driver's seat of her silver car, chatting to Dad who is sitting in the front passenger seat. In the back, Chris looks bored and keeps giving me evil stares. I'm not sure if it's because he's fed up of the long goodbye, or if it's because he wants me to go with them.

"We've got a lot of revision to do," I say.

"Besides, Dad will bring us in time for Christmas," Sophie says. "So we'll see you in a few days."

"I know," Mum breathes. "I'm just worried, that's all."

"Don't be," Sophie says. "Dad will keep an eye on us. We'll be fine, promise."

"You'd better go," I say, half pushing her towards the car. "Or it'll be midnight before you get there."

Mum nods, gives me another hug and then gets into the car. She puts the window down and leans out. "Call me."

"I will."

"Study hard." She waves at me as Mrs Jenkins starts the engine and backs out of the drive and onto the street.

It's weird seeing Mum and Dad going away on a holiday together, but I try not to let it give me hope they might one day reconcile. Mum made it quite clear that she had fallen out of love with Dad. She never was able to explain why, even when I pressed her on the issue.

"So," Sophie says, looping her arm around my shoulders once the car has vanished round a corner. "What's the plan?"

We head inside, where I explain the vague plan AJ and I had come up with earlier.

"We got a good way towards working out a potential ritual, but it's not really something we can try out. We're not even positive there really is a void between our two worlds."

Sophie pours us both a drink of cold lemonade. "Sounds like we need to do some research. Open a gateway and *look*."

I accept the drink and sip at it, wrinkling my nose as the bubbles tickle me. "We don't know how long a gateway is open for. AJ said it depends on how long it takes for the magic to disrupt the pictographs. If we used ink, rather than charcoal or pencil, it might last long enough to investigate what really lies in between the entrance and the exit. We also don't know how to make the spell permanent," I say.

"What if you don't have to?"

I stare at her, not understanding.

"Let's just say I've been opening gateways for a Baneem," she says. "I go to open one and it doesn't work. I try again and it doesn't work. How many times am I going to try before I decide it's not possible anymore?"

I shrug.

"And once I believe it's not possible, I'm not going to bother teaching anyone else, am I? In fact, I'm probably going to screw up the instructions and throw them away." She smiles. "We don't live in an age where people are trying to discover magic any more. We have technology. We have things our ancestors couldn't even have dreamt of."

"The spell just has to last long enough."

She nods. "Use chemicals to etch the spell into metal. If you do it deeply enough, it should last a good amount of time. Possibly months, or even years."

I put the glass down on the side and hug her.

"What was that for?" she asks once I've let her go.

"You're brilliant."

She laughs. "Hardly. You just needed a fresh perspective." Her eyes light up with excitement. "Let's go on a magical field trip."

*

Two hours later I'm standing in the warehouse, clutching a length of metal, with pictograms scratched into the end. They aren't deep and they're crooked, but I hope they'll be good enough for a test in the space between earth and Uralahnd. They're also not my handiwork, but AJ's, using the now blunt camping knife.

"Do you think this will work?" I ask.

He was silent whilst Sophie and I were explaining our *magical field trip* plan. Matthew voiced concern, held back rage making his voice gravelly. Right now, he's pacing up and down close to the entrance, shaking his head every so often as though he's formulating arguments and then dismissing them. By now, he should have realised I'm stubborn, especially where the safety of my friends and family are concerned. It doesn't matter what he says, I won't listen. We have to find out everything we can about the space between the worlds, so we can stop gateways being opened.

"I don't remember enough from using the gateway to know," AJ says, his words measured. "There was something there, but it felt like nothing. What if by trying to stay there, if only for a few minutes, you get trapped?" He chews on his lower lip. "I'd feel better if I were going with you."

I shake my head. "I need you to open the gateway and keep it open, so we can get back."

He frowns, wrinkles forming across his brow and slashing down the top of his nose. "What if you *can't* get back?"

I widen my eyes and shake my head. I hadn't wanted to think about that possibility, but now that AJ has voiced it, my skin crawls with goosebumps.

"Who says it's a two-way door?" AJ asks.

I shrug his concern away, even though I feel it acutely myself. "It has to be? Humans open gateways so Baneem can come through from the other side."

"That doesn't make it a two-way door, Kim."

My brow crumples in confusion. "I don't understand."

He rubs the back of his head. "I'm being stupid. Ignore me. We've seen nothing to suggest we can only travel one way, rather than either way, through the gateways."

I could leave it there. His words suggest he's brushed away he's fears, but concern is still etched on his face, marring his forehead with deep worry lines.

"We need to be as prepared as possible before Sophie and I step through the gateway." I hesitate and jerk my head back. "What if we stop thinking of it as a gateway, and think of it as a tunnel?"

AJ tips his head to the side a fraction.

I point to the door. "Calling it a gateway suggests it's an entrance. One step and you pass through it, but that's not the case, is it?"

"No. There was *something* between. I had to move through it." Regret tugs his mouth down. "I wish I'd paid more attention."

I touch his face with my fingertips. "You were injured, frightened and trying to escape Saul. You were hardly on an information gathering mission. That's what Sophie and I are about to do."

"A tunnel..." AJ mutters. "Like the ones that go under rivers, or through mountains. They have lane control. The lights show which lanes you can and can't use and they never have green lights on the same lane from both directions."

"That would cause an accident." I scrunch up my lips, remembering holidays to Kent and Wales when I was younger, before my parents' divorce. "Sometimes, they only ever allow traffic to flow in one way. Vehicles in one direction go through the tunnel and vehicles travelling in the other direction are sent a different way, like over a bridge."

AJ chews the inside of his lip. "If that's the case, the person opening the gateway is effectively in charge of lane control. They choose the direction of travel and it doesn't matter what their starting point is."

"*If* we're right. Sophie and I could walk through the gateway and find there's nothing to stop us turning round and coming back again."

He blows a breath over his lower lip. "I'm jumping to worst case scenarios. I'm probably wrong."

"But in case we are right, maybe you should open the gateway to somewhere here. My house, for example."

"Okay."

I stare up at him as he takes hold of my free hand and begins to stroke the back of my hand with his thumb.

He sighs. "It's hard to be positive. Everything we're doing is dangerous. You've had to send your family away." He squeezes his eyes shut. "The Baneem have already taken so much from you, from us both. I don't think I'd cope if we lost more by trying to stop them." He opens his eyes and stares into mine. "If I lost you."

His concern takes my breath away. I push up onto my tiptoes and kiss him. "It'll be fine, I promise. Open a gateway to my home. If it is a one-way door, at least Sophie and I won't be stuck in Uralahnd. Either way, we'll know for sure which theory is right. Are you ready?"

"No, but I'll do it."

I smile, ease my hand away from him and stroke his face. Then I wave the metal rod at him. "How do I make the spell work?"

"Believe in it and tap it?" The corners of his mouth droop. "I don't know, for sure, Kim. I know I said understanding how magic works for us didn't matter, but I'd like to know a little more."

"Maybe we *do* have magic inside us," I say. "Just not as much as the Baneem do. Or maybe there's magic in the world around us. Maybe that's the *real* reason the Baneem set their sights on earth a couple of thousand years ago. All I know is, we *can* use magic through the use of pictograms and ritual. I'm not even sure the pictograms are important. I think they're a focus."

AJ's frown deepens.

"Gage taught Tia how to work magic through music that she then recorded. Her playing the cello, concentrating on the effect she wanted to achieve, what was that if it wasn't a ritual? The pictograms are the same as her music. They're a tool. A focus. A way to channel the magic to do what we want it to do." I glance at Matthew and then lower my voice to a whisper. "Which is exactly how Matthew uses the pictograms, only he can do it faster and with only one to represent the concept of what he's trying to achieve."

"You think it is magic, then?"

I nod in agreement and then clear my throat, turning from AJ to Sophie. "Ready?"

She nods, grinning from ear to ear. "Magical field trip time."

I doubt she's as confident as she sounds, but I'm glad she's pretending to be.

"This is a stupid idea," Matthew growls.

"You've said that," I say in a bored tone. I glance at AJ. "To my house, okay?"

He nods and starts drawing a gateway on the wall in a permanent marker pen that Sophie grabbed from her art supplies at home. She holds my hand whilst we wait for AJ to complete the diagram. He hesitates when he's finished, holding his palm over the final glyph in the very centre.

"I don't know if I'll be able to find a way to keep it open," he says.

"Just do your best," I say with a smile.

He nods and presses his palm against the glyph. Nothing happens. His eyes widen in shock as he tries again and again. Behind me, Matthew snorts.

"Not helpful," I mutter. "What's wrong?" I ask AJ.

He shrugs. "I don't know."

"Maybe you can't open gateways within the same world?" Sophie says.

Both AJ and I stare at her, making her squirm.

"What? Did I say something stupid?"

"No," AJ says in a glum tone. "I suspect you're right."

"Even more reason to give up this stupid idea now," Matthew says.

AJ knits his eyebrows together as he turns to me. "Maybe he's right."

I roll my eyes, grab his hand and pull him as far away from Matthew as possible. Although the warehouse is vast, I'm sure Matthew's hearing is better than that of a human, though I can't be sure.

"It will be fine," I say.

"What if you get stuck in Uralahnd?" AJ says. "Or in the space between here and there?"

"I know you're scared. You've every reason to be. But it will be fine." He starts to shake his head, but stops when I place my finger over his lips. "Don't open the gateway to Uralahnd."

He jerks his head back a little, takes a deep breath and then waits for me to continue.

"Open it to heaven." I'm not sure what's going through his mind, but the worried expression drains from his face, replaced by stoic blankness. "If Sophie and I get stuck there, you and Matthew will *have* to come and get us."

"He'll hate you for it," AJ breathes. "He'll hate us both."

"I don't need him to like me, I need him to survive. I need him to not be trapped inside the golem."

"What if you can't survive there?"

"Why wouldn't I be able to?"

"Because... Matthew doesn't have to breathe, does he?"

I almost laugh, but hold the sound inside, even though it hurts my chest to do so. "But the Baneem *do*. Believe me, if I have to be stuck on another world, I'd rather be with the Shamari than with the Baneem."

AJ stares at the floor between us. "Okay."

It wasn't the answer I was expecting. I almost want him to object, but the fight seems to have drained out of him.

"Okay," he repeats, striding away to the gateway.

I hurry after him, taking my place beside Sophie again as AJ squeezes his eyes shut, concentrates and then slams his hand against the final pictogram.

The pen marks glow brightly. A rush of energy pushes towards us, almost knocking me over. Sophie and I steady each other.

"Go," AJ says through gritted teeth. "And be fast."

Holding hands, Sophie and I step through the gateway.

# CHAPTER THIRTEEN

One step changes everything. I'm standing in a vortex of wind and light, which forms a brief tunnel in a sea of endless black. The only thing holding me in place is Sophie, who turns and grabs onto me, her teeth clenched as she fights against the pressure to move the couple of steps to the other end of the gateway. We both sink to our knees to stop ourselves from being pushed along by the relentless onslaught of magic. I make the mistake of glancing down, only to realise there's nothing but a rush of light beneath us. Around the corridor of light, there's nothing but an endless void of darkness. My stomach somersaults and I dry heave. Sophie clutches onto me even tighter.

"Do it," she yells above the screech of the wind.

We're both starting to slip, the weight of our bodies not enough to truly anchor us. Already, I can see the gateway in front of us starting to close as it becomes smaller, like watching a camera shutter in slow motion. I nod and raise my trembling hand, which is still clutching the long piece of metal. The wind threatens to rip it from my grasp. The pressure of holding it makes my hand ache and the sharp edges dig into my skin, drawing blood. Trusting Sophie not to let go of me, I raise my other hand. I concentrate on the desire to create light, and press my palm against the glyphs AJ scratched into the metal. Light blooms from the end of it, a soft blue glow that's less intense than the magic around us and almost melancholy in its shade.

"Let it go," Sophie says.

I shake my head. "It'll get dragged through the gateway."

I thrust my hand out of the vortex, screaming as pressure whips against my wrist. There's an awful snapping sound. Pain tears up my arm. My fingers become numb and useless and the metal slips from my grasp. Sophie pulls my hand back in and I hug it to my chest, sobbing.

"Look," Sophie says, staring wide eyed at the length of metal.

It hasn't plummeted into the darkness. Instead, it's floating, drifting further away from us, the mournful blue light providing a beacon in the darkness. Despite the pain, a brief flicker of a smile crosses my lips.

"It worked," I whisper, even though I know Sophie won't be able to hear my words. Relief floods through me, which helps to dampen the pain in my wrist a fraction. Our crazy plan might actually work.

"We have to go back," Sophie says.

She helps me stand and we try to step back into the decreasing gateway, to return to AJ and Matthew. We can't. It's like bumping into plate glass that's so clean and clear you can't even tell it's there. Sophie's face drops in horror. I share her terror. Even though AJ and I had discussed this possibility, I hadn't wanted to believe it. Suddenly, my request for AJ to open the gateway to wherever Matthew is from seems terrible. We know nothing about Matthew's home, not even its name. I keep calling it heaven, but could just as easily be hell. How will the Shamari react to a pair of humans turning up in their world, using a ritual spell?

"Kim?" Sophie asks. "Why can't we go back?"

"It's a one-way gate," I shout, forcing myself to remain calm for her sake. "We have to go forward."

Sophie grimaces. "I guess Uralahnd is better than being trapped here."

I wonder what will happen if the gateway closes and we're still standing here between the worlds? Will the pathway of light vanish from beneath our feet, leaving us drifting endlessly in the darkness?

"Not Uralahnd," I shout. "Heaven." I hope I made the right decision.

Sophie's eyes widen. "Better than being trapped here," she repeats.

She takes hold of my good hand, turns and, together, we allow ourselves to be pushed the couple of steps through the gateway.

As our feet tough solid ground, we both collapse. Oppressive heat beats down on us, making my skin prickle. I'm still sobbing, though it's now from relief as much as from pain. The ground beneath us is solid and covered with thick bladed grass. Flowers are dotted here and there. Somewhere close by I can hear the trickle of water, but I'm not sure if it's from a stream or a fountain. I breathe in and out a few times. The heat is dry and hurts my throat, but it's fresh and helps me feel less queasy. I look up. We're in a garden, which is hemmed in by a massive wall.

"Green," Sophie mutters staring at the way the sunlight plays over her hand, creating a green sheen.

I look up, dragging my good hand away from Sophie so I can shade my eyes. She's right. The sky isn't blue and the sun isn't yellow, both are green. Except they aren't, not really.

"It's some sort of dome," I gasp, not understanding.

Sophie grabs my hand and squeezes it hard. "Kim."

I drop my gaze and stare in the same direction she is. A Shamari is striding towards us from the direction of a single storey building. His huge wings are folded along his back but I can still tell that they're a perfect shade of white, unlike Matthew's mottled feathers. His skin is golden, his hair and eyes dark. Already I can feel the enormity of his presence. As he draws closer, my mind is robbed of all its sense. I can't speak, can't move and I can barely breathe. He stops a pace in front of us, folds his arms and stares down at us, his eyes narrowed. The only thing I can think, is that I must be staring at a true Shamari.

"Who are you?" He demands, his voice a powerful command.

My mouth flaps open and closed as I try to force words into it. I need him to use the glyph of clarity, like Matthew did once, so I can think and talk. I can't answer his question when I'm caught in the intense power of his aura. He doesn't move to help me.

"Why are you here?" he asks instead, even though he must know Sophie and I are paralysed by awe.

"Matthew," I manage, my voice little more than a pained squeak. "Needs help."

The effort of breaking through the power of his aura leaves me breathless. Dark spots form in front of my eyes. The pain in my wrist feels more intense than it had felt seconds before and I find myself falling to the ground. The Shamari saves me from face planting and pulls me to my feet. Next, he drags Sophie up.

"Come with me," he orders.

Even if I wanted to resist, I couldn't. Caught in the power of his aura, Sophie and I have no choice but to follow the Shamari towards the building.

# CHAPTER FOURTEEN

I watch in horror as the magic begins to smudge the permanent ink, slowly disrupting the pictograms. The bright entranceway begins to flicker and shudder, threatening to collapse shut at any second.

"Do something," Matthew hisses.

I clutch the marker-pen tightly and, bracing myself against the tug of the gateway, try to trace over the pictograms to refresh them. But even though I'm sure the wall is still physically there, I can't see it or touch it. I try to draw on the light itself, but there's nothing to press against, nothing physical to make a mark on. For a second I can't breathe and it feels like my heart has stopped beating. Pain clutches my chest, but I refuse to give into it. There must be something I can do. I just have to think. My eyes widen. If I can't refresh the current gateway, maybe I can open a bigger one to envelop it.

I begin to redraw the pictograms in a larger circle around the first. I work as quickly as I can, not wanting my penmanship to be so sloppy that the spell doesn't work. I have to draw those on the bottom quadrant of the circle on the floor. I'm practically laying down as I do so, pressing my toes against the floor to avoid being pulled in. It won't help Kim and Sophie if I end up with them. With only the final, central, pictogram left to draw, I get to my feet and step backwards, staring at the swirling white energy. I can't draw it, let alone activate it. All

I've done is waste time as the gateway loses power. It's so weak now, I'm no longer in danger of being drawn into it.

I throw the marker away with a growl, watching as it bounces on the floor and then rolls into shadow. I grip my hair in my hands. There has to be something I can do. My heart is pounding so hard, it's like my ear is pressed against a large shell, amplifying the frantic rush of my blood through my body.

"It's closing," Matthew says.

"I know that!" I snap. What does he expect me to do? I don't know enough about magic to keep it open. I tried and failed. "Kim!" I yell. "Sophie! You have to come back." *If* they can. And if they can't? I know I've opened the gateway *somewhere*, I'm just not sure where.

Matthew has never told us where *home* is. I certainly wasn't thinking of *heaven* when I opened the gateway, at least not in the way that Kim would think of heaven. Mum taught me it wasn't a permanent place of rest, but a temporary reward for good deeds done in life. For her, *heaven* wasn't a single place, experienced in the same way by everyone. There definitely weren't angels playing on harps and a single, all-seeing god ruling over it all. Focusing on something so unique, fleeting and ethereal would have been foolish. I could easily have dumped Kim and Sophie into outer space. Instead, I concentrated on Matthew and *his* home. A real, physical, tangible place that Kim only calls *heaven* because Matthew has never offered her an alternative explanation.

I scream their names again, louder and louder, over and over, until my throat aches and my voice is hoarse. It feels like a lifetime is passing, when really it's a matter of seconds. I kept calling, even as the gateway gives a final shudder and snaps shut, leaving me staring at the smudged glyphs and lines I'd drawn. Guilt floods through me, making my shoulders sag and tears sting my eyes. I should have found a way. I should have tried harder.

Matthew slams into me like a locomotive, pushing me backwards until I crash against the unforgiving concrete walls.

He closes his fist around my neck, tightly enough to make it uncomfortable to breathe, but with enough slack that he doesn't actually strangle me. I grab at his arm, but he's too strong. Matthew raises his other arm, curling his hand into a fist.

"What happened?" he demands.

"It closed?" It's a stupid thing to say, but they're the only words I have to offer.

My words make his mouth curl into a snarl and he drags his eyebrows down sharply over his eyes. "Why didn't they come back through?"

"It must have been a one-way door. It's why I tried to open a gateway to Kim's house, remember? But I couldn't."

He growls at me. "And now what? They're stuck in Uralahnd?"

I manage to shake my head, despite the pressure on my neck.

"Then where?"

"Kim asked me to..." I gasp as he tightens his grip. "Home. *Your* home." I hope.

Matthew's fist slams into my face, smacking my head against the wall. I feel the warmth of blood smearing from my nose and across my cheek in the wake of his knuckles. My nose throbs and it's hard to breathe through it, like each time I drag air in, I also inhale a dozen razorblades. There's a chance it's broken, not that it matters. I can already feel the tingling sensation that signals that my magic is kicking in to heal me, whether I want it to or not. But thanks to Saul, I know I can fight through it and stay awake and aware, no matter how much it has to heal.

I glare at Matthew. "Feel better?"

He clenches his teeth and raises his fist again. "You don't know where I'm from," Matthew spits through his clenched teeth. "They could be anywhere. They could be dead." He inches forward, so we're nose to nose. "If *anything* has happened to them—"

"You'll do what?" I retort, anger bubbling up inside me. "Kill me? I thought you weren't allowed to hurt humans *or* Baneem."

His lip hooks up as he snorts.

"I guessed the gateways might only be a one-way trip and I told Kim as much. She suggested I open the gateway to wherever you call home. And you know what? She was right. Being with the Shamari has got to be safer for them than being with the Baneem."

The anger and concern doesn't dissipate from Matthew's face. I'm almost amazed he's forced so much emotion into the golem, except it's far more terrifying than awe-inspiring.

I narrow my eyes. "Unless for some reason you've never told us, they're not safer with the Shamari at all."

Matthew releases me and stalks away, both fists clenched, his arms clasped by his sides. I sink to the ground and tilt my head back against the wall, breathing slowly and steadily as my magic completes its work preparing my damaged face.

"I'm worried," Matthew says eventually. "How could you send them to a world you've never even been to?" He turns to face me. "Besides, I didn't believe you could even open a gateway to my home."

I force my own hard expression to soften. "I know you didn't want to believe that magic of any kind could reach the Shamari, but what if it can and did? Kim and Sophie need us to go and find them. Kim's never drawn a gateway, remember? I doubt she could remember every pictogram in the right order, even *if* the Shamari allowed her to use magic."

Matthew unclenches his hands and stares at them. "What makes you think the Shamari will allow *you* to open a gateway back here?"

"I was hoping you'd persuade them to let us come home. Either by our own means or theirs. You can—could—travel between the worlds and you must have done it physically, in order to take the Baneem you captured with you. Right?"

Matthew nods. "The Shamari will probably bring Kim and Sophie home, then."

I use my arms to push against the wall and help me stand, even though my limbs are still shaky from my magic. "Probably? Why risk that when we can go and make sure ourselves. And, at the same time, you can get healed."

He presses his lips together.

"You still don't want to use human magic," I say, my voice filled with venom, even though I hadn't meant it to be.

Matthew scowls. "Do you blame me? Magic has never brought anything other than grief."

I stride towards him, squaring up to him. "Really? I saved Kim's life with magic, remember? Magic was the reason I escaped Saul and Uralahnd, to get back here. And magic is going to be the thing that stops the Baneem from travelling between the worlds."

"And maybe the Shamari too," Matthew says in a quiet tone.

I jerk my head back and stare at him.

"If gateways can be opened to my world, then putting something destructive in the space between the worlds will stop us travelling too, won't it?"

I nod, feeling numb. "But you won't be needed anymore." I wince at how crass and insensitive my words sound. "I didn't mean it like that, I'm sorry."

"But you're right."

I blink and miss a breath. I don't think Matthew has ever agreed with me on anything.

"We exist to stop the Baneem interfering with humans. But if the Baneem are trapped in Uralahnd, what purpose would the Shamari have?"

My jaw becomes slack and I feel a sense of anger at myself. In our desire to stop the Baneem, neither Kim nor I had paused to think about what it would mean for the Shamari.

"Open the gateway," Matthew says, turning his back on me again. "Making sure Kim and Sophie are safe is the most important thing." He glances over his shoulder. "More important than my apparently fragile ego." He forces a smile to his lips, but it only makes me shudder.

I traipse to my bags of supplies, my feet heavy as concrete, and find a pencil with which to draw the gateway. There's no sense in making it last longer than it needs to, Matthew and I will only need seconds to pass through to the other side. My body is numb as I draw the wheel and then the pictograms. It's hard to admit that I've been so wrapped up in myself, that I've ignored Matthew and his suffering. I've felt *guilt* for what happened to him, but no empathy for his situation, now, or in the future.

"I'm sorry," I say, as I hold my palm over the final glyph, refusing to touch it.

"For what?"

I shrug. "Everything? It's my fault you're trapped in the golem. Saul was only able to execute his plan to try to kill you because I helped him." I tense myself, waiting for Matthew to attack me.

"To save your mother?" he asks, voice quiet.

"I was stupid."

"You were human." He curls his hand around my shoulder. "I couldn't save my family, either. But we can help Kim and Sophie. Open the gateway."

I clear my throat and do as I'm told, pressing my hand against the final glyph as I hold onto the thought of taking Matthew home in my mind.

The gateway flares open and I step through, helped by a not so gentle shove from Matthew. I don't hesitate, don't pause to look at what lies between, I just keep walking. I'm briefly aware of light and darkness and nothingness and then we're through, standing in a lush garden, with a single storey building a hundred feet or so away. The quality of the light is odd and it's only when I look up that I realise why—a delicate green dome covers the whole compound.

"You did it," Matthew whispers. "You really brought me home."

"This is..." my voice trails off as I stare down at the ground. There was already a scattering of pretty white flowers on the lawn, but, around my feet, more are blossoming in response to my presence. My heart thunders in my chest and my eyes widen as I spin round to stare at Matthew. "This is Uralahnd."

Matthew's expression contorts in confusion.

I'm aware of footsteps crunching across the grass towards us, but I ignore whoever is coming and direct all my anger at Matthew.

"You lied to us. No wonder you didn't want us coming here. Your home is in fucking Uralahnd. You—"

My words are cut off as something heavy slams into the back of my head. I waiver for a second and then plummet to the ground, my magic unable to respond fast enough to stop me from slipping into unconsciousness.

# CHAPTER FIFTEEN

Sophie and I were led to a small room, where we've been left alone for long enough to feel frustrated, fed up and more than a little afraid. There are no windows, no furniture, just cold green walls that feel like some kind of stone. My broken wrist hurts like hell, but it's not stopping me from using my good hand to hammer against the door, in an effort to make someone come and talk to us.

"I thought the Shamari were on our side," Sophie mutters. She's sitting with her back against the wall, her arms wrapped around her knees.

"They are." I pause from banging my fist against the door long enough to turn and offer her a pained smile. "But we're not meant to be here. I don't think the Shamari who found us knew what to do with us."

"Not treating us like prisoners would have been a good start."

I raise my eyebrows in agreement and go back to bashing the door, hoping it'll make someone come and talk to us sooner.

"That's not helping," Sophie says.

I want her infectious positivity back, not glum defeatism. I hold in sharp words that might upset her.

"I have to do something," I say. "Do you have any other ideas?"

"No."

I stop, turn and press my back against the door. "Matthew and AJ will come and get us."

Sophie looks up at me, her eyes wide and shimmering with tears. "I hope so, Kim, I really do."

I wander across and sit beside her, wrapping my arm around her shoulders, whilst hugging my broken wrist against my chest at the same time. The pain is severe, but I have to fight through it for Sophie's sake. Her excitement at our *magical field trip* has vanished, replaced by fear and defeat. I can't blame her. I'm scared too. Besides, for all the times Sophie has held it together for me, I owe her the same now.

"It'll be okay," I whisper, as I encourage her to drop her head onto my shoulder.

She nods and sniffs. I hug her tightly, as the realisation that we can do nothing but sit and wait sinks in. I rest my head against Sophie's and allow my eyes to drift shut. The pain in my wrist stops me from falling asleep or truly resting, but doesn't stop me trying to relax.

We're both shocked upright when the door opens. I scramble to my feet, expecting to be hit by a Shamari aura at any moment. Instead, Matthew strides into the room, holding AJ's limp body in his arms. He lays AJ down in front of us, before standing straight. I press my hand to my mouth to supress a gasp of relief at seeing them. How AJ came for us and, somehow, he managed to persuade Matthew to come too. My joy is shortlived as I realise AJ is unconcious.

"Are you both all right?" Matthew's gaze drifts to my wrist. "What happened?"

"Long story," I say through a tearful grimace. "What happened to AJ?"

Matthew stares at AJ and then glances over his shoulder, to the doorway, where the Shamari who found Sophie and I is standing.

"He was aggressive," the Shamari says, stepping into the room. "He needed to be subdued."

"AJ... aggressive?" I glance at Matthew for confirmation, just as the Shamari's aura knocks me to my knees again and robs me of my ability to speak or form coherent thought.

"Matthew?" A soft and musical voice filters to me from the corridor, a moment before a beautiful woman enters the room. "I was told you were back," she says, absently touching the male Shamari on the shoulder in a dismissive gesture. "What has happened to you?"

Matthew turns to face her and bows his head as she approaches him. "It's a long story, Elizabeth."

She raises her hand to his face, tracing the contours of the golem's cheeks and jaw. Her expression twists in shock. "What is this thing you're trapped inside?"

"A golem." He motions towards me. "Kim created it to save me. My soul was badly damaged by magic and was decaying. I was unable to access any of my abilities, not even to contact anyone else."

Elizabeth presses her fingertips against her lips. "We must heal you." She shifts her gaze to Sophie, AJ and I, scrutinising us, as if truly seeing us for the first time. "How is it possible that humans have come here? I know this one," she gestures to AJ, "arrived with you. But the other two?"

Matthew grimaces. "We all came via human gateway rituals."

Elizabeth gasps, her dusky skin paling. "How can that be possible?" she asks in a shaky voice.

I want to speak, but I'm utterly paralysed by her aura.

"You allowed them to do this?" Elizabeth asks Matthew, her eyebrows slashing down in an angry expression.

"It was the only way for me to return home." Matthew gestures at his body. At the golem. "Without my abilities, I was trapped on earth."

"You brought humans here?" Elizabeth backs away from Matthew, shaking her head as her eyes widen in horror.

"They need our help, Elizabeth."

"But using magic... Matthew..." The shock in her voice is clear, proving to me she holds the same—possibly false—beliefs as Matthew.

"AJ thinks we're in Uralahnd," Matthew says, his words rushed as though he doesn't really believe them, but needs confirmation AJ is wrong.

I manage to glance at AJ, despite Elizabeth's aura. He's starting to stir, although I doubt he can wake up fully whilst any of the Shamari are present. I wish I could move to him. He's so close to me, but it's still too far for my paralysed limbs.

"Uralahnd?" Elizabeth asks. "Why would he think that? How could a human know anything about Uralahnd?" She narrows her eyes, scrutinising first AJ and then Sophie and I more closely. "Unless one or all of them have been consorting with the Baneem. Is that how they know of gateways? Did any of them open them for the Baneem?"

"No," Matthew says. "They're not in league with the Baneem, I swear to you." He raises his hand to his throat. "Release them from the power of your aura, and then we can all talk."

Elizabeth tilts her head to one side, pursing her lips. "I'm not sure that's a good idea. We should wait for orders from our Elders."

Elders? Could she mean the true Shamari? If she does, that would mean neither she nor the male Shamari are any different to Matthew, even though they both felt more powerful.

"How long will that take?" Matthew asks. "I told you, they need our help. They're fighting against the Baneem, just as we are. Only they might have found a way to end the fight."

"End it?" Elizabeth's voice comes out in a barely audible whisper, like she can't dare to believe what Matthew is saying.

I try to nod, but can't. I try to speak, but can't. All I can do is focus on how much I hate the Shamari's powerful aura.

"Give them clarity," Matthew pleads.

"All right."

Elizabeth steps up to me, running her thumb over my forehead in two, long, shallow curves, which touch each other at the points. Inside the cold imprint, she traces a small circle, completing the eye. "Clarity." She smiles as she speaks, but the action is nowhere near as warm and comforting as Matthew's smile was before we bound him inside the golem.

I gasp in a breath. I still feel weak, my mind still confused. As Elizabeth turns her attention to Sophie, Matthew helps me to stand.

"Are you all right?" He touches my broken wrist, which elicits a pained hiss from my throat.

"I will be." My gaze drifts to AJ, although I'm not sure when he'll be able to heal me.

Sophie, now free from Elizabeth's aura, staggers to her feet beside me. Elizabeth crouches beside AJ and repeats the gesture and command. As soon as she finishes, his eyes pop open and he gasps for breath. He stares at Elizabeth for several long seconds, his face rigid with fear. Then he rolls to his feet, moving away from her. He opens his mouth as if to speak, but then clamps his lips together.

"Thank you," I say to her, trying to draw her attention away from AJ. "You're Shamari, aren't you? Changed, like Matthew?"

Elizabeth nods. "You've obviously been quite liberal with what you've told them." Her tone is scolding, like she's talking to a naughty child. "I should organise healing for you, Matthew, and the Elders must be informed of what has happened to you and of the presence of these three humans."

"And what will happen to them in the meantime?" Matthew asks.

Elizabeth shrugs. "They'll have to stay here. Come along, Matthew."

He hesitates and I assume he's torn between following her order and staying with us.

"Matthew," Elizabeth says, her tone stern. "They will be quite safe here, I promise."

He nods hesitantly. "I'll be back soon," he promises us.

"Like hell you will," AJ mutters under his breath. He stares at Matthew, anger flaring in his eyes until it looks like he's ready to murder Matthew.

"I've never lied to you," Matthew says. "You're confused, AJ."

"Of course I am," AJ snaps. "Is that why I was hit over the head by one of your *friends*?"

Elizabeth sighs loudly. "Matthew tells me you believe you're in Uralahnd."

AJ's gaze snaps to her and I can see him visibly shaking.

"If that is the case, then you truly are confused. I would also be interested to know *how* you come to have any knowledge of Uralahnd whatsoever. However, that conversation can wait. For now, the three of you will remain here whilst Matthew is healed and we discuss what is to be done with you."

"What's to be done with us?" I demand. "You'll allow us to go home, that's what."

A ghost of a smile flickers at the corners of Elizabeth's lips. "Hopefully, child, hopefully."

Her words make me shudder. I realise our fate is in her hands and we're not really in any position to make demands. All we can do is hope she'll set us free.

From the corner of my eye, I see AJ move towards her, teeth and fists clenched. I step in front of him, physically blocking him, gasping as fresh pain shoots through my wrist. Instantly, the anger drains out of AJ as he focuses on my injury. It gives Elizabeth enough time to usher Matthew out of the room, close the door and lock it behind her.

AJ takes my wrist and cradles it in his hands.

"You can't heal me," I whisper. "Not here."

"I know."

"What makes you think this place is Uralahnd?" Sophie asks.

"The flowers..." he mutters. "They blossomed around me. I saw the same thing happen in Saul's compound. The grass and plants were all withered when I first arrived, but within hours they were lush and blooming. Saul told me that Uralahnd can be shaped by magic. It can be as beautiful or as barren as they wanted it to be." His expression becomes distant. "He said it was too easy."

"Maybe this place behaves the same way?" I ask.

He shakes his head, anger flashing in his eyes. "It behaves the same because *it* is the same. This is Uralahnd." He releases my wrist and crosses his arms, using them to clamp his hands against his sides. "We've come to the worse place possible." He glares at the locked door. "It also means Matthew has been lying to us all along."

"AJ..."

"Why else would he be so against us using a gateway to come here? He knew I'd recognise this place. He knew."

I reach out to comfort AJ, but he back-steps away from me. "Matthew has never lied to me."

"Really?"

"You know why Matthew didn't want us using magic, especially not to try to bring him home. It goes against everything he believes."

AJ shakes his head, his top lip curling.

I grab his hand, wresting it away from his side so I can hold it tightly. "Let's assume you're right and this is Uralahnd... I don't believe Matthew knows it is."

"So why did he tell that woman that I think it is?" AJ demands.

"I don't know..."

"For what it's worth, he didn't tell her you were... you know..." Sophie says. "He didn't betray you. I think he was as confused as you are."

"I'm not confused, I'm angry."

"Matthew wouldn't betray me," I say, tears prickling my eyes. A lump has formed in my throat. I can't stand the thought of AJ being so angry at Matthew, any more than I can allow myself to believe that this is Uralahnd and that Matthew has known it all along. "He hates the Baneem. He's fought against them for over four hundred years."

AJ hisses in a breath and I half expect him to tear his hand from mine and turn his back on me. Instead, he plunges his teeth into his lower lip, drawing a bead of crimson blood, which he wipes away with the back of his free hand. He takes three deep breaths, which seems to help the tense anger drift away from his body a little.

"Fine. Matthew doesn't know. But I'm not wrong, Kim. I'm not."

I nod and stroke the back of his hand with my thumb. I believe him, even though I don't want to. He's too worked up for it to be a hunch.

"What do we do now?" Sophie asks.

I sigh. "Nothing. We have to wait for Matthew to come back, however long that takes."

# CHAPTER SIXTEEN

I don't know how long we've been waiting for Matthew to return, or how long AJ has been pacing back and forth. I watched him until the effort of doing so made me dizzy. A hug isn't going to erase his fear, nor are words, leaving me with nothing to do but nurse my broken wrist as I sit beside Sophie. I hope AJ is wrong and that this isn't Uralahnd. But the more time slips by, the less certain I am and the more afraid I'm becoming. Elizabeth was less than comforting. If anything, the things she said make me feel more on edge.

"How can you just sit there?" AJ asks.

"I don't think there's much we can do but wait," I say. "Unless you think you can break the door down." I suck in a breath. "I'm sorry. I didn't mean to be so snarky, it's just... I'm scared." I stare down at my broken wrist.

Beside me, Sophie lets out a small sob.

"And you're in pain." AJ stops in front of me, his eyebrows pinching together in concern. "I can't he..." He shakes his head and rubs the bridge of his nose. "Despite the fact we're basically prisoners, you don't believe we're in Uralahnd, do you?"

I push my hair back from my face with a sigh. "It's not that I don't believe you, AJ. I can't understand how we could be there. The Shamari work against the Baneem. How could we be in Uralahnd? Don't you think they'd sense it every time a Baneem did magic here? There's no way they wouldn't know if this compound was really in Uralahnd."

His mouth twitches into a grimace. "Unless Matthew has been lying to us."

I shake my head. "No," I say, unwilling to accept that. "Besides, if he had been lying, don't you think we'd be prisoners now?"

AJ snorts and gestures to the locked door. "Aren't we?"

I rub my wrist. My fingers are tingling, but the pain seems to have lessened. Or maybe I've gotten used to it. This room feels like a cell, but I can understand Elizabeth wanting to keep us away from the other Shamari. We're not supposed to be here. We're probably the first humans to have ever found a way to their home. The fact we came here through magic only makes things worse.

I cup my hands over my mouth and take a few deep breaths to try to squash down my fear. It doesn't matter how much I try to justify why we've been left alone in a locked room, something feels very wrong. "It doesn't make sense. We can't be in Uralahnd." My words are a way of denying the possibility that AJ is right. He can't be right. I squeeze my eyes shut, letting out a squeak of surprise as AJ wraps his arms around me and holds me tightly, careful not to bump my wrist. "I can't believe Matthew was lying to me," I whisper, my voice cracking.

"Maybe he's wasn't lying to you," AJ says, settling down beside me. He runs a finger over my broken wrist, regret filling his eyes.

I know he wants to heal me, but I can't let him.

He frowns and pats his hand against the wall. "Jade is an odd material to make a room from, don't you think?"

I turn my attention to the walls. I hadn't really noticed what they were made of. "How do you know it's jade?"

"When I was younger, Mum had lots of little trinkets carved out of jade. Dragons and such. Most of them got lost as we moved around." He bows his head, his eyebrows squeezing together, his expression full of raw pain.

"The corridor we were led through was made of the same stuff," Sophie says, leaning forward so she can see both AJ and

I. "I figured they had an emerald city vibe going on. Shame we don't have three pairs of ruby red slippers to get us home," she adds with a wry grin.

I find myself chuckling at her words.

"Did you notice the dome outside?" AJ says, barely pausing for us to nod. "It must have been made from jade, too, though I'm not sure it would be possible to craft something like that on earth."

I nod. "It surrounded the whole compound. It can't be for show. It must have some kind of purpose. But what?"

AJ tenses beside me. He draws in a shaking breath. "My cell in Saul's compound was made from obsidian. It dampened my magic, making it impossible for me to actively use it."

I frown. "Is the jade having the same effect on you?"

"No. But that doesn't mean it isn't doing *something*."

"Like what?"

He shrugs. "I don't know."

"Matthew wouldn't have lied to me." I stand. "The Shamari shouldn't have a problem with opening the door and answering our questions, should they?" I stand and start to smack my good hand against the wall, but the jade dampens the sound.

I ball both my hand into a fist and pound it against the door. "Hello? Is anyone out there?"

Sophie and AJ join me. In the small room, our shouting and pounding makes my ears ring painfully.

No one responds. No one comes. I'm not sure how long we continue to make as much noise as possible, but by the time I stop and slump against the wall, my fist is red raw. The pain in my hand only amplifies the pain in my other wrist and it makes me feel sick.

"No one's listening," I say, causing the other two to stop. I rub my arm, trying not to vocalise the fear I'm feeling—what if AJ's right and we are prisoners? "Maybe the jade is too thick for anyone to hear us."

"That's great," AJ says, pacing again. "Just great."

"You're not helping," I snap.

Sophie hugs me. "Getting angry won't help either," she says.

I run my hand over my face, taking deep breaths to calm myself. It's only been a couple of days since AJ escaped Saul. Of course being stuck in this room is stressing him out. I've been busy trying to convince myself that everything is fine, and that I can't see AJ crumbling under the pressure of our situation. I remember how much I freaked out when AJ and I were alone together, in my bedroom, for the first time. It had been a year since the incident with Gage and I still freaked out. AJ's ordeal hasn't really ended and it won't until we stop Saul from being able to reach him again.

I pull away from Sophie so I can embrace AJ, forbidding him from continuing his pacing. Fresh pain shoots through my wrist as I hold it against his back, but I clench my teeth in an effort to ignore it. "It'll be okay."

"You don't know that. You can't know that. It was my idea to try to come here."

"I was the one who asked you to open the gateway here," I reminded him. "If anyone is to blame, it's me."

We all snap our heads round to stare at the door as it scrapes open. A male Shamari is standing in the doorway. He smiles at us, even though it must be obvious how worried we all are.

"Where's Matthew?" I ask. "Is he okay?"

"Come with me and I'll take you to Matthew."

I shake my head, standing my ground. "Not until you answer some questions." I'm buoyed as AJ and Sophie both stand beside me.

The Shamari's smile broadens. "I am sure you have a lot of questions; however, this is not the place to answer them. Come with me, please."

I hesitate. I'd feel a lot more positive if Matthew were with him.

"If you want answers, the only way you will get them is if you come with me. I apologise that Elizabeth chose this room for you to rest in. She is..." he rolls his dark eyes upwards. "... quite out of touch with humanity. It has been a long time since she died and her soul was revived. Unlike Matthew, she has made no attempt to maintain relationships with humans. She is effective in her mission against the Baneem, but she remains somewhat cold."

"You're not exactly Mr. Charisma yourself," I snort.

He purses his lips. "No, I suppose I'm not. I have also been Shamari for a long time, but not as long as Elizabeth. She is the oldest of us."

I gasp. "Is she a True Shamari?"

"No. Now, come with me." He starts to stride out of the room, not giving me time to process his clipped response.

I scrunch my lips up tightly. "We don't have much choice, do we?"

His smile only deepens. I sigh and together, AJ, Sophie and I follow the Shamari out of the room and into the corridor.

*

Elizabeth meets us at the end of another corridor and, after bidding farewell to her companion, leads us to another jade room with a semi-translucent, orange-brown box in the centre. Peering at it closely, I can see there's someone within it. I clap my hand to my mouth as I realise it's Matthew, still encased within the golem. I turn to Elizabeth and slam my fists into her chest.

"What have you done to him? You said he would be healed."

"We've been trying to," Elizabeth says. "However, the damage done to his soul is very severe and the methods we have of being repaired are, regrettably, falling short."

"Why? What is that thing?" I demand, jabbing my finger towards the coffin.

When she doesn't respond, I stride over to the coffin and run my hand over it. It isn't stone and it's warmer to the touch than the jade. I raise my eyebrows at AJ as he joins me and also places his hands on the coffin.

"Amber," I breathe, as I remember a necklace my mother sometimes wears. It's a black cord, threaded with several pieces of unpolished amber.

I glance up at Elizabeth, who nods to confirm my statement.

AJ, who has positioned himself so his back is to her, touches my fingertips to draw my attention to him. "Magic," he mouths, tapping his finger twice on the box.

I frown. "Why have you put Matthew in an amber coffin?" I demand.

"It is not a coffin," Elizabeth assures me. "It is a vessel that contains the power used to heal damage done to the souls of the Changed, so none of the power is lost. It is also used to transform a human soul into one of the Changed. Each of us was reborn within this vessel, though none of us can remember the metamorphosis."

AJ moves his head a fraction in an almost imperceptible shake.

"Why not?" I hope my voice sounds casual, like I'm asking out of idle curiosity, rather than distrust.

"The soul forgets what it does not need to remember."

AJ's eyes narrow.

"Does the soul also forget being healed?" Sophie asks.

Elizabeth nods.

"And do they forget being in this room?" Sophie presses on.

"Why would they need to remember?" Elizabeth asks. "They are made whole again, that is all that is important."

The Shamari who were brought to this room to be healed would have been able to sense the magic radiating from the box, just as AJ can. Probably more acutely than he can. That's why Elizabeth makes them forget. She knows more than the others and is hiding things from them all, inlcuding Matthew.

"You said the... power... is falling short of healing Matthew. Why?"

"I believe I have already explained. The amount of damage done to his soul is too great."

I shake my head firmly. "I'm not buying it, sorry." I flatten my hand against the top of the box. "If this thing is capable of turning a human soul into one of the Changed, it can heal Matthew. Either that, or there's something you're not telling us."

There's plenty she's not telling us and so much I want to ask, for AJ's peace of mind as well as my own. Except I'm no longer sure the truth is anything I want to hear.

"If there's something I'm not telling you, it's because it's not for me to say."

I stride round the box until I'm standing in front of her again. "Then who can we talk to? Is one of the True Shamari here?"

The way she smiles sends a shiver down my spine. It's not that it's patronising—although it is, like she's looking at someone very, very stupid—but that behind the smile she's obviously hiding something. A secret she's taunting us with.

"If it's not helping him, let him out," I say.

"I didn't say it wasn't helping," Elizabeth says. "It is stabilising him."

"Which means he'll be able to leave the golem?"

Elizabeth grimaces. "I'm not sure."

I twist my fingers round my hair. "Is there anything you are sure about? Because you seem keen to dance around every question I've asked. But you must have brought us here to see Matthew like this for a reason."

"I asked Elizabeth to bring you here," a woman says, stepping into the room.

She's old, with snow white hair and deeply lined skin. Unlike the Shamari, her eyes are a pale, watery blue. She's a lot shorter than Elizabeth and not at all imposing. I feel no sense of awe in her presence. If anything, she's entirely normal.

"You've created quite a stir, both with your presence here and your mode of transportation to this place," the woman says.

"Who are you?" I ask.

"I am Tanith," she extends her hand to me, but I don't make any effort to move closer to her so I can shake it. Her mouth tugs down at the corner, as she retracts her hand and moves it to stroke the amber pendant.

I asked the wrong question. "*What* are you?"

"I suppose you would think of me as a True Shamari."

"But you're not, are you?" AJ asks.

Her eyes sparkle, as though she's about to let us in on a private joke. "It's exactly what I am. Perhaps it's your definition of what a True Shamari is that needs to change." She waves her hand in the direction of Elizabeth. "Elizabeth was the first Changed. As such, she knows things the others do not," Tanith says.

She shuffles further into the room closing the door behind her, her back bent as she moves. She gazes around the room, her expression regretful and then lets out a long, loud sigh as she lowers herself awkwardly down to the floor. I assume she was searching for a chair in the barren room. She leans back against the wall, her legs stretched out in front of her and her hands loosely clasped in her lap. Elizabeth moves to stand beside her, her hands clasped behind her back.

"I heard your conversation," Tanith said. "Whilst you were alone."

AJ pales and sags against the amber tomb.

"How?" I ask.

"Magic," AJ says. "She's Baneem. That's why we're not in awe of her. There's nothing to be in awe of."

Tanith chuckles. "Not *my* magic, but yes, one of our number is able to listen across distances and share what he hears with others. It's an incredibly useful talent."

"You're Baneem?" I ask, not wanting to believe it.

"Yes," Tanith says. "Although we have not gone by that name in a long time. We call ourselves Shamari, because it more aptly portrays our goal to guard humans from the influence of the Baneem."

"I told you we were in Uralahnd," AJ says, balling his hands into fists.

"I'm curious as to how you came to that conclusion. I suppose it's tied in with whatever you're desperate to hide from us."

It feels like my legs are turning to jelly. I slip to the floor, despite Sophie's efforts to catch me. Instead, I bring her down with me and we land, side by side, both staring at Tanith. I hadn't wanted to believe AJ.

"And Matthew doesn't know?" I ask, needing her to explicitly state that he didn't lie to me. "He doesn't know he works for Baneem?"

"No. None of the Changed do."

"Except Elizabeth," Sophie says, shaking her head. "Does that mean everything Matthew believes is a lie?"

Before Tanith can reply, AJ turns and glares at her.

"They must *all* know. They *must* be able to feel your magic," he says accusingly. "They must be able to feel the magic contained within this," he points his finger at the amber box. "And they must be able to sense every time a Baneem uses magic within Uralahnd."

Tanith shakes her head. "Only Elizabeth interacts with us. She alone keeps our secret. Besides, I no longer have any magic, so there is nothing for anyone to sense. I am no different from a human." She sighs. "Those of my number who do still have magic would never risk encountering any of the Changed."

"So... your magic has been stripped from you?" I ask.

Her eyes widen slightly. "I wouldn't use that term and I'd very much like to know where you have heard it. To my knowledge, no one outside of this compound knows it's even possible for the magic of a Baneem to be given up."

"Or taken forcibly," I say.

Her mouth twitches. "We would never do that. I, like many others before me, gave my magic freely to help create and maintain the Changed. I am old, soon I won't have any use for magic anymore anyway. Who else has spoken to you about this?"

"Gage," I mumble. "He said the Baneem he was working for was going to strip someone's magic."

Tanith leans forward, pinning me with her watery blue stare. "Who was he working for? Whose magic was going to be taken from them?"

"It's the jade, isn't it?" AJ asks.

I'm glad of his unsubtle change of subject. Tanith glares at him, nostrils flaring, but AJ ignores her and ploughs on.

"From the dome we saw when we were in the garden, to the walls and the building. This whole place is made of jade because it somehow hides magic. I already know that obsidian dampens Baneem magic to the point that they can no longer actively use it. So, if jade hides magic and obsidian dampens magic, then... maybe amber can... *confine* it?

"Very astute," Tanith says, her mouth quirking upwards in a look of admiration.

"Magic created the Changed," I say. "And it maintains their souls when they're damaged. It's why they can use magic, even though they don't believe it's what they're doing."

"Yes. So you see, you were absolutely right when you said Matthew would never lie to you. He told you the truth as he knows it. The truth we instructed Elizabeth to tell him and the others."

"But why?" Sophie asks. "Why all the lies?"

I glance at her. She looks as upset as AJ. I don't blame her. My lies nearly tore our friendship apart. She felt betrayed I wasn't able to confide in her. She was right to feel that way. The Shamari have been lied to for far longer than I lied to Sophie.

"Do you think Matthew would help us if he knew we were Baneem?" Tanith asks. "Do you think any of the Changed would? They all died because of Baneem. Many of them lost loved ones before they lost their own lives."

I shake my head and gaze miserably at the golem within the amber tomb. The truth is going to destroy him. "I still don't get why the magic contained within the box can't heal his soul. Or even why magic was able to damage his soul in the first place. Surely magic is magic? How can it both hurt and heal him?"

I saw what it did to him when Gage attacked him with magic. It opened black welts on his manifestation. When Stella attacked him, it made his soul start to unravel.

"Intent," Tanith says. "In your world, you have many drugs that have been created to heal in one way or another. But those same drugs, if used incorrectly, can also have the power to kill. Magic is the same. When it is wielded against the Changed, the intent is for it to harm. But the magic in that box has no wielder and therefore no purpose."

"And yet it heals," I say.

Tanith sighs and shifts her position, her knees clicking as she does so. "Not exactly. And that's the problem. It supercharges their souls and yes, it's more like it gives them renewed strength and covers over the damage that has been done. There is no healing power within that box. No Baneem has ever been blessed with that gift." She glances at AJ as she speaks, reminding us all that she heard *everything* we said while we were alone. "In Matthew's case, so much damage has been done it cannot simply be smoothed over. No amount of strength given to his soul will repair it." She gazes regretfully at the amber tomb. "He has been stabilised, but I doubt he will ever be able to leave the golem. He will not be able to stand against the Baneem."

"It's why you haven't let him out to hear this conversation, isn't it?" AJ asks. "He has to stay here, so you don't want everything he believes to be destroyed." He crouches down next to me and places his hand over mine, allowing me to feel that he's shaking. "So why are you telling *us*? Why are you letting us in on your secret?"

"Elizabeth said you needed our help. For Matthew to allow you to use magic to come here, your need must be great." She inclines her head. "And your conversation earlier fascinated me."

AJ presses his lips together and shakes his head.

"You don't trust me." Tanith sighs. "Honestly, I don't blame you. You have no reason to trust me and I can see my behaviour must look odd to you. However, if you are to trust me, I must be honest with you. That is all I am trying to do."

"Matthew deserves to know," I say through my still gritted teeth. "He's given you four hundred years. He deserves to know the truth."

"I do not think that is a good idea," Elizabeth says.

I glare at her. "How can you lie to all of them?" I realise my question is hypocritical. I lie to my family every day. I lied to Sophie. I even lied to AJ. I'm no better than she is.

Elizabeth shrugs. "We do it to ensure their loyalty to our cause. The True Shamari are quite unlike the Baneem you have encountered. They do not wish humanity any harm."

"And if you understand that, don't you think the rest of the Changed would as well? Don't you think Matthew would?"

AJ wraps his arm around my back, forming small, calming circles with his thumb. "Theoretically, if healing magic did exist, could he be healed?"

Tanith regards him cooly. "In theory, yes. It would take more than the amount that could be spared in a single burst. It would need to be sacrificed freely by the Baneem, in the same way I have sacrificed my own. But it doesn't exist. Not once, in all our history, has there been a record of a Baneem who can heal."

AJ shrugs. "We've encountered a Baneem whose magic can destroy, why shouldn't the opposite magic exist?"

Tanith visibly shudders. "That is not a Baneem I would like to meet," she says. "Is he the one who was intending on... *stripping* magic?"

I nod. "Would you be able to put his magic in there? Could his magic do some good?"

She shakes her head. "No. If its nature is to destroy, it would continue to do that with or without intent."

I shudder. Is it the nature of Saul's magic that makes him do such hideous things? "Can you teach us how to strip magic?"

"Why would you want to know such a thing?"

"To take Saul's magic away from him." I clench my fists. "He's planning on destroying all the Changed. Attacking Matthew was a test, to see if his plan would work. If he succeeds, you'll lose them all."

Tanith frowns. "Was it...?"

"Saul," AJ mutters. "His name is Saul."

"Was it Saul's magic that did this to Matthew?"

I hesitate. "No, not exactly. It's his plan." Finally, I look to AJ. He's the only one who can answer these questions, only he doesn't offer any words to help me.

"Then why do you want to know how to take his magic away?" Tanith asks.

"To stop him hurting anyone else," AJ says. "Whether he goes through with his plan or not, he's dangerous. Not just to the Shamari and humans, but to other Baneem as well." He lifts his head and meets her gaze for the first time. "He wants to be a god."

Tanith raises her eyebrows. "Delusions of grandeur," she breathes. "Forgive me. It's been a long time since anyone in our group had any direct contact with the rest of the Baneem. I suppose I'd hoped that they were starting to see sense and change their ways." She shakes her head, her eyes downcast. "But I suppose if they had, the Changed wouldn't be kept as busy as they are."

"Why aren't you the same as the other Baneem?" Sophie asks. "Why don't you want to corrupt humans too?"

"Call it a difference of ideals. I'm sure not everyone agrees on how to live and act on earth, do they?"

Sophie shakes her head. "No. If they did, we wouldn't have wars and acts of terrorism."

"We have a lot to talk about," Tanith says. "But not here. I will take you to where I reside. There I can organise food and water for you and something comfortable to sit on. I can probably find a sling for your arm. If you'll trust me enough to come with me, of course."

"You're going to take us to the other Baneem?" I ask.

"I really do prefer the term Shamari," she says. "We took a decision to stand apart from the Baneem. To work against their selfish desires to corrupt humanity. When we did that, we named ourselves Shamari."

"How old are you?"

She laughs. "How old do I look?"

"Seventy? Maybe Eighty?"

"Eighty-three," Tanith says. "So no, I am not an original Shamari, far from it. Our group broke away a little over two thousand years ago. Anyway, will you come with me?"

My gaze drifts to the amber box and Matthew, still motionless within it.

"Would you really have him know the truth, even though it might destroy him?" Tanith asks.

I pick myself up and go to the box, running my palm over the smooth, warm surface. I can see the blurred features of the golem through the orange-brown surface. The face is completely void of emotion and, even though it's only a vessel, it's still Matthew's likeness and his soul is still within it. Tears sting my eyes. I'm not sure I have the right to make this decision for Matthew, but it's not one he can make for himself. AJ joins me, placing a hand over mine.

"Would you want to know?" I ask, searching his face for answers. "If we don't tell him the truth, I'd have to say goodbye to him and I'm not sure I can do that, AJ. I know it makes me selfish." I sniff back a sob as tears threaten to spill from my eyes.

He grimaces. "If Matthew's not at full strength, he can't help us anyway."

"You think he shouldn't know?"

"That isn't what I said." He looks me directly in the eyes. The reflection of the amber box illuminates the gold flecks in his eyes, bringing an intenseness to his gaze that drives a lance of realisation through my mind.

"No," I hiss, understanding what it is he's offering to do.

To heal Matthew, he would have to betray himself to Tanith, Elizabeth and the other Shamari. He'd have to sacrifice all of his magic. And yet, I can see why he might be willing to do it. Without magic, he'd be useless to Saul and healing Matthew would go some way to alleviating him of his guilt. And, unless Matthew is fully healed, we can't ask him to help us any further. He'd have to stay here, trapped in the golem forever. I doubt AJ's guilt will allow him to do that, whether we decide to tell Matthew the truth or not.

"Matthew needs to be given the choice," I say. "It's not up to any of us to decide if he should know the truth."

"That's impossible," Elizabeth points out. "If you knew a secret was being kept from you, would you be content not to know it?"

I shake my head.

"And how do you think he will react?" she asks. "With acceptance, or anger?"

"Anger," I mutter.

"So it is better he remains in blissful ignorance."

"What about you?" Sophie asks. "You don't seem bothered by the fact the True Shamari are actually Baneem, or that magic made you what you are. When did you find out?"

Elizabeth smiles. "I've always known. Using magic to turn human souls into powerful weapons... it was my idea."

# CHAPTER SEVENTEEN

"Your idea?" I ask, caught between disgust and awe.

"I had to find some way to atone for my sins," Elizabeth says. Beside me, AJ stands and stretches out his legs. "What sins?"

Elizabeth stares down at her hands. "I was the one who worked out how to open a gateway to Uralahnd. I was the one who first allowed Baneem through. Without my curious meddling, the Baneem would never have been a threat to humanity." She drops her hands to her sides and focuses her gaze on the floor. "The first Baneem I encountered were curious. I saw no harm in showing them the lands in which I lived. Besides, I was swayed with promises of being taught magic."

"Idiot," I breathe. "You were naive."

"Yes," Elizabeth agrees. "However, please remember I was a learned woman in a time when women were little more than the possessions of men. My entire lot in life was to bear my husband's children and look after our home. I wasn't content with that. I learned how to read and write and yes, I meddled with things I shouldn't have." She tilts her head to the side and smiles sadly. "Besides, I'm far from the last human to be cajoled by promises of power."

I suck in a breath and shake my head.

"But at some point, you realised the Baneem had bad intentions?" Sophie asks, as she hugs me tighter.

Elizabeth nods. "Yes. But not before I had allowed other humans in on my secret. It's amazing how quickly word of the gateways and magical beings spread beyond my power to control. Then the Baneem who had come through to earth started to do more than explore and teach. They started to wield their power over humans. One bewitched my husband and enticed him to commit the atrocity for which he was executed." Her expression becomes distant and full of regret. "We might not have loved one another, but he did not deserve that fate." She rolls her gaze upwards, to the ceiling. "At that point, my life was essentially over as well. I had no home and those who had sought my favour in order to learn from me, turned their backs on me. They couldn't see how poisonous the Baneem were." She curls her hands into fists. "They had to be stopped, but I was the only person who seemed interested in doing so."

"But how?" I ask.

Elizabeth smiles. "Exactly. How? Do you think working out how to open a gateway between the worlds was easy?"

I shake my head.

"Of course not. I had to learn how to harness the energies of this world. First, I tried to reason with everyone I knew I had taught to open a gateway. I implored them never to do it again."

"But they didn't listen?"

She lets out a bitter laugh. "No. Why would they? Even if they had, as I've already said, the knowledge had long since slipped beyond my control, spreading like a forest fire between people eager for power. I had to find a way to fight the Baneem, that would make up for the fact that I was one person, standing against their entire race." Her gaze takes on a misty quality. "It was then that some of the Baneem who had come through approached me. They were as appalled by what their brethren were doing as I was. They had tried to persuade all of the Baneem to return to Uralahnd, but had been unsuccessful. Together, we worked out how to create a weapon against the Baneem, but it required the sacrifice of a human life and of the magic of a Baneem."

"You sacrificed yourself?" I ask, horror contorting my voice.

"Yes." She stares at me, the dark depths of her eyes catching hold of my gaze so it's impossible for me to look away.

It feels like I'm falling. I should be used to this sensation from staring into Matthews eyes and being caught in his aura, but this is somehow more terrifying.

"As I said, I had to atone for my sins. I have spent two thousand years doing so."

"And the others?" I ask, struggling against the pull of her aura. "All the other Changed? Were they sacrifices, too?"

She shakes her head. "As Matthew will attest to, the others were changed at the point of death. They were given a choice." She looks away, releasing me. "The first soul we changed turned against us when he realised the Baneem had helped to create him. He was too bent on revenge for what the Baneem had done to him whilst he had been alive. He... had to be destroyed."

"And after that?" AJ asks.

Elizabeth sweeps her hand to indicate the jade walls. "We found a way to lie to them." She nods to AJ. "Your friend has already guessed correctly about the effect jade has to mask magic. It might not have been ideal, but it worked."

"And all the restrictions placed upon the Changed?" I say. "Making them believe they couldn't hurt humans *or* Baneem?"

"All lies," Elizabeth confirms. "The Baneem helping me would only do so on that condition. They might not have liked what their brethren were doing, but they did not want to see them dead, either."

"And Baneem not being able to open gateways, is that a lie too?"

Elizabeth's lips curl into a smile. "I had to have some modicum of control over the creatures I was bringing to earth." Her lips droop down. "The Baneem believed me, but it gave them one more thing to hate humans for. Why could humans use a more flexible form of magic, when they were bound by their individual power sets?"

It also gave the Baneem one more reason to hurt and manipulate humans, convincing them to open gateways. Good people like Phailin and Sophie's dad.

Tanith stands, her joints creaking. "This is a wonderful history lesson, but could we please go somewhere more comfortable?"

I glance over my shoulder at the amber vessel, within which Matthew lays. I'm loathe to leave him for any reason. He has a right to know the truth, all the Changed do and yet... I do understand why Elizabeth and the True Shamari have lied to them all this time. To protect them, just like I've been trying to protect my family since I discovered the truth about how Charley died. I look at Sophie. Despite hugging me, her gaze has been fixed on the floor the whole time, anger making her rigid. She's been lied to her whole life. First by her father and her aunt, and then by me.

"It's wrong," she whispers. "They're risking themselves and fighting because of a pack of lies."

"No," Elizabeth snaps. "They do it because the Baneem have destroyed their lives. They don't want to see other humans hurt, and they want to see an end to the suffering the Baneem have caused."

"Some of the Baneem," Sophie yells. "*Some* of them. What I don't get, is that despite everything you've accomplished—opening the first gateway, taking magic from Baneem *and* fusing it with human souls to create walking talking, wepons—you can't figure out a way to stop the Baneem for good."

"Maybe she stopped trying," AJ says quietly.

We all turn to stare at him. He's leaning against the back wall of the room, hands thrust into his pockets, head bowed.

"She had a solution."

"Not a very good one," Sophie mutters. "Two thousand years and you're still fighting a losing battle."

"Judge me as you will," Elizabeth says. "I believed I was doing the right thing. I still do."

I look to Tanith. "And the True Shamari? You all agree with Elizabeth?"

She nods. "If we didn't, we wouldn't sacrifice our magic so willingly to create and restore the Changed, would we?"

"You're as bad as Saul," AJ says accusingly, staring at Elizabeth. "He wants to be a god and you effectively are one." He gestures to Tanith.

I hiss in a breath as I realise he's right. She's created one race and has another, albeit originally a breakaway faction, willing to sacrifice everything for her cause. I press my palm against my forehead. It's all too much to take in and I can't help but feel Elizabeth's revelations are partly designed to distract me from Matthew. I shrug away from Sophie and go to stand beside the amber vessel again.

"He must not know," Elizabeth says. "It would destroy him."

"It's not your decision to make," I mutter.

"Isn't it? I created him. Besides, what makes you think it's your decision?"

I shrug. "It isn't." But she was right about one thing, we can't give Matthew the choice of knowing the truth or remaining oblivious.

"His soul is being repaired," Elizabeth says, as she comes to stand behind me.

My instinct is to flinch away from her, but I hold myself rigid, barely even breathing as she continues to stand uncomfortably close to me.

"He must stay here, within the golem," she says. "I can put him to good use, but only if he remains blissfully oblivious to the truth."

"I can heal him," AJ says, pushing away from the wall.

I gasp and shake my head, but there's a look of determination in AJ's eyes that makes me freeze.

"I can heal him," AJ repeats.

# CHAPTER EIGHTEEN

"What?" Elizabeth hisses, staring at me, narrowing her eyes as though she's trying to pierce through my soul.

I'm glad Kim is beside me; she's a solid and comforting presence when the ground beneath me feels like it could open up and swallow me whole if Elizabeth wanted it to.

"You're human," Elizabeth concludes.

"AJ," Kim says in a warning tone.

I don't listen to her. What difference does it make if they know I'm half Baneem? Tanith is Baneem and we know she's not alone. If anyone should understand shades of grey, it's Elizabeth.

"Half human," I say, not allowing myself to look away from Elizabeth's gaze. I hate the way it pulls me in. "Half Baneem."

"And you can heal?" Tanith asks incredulously. "Impossible. No Baneem has ever had the gift of healing."

"I do." And for once, my magic doesn't feel like a burden or a curse I have to keep hidden away.

I walk over to Kim and take hold of her broken wrist. She tries to pull away, but I offer her a comforting smile and she slowly relaxes into my grip.

"It's okay," I tell her. "They're not going to hurt me."

She nods and sniffs as I begin to heal her wrist, taking the damage onto myself so that my magic can heal it. I feel the familiar tingling sensation in my body and darkness pressing against my mind, but I block it all out, focusing on my task and on staying very much awake. When I'm finished, Kim flexes her wrist and fingers. All trace of the bruising and swelling is gone. I glance up at Tanith and Elizabeth. They are both standing, staring at me with wide eyes. Tanith's jaw has dropped in shock.

"I can heal Matthew," I repeat.

Elizabeth shakes her head. "Only if you give up your magic."

"Which I'm willing to do."

"AJ..." Kim wraps her arms around me. "You can't."

"Why not? My magic has been nothing but a curse to me my whole life. Because of it, I've spent my life running, and my mum is dead. Because of it..." I breathe in and out harshly as I stare at Matthew through the amber. "It's my fault Matthew is trapped in the golem."

"How?" Elizabeth asks. "Did you attack him?"

I shake my head.

"It wasn't your fault," Kim says. "It was Saul's. He did that to Matthew, not you."

"Explain," Tanith says, settling down on the floor again with a heavy sigh. "Explain everything. How does Saul plan to destroy all the Changed?"

Kim glances at me. Whilst she could explain—to a point— we both know it's better if the explanations come from me. I sit down, resting my back against the amber vessel.

"He has another Baneem working with him, Adele. She can transfer souls from one body to another."

Tanith purses her lips, waiting for me to continue.

"She learnt that, if she places a Baneem soul inside a human body, the Changed can't sense them. Like that, a Baneem can walk straight up to a Changed and attack them with magic."

"And that's what happened to Matthew?" Elizabeth asks.

Kim nods.

"How did she discover this?" Tanith asks.

"She studied me," I say, squirming under the intensity of Tanith and Elizabeth's stares. "Like I said, I'm only half human. My father was a Baneem."

"You cannot tell this by looking at him?" Tanith asks Elizabeth.

She narrows her eyes in annoyance. "No. He *looks* human. I can't sense any power in his soul at all."

"My human body masks it," I say, shivering at the memory of what Saul and Adele did to me. "Like a thick shroud covering a flame." I press my fingertips against my palm. It might have healed instantly from the damage caused by Flame Guy's fire, but for a moment, I can almost feel the prickle and heat of the burn again. I suck in a deep breath, knowing I have to continue. "But the transfer process is brutal. Adele also discovered that a Baneem soul burns too brightly for a human body. It destroys it from the outside in." The words hurt as I say them and bring with them memories of the homeless girl and Mum, burned, broken and dying. I brush fresh tears from my eyes. Now isn't the time to fall apart.

"That makes sense," Tanith says, nodding. "The magic would be too powerful." She frowns. "But that doesn't happen to you... you do not seem to be in any pain."

"My magic is constantly working, repairing the damage it does my body." I grimace. "I didn't know that until Adele figured it out."

Tanith stares between me and Elizabeth. "Yet you cannot feel his magic at all, even knowing it's working?"

Elizabeth rolls her shoulders back and lifts her head high. "When he healed the girl, I could sense it then."

Kim sits beside me and strokes my arm. I wonder how she feels, hearing things tumble out of my mouth that I haven't managed to tell her yet. I can't look at her. I don't want to see hurt in her eyes. But her touch is gentle, comforting and supportive. She's helping me continue even though each word threatens to choke me or make me break down in tears.

"Saul didn't tell me exactly what his plan was before I escaped," I say.

"But Gage, who worked for him, told me that Saul was going to create a hidden army to strike against the Changed in one go," Kim says. "He said that Saul was going to strip AJ's magic from him."

Tanith nods. "He'd have to do the same to Adele, as well."
I gasp. "What?"

"Can you imagine how much magic would be needed to create such an army? To transfer that many souls and to keep them all alive at the same time? Within us, our magic is a limited but replenishing source. There's only so much we can expend at one time before it exhausts and weakens us. But as our strength returns, so our magic grows again. Outside of us, that same magic is a limited pool that can be used in its entirety, or, if stored, slowly."

"Like the box Matthew is in?" Sophie asks.

"Yes. Adele wouldn't be able to transfer enough souls, any more than you could heal enough people."

I shake my head. "She didn't strike me as the type who would sacrifice all her magic for Saul's crazy plan."

"Maybe there's a reason he never discussed his full plans in front you," Tanith says. "Tell me, was she always present?"

"Nearly always."

"Saul is going to betray her," Kim says.

I don't feel sorry for Adele. She wants Saul's plan to succeed. She enjoyed hurting me and took pleasure in Mum's death.

"It would also take co-ordination with humans in thrall to Saul," Tanith continues. "Presumably, he would make the army here, in Uralahnd, but then he'd need humans in several locations across earth to open gateways for him as close to the same time as possible. He'd also need to know where all the Changed were."

"He could lure them," Kim says. "By having Baneem use magic."

Tanith nods in agreement. "But can you imagine how many people he would have to have working for him? The humans to open the gateways. Baneem on earth to lure the Changed to certain locations and then the Baneem in Uralahnd, willing to risk their lives for his plan." She shakes her head. "Let's assume that the human vessels are not willing. It's still a lot of people. Does Saul really command that much power?"

I shrug. "I have no idea." I'd like to think he doesn't. I didn't see that many Baneem in his compound, but I can't guarantee he doesn't.

"Is it possible he was making sure his plan would work before rallying Baneem to his cause?" Sophie asks. "He wouldn't need that many humans working for him. Each Baneem who agrees to help him would probably have a human who opens gateways for them, right?"

"That's plausible," Tanith says. "But as far as I can see, if you stay beyond his reach, AJ, he cannot go through with his plan. You're safe here."

"I'm not staying here forever," I say, gritting my teeth. "I'm not hiding. I'm done hiding."

Tanith rolls her eyes upwards. "Even if that's the most sensible thing for you to do?" Her expression softens. "Allow me to show you where I live. You'll see it is beautiful, a place where you could be happy."

My voice catches in my throat. I know the potential Uralahnd has, a potential that Baneem like Saul have ignored. But Uralahnd isn't my home. I grimace. Not that I have a home on earth, either. Not anymore.

"Saul murdered AJ's mum," Kim mutters.

"So you're seeking revenge?" Elizabeth asks, her lips quirking upwards.

"No," I say quickly. "But I won't hide forever."

Tanith splays her fingers on the table. "I see."

"Even if I did... Saul isn't the only Baneem who means humans harm, is he? You've been fighting against them for two thousand years and they haven't given up."

"Despite the threat of being dragged to purgatory," Kim mutters bitterly.

"What can you do that the Changed couldn't?" Elizabeth asks.

Kim puffs out her cheeks. Her hand, still resting on my arm, tenses. "We want to stop the gateways being opened. And we think we know how to do it."

Elizabeth stares at us all.

"You stopped trying to find answers," Sophie reminds her. "Don't look so shocked that we figured out a better solution than you."

Elizabeth shakes her head slowly. "Forgive me. You are right. I suppose immortality made me stuck in my ways, rather than inventive, as I had been whilst I was mortal. I had a solution, I looked no further." She edges closer to us. "But you three... you have a way to stop the gateways being opened?"

Kim nods. "We were testing whether our idea would work. That's how we ended up here. The gateways are one-way doors."

"But you'd all be trapped too," I say, remembering Matthew's fears. Except he hadn't known that his home was in Uralahnd. I wince internally, angry at myself for not believing he had been telling us the truth, even if it was just lies that he'd been duped into believing.

"Even more reason for Matthew to remain here in ignorance," Elizabeth says. "And if there is no longer a battle to fight, healing him will not be necessary."

"Being stuck in the golem isn't a life," Kim cries out. "He hates it in there."

I nod in agreement. "Whatever happens, whether we succeed or fail, Matthew deserves to be healed." I inhale deeply. "But I won't do it without his knowledge. I know how he feels about magic. It has to be his choice. Maybe once he understands—" I clamp my mouth shut as Elizabeth glares at me through narrowed eyes.

"None of you have the right to destroy or undermine what I have created here. Give up your magic if you wish. It makes no difference to me. I will gladly use it to heal Matthew, but I will not curse him with the truth. He will not understand."

I sigh and wipe my hands over my face. Maybe she's right.

"Did Matthew know about you?" Tanith asks.

I jerk my head up to look at her and nod.

Tanith smiles, trying to placate me as she turns to Elizabeth. "Then it seems to me that Matthew already understands that things aren't black and white." She purses her lips. "Besides, if these children are successful, the Changed will lose their sense of purpose. They will need to build a new life and they could do that alongside us." Her expression becomes dark. "Unless you are planning on destroying them once they are no longer of any use to you?"

"No, of course not," Elizabeth snaps.

"Perhaps Matthew can be the bridge between the old and new way of life," Tanith says. "Once he understands, he can help the other Changed to understand and be at peace with the truth."

"He'll have felt the magic in the box already," I say. I can't help but wonder how they managed to convince him to get into the box, given how vehemently he's been rejecting accepting the use of human ritual magic to help him.

"No," Elizabeth says. "He was sleeping before I carried him in here and placed him inside. There will be a brief moment, when he is realeased, where he will be aware of it."

"And then you'll make him forget," Sophie says through gritted teeth.

"You can't make him forget this time," Kim says. "I know he can help us. He'll understand. I know he will."

I'm not sure Matthew will be receptive to the truth or my offer of healing, but I hold my concerns inside. It would be too easy for me to side with Elizabeth, only I've seen the damage lies can do. I know how cut up Kim is about lying to her family.

Elizabeth stares at all of us. She has no reason to bow down to our wishes. She's more powerful than any of us and could crush us all if she wanted to. But strangely, I'm not afraid of her. I understand her desire to atone for her sins. I need to do the same, except I haven't had two thousand years to dwell on mine.

"All right," she says finally. "I will let him out. I only hope he is as receptive to the truth as you believe."

She steps up to the vessel and traces a glyph on the surface: two broken U's, one nestling within the other. The top slides back, until its edge is resting on nothing but the thick lip of the chamber. By rights, it should topple to the floor, but it hangs as though suspended on wires. I bite my lower lip to stop myself from reacting as the glowing cocktail of free magic within it calls out to my soul, enticing me closer. I grasp Kim's hand, hoping the solidity of her grasp will ground me and keep me stationary. Matthew opens his eyes and blinks at Elizabeth. Wisps of magic escape the box in the few seconds it takes her to help Matthew climb out. She then traces a second glyph on the lid, a square spiral, which prompts it to slide shut, nullifying the pull of the magic. I release the breath I'd been holding in a loud gasp.

Matthew stares at Elizabeth and then his gaze shifts to each of us, finally coming to rest on Tanith. "Who are you?" He stares down at the box. "Magic? I don't understand." His voice is cold, the golem's face expressionless.

I release Kim's hand, allowing her to pull away from me so she can go to Matthew. She tries to touch his cheek, but he flinches away from her.

"Do you still want him to know the truth?" Elizabeth asks. "It isn't too late for me to make him forget what he's seen."

"What's going on?" Matthew asks, focusing on Elizabeth. "What truth?"

"He needs to know," Kim mutters.

"What do I need to know?" Matthew asks, contempt leaking into his voice. "Why is there magic in that box?"

"She's True Shamari," Kim says, pointing at Tanith, the words rushing out of her. "Or rather, she's Baneem. She's part of a group who broke away from the rest of the Baneem, because they didn't want to see humans getting hurt or corrupted. Elizabeth created the Changed with the help of the breakaway group of Baneem." She shakes her head. "I don't get it. With not-angels capturing them on earth and dragging them to imprisonment, why didn't the Baneem just give up? Why bother taking the risk all these years?"

Tanith shrugs. "I wish I knew. My ancestors spread the word that the Creator was unhappy with the actions of our people and that He had created the Changed in order to punish them. The hope was that they would stop their actions immediately. But they didn't. And here we are, two thousand years later, still fighting a losing battle. The Baneem have far greater numbers than we do. Our numbers have diminished over turn and so, in turn, has our ability to create and maintain the Changed."

"I was created by magic?" Matthew says slowly, his face crumpling into a devastated expression. "How could I not have known?"

"Because you were lied to," Sophie says, anger bubbling in her voice.

"We believe what we're told," I say quietly. It won't help if Sophie or Kim lose their tempers now.

Matthew stares down at his arms, as though if he peers long enough he'll be able to pierce through the bulk of the golem, to his soul and see magic.

"Does knowing the truth change what you do?" I say. "Or why you do it?"

He cocks his head to one side, staring at Elizabeth. "Why didn't you tell us? Why lie to us?"

"I didn't think any of you would accept the gift of immortality and power, if you knew it was coming from Baneem, the very creatures who led to your deaths."

"Wasn't that our decision to make?"

Elizabeth presses her lips together.

"Evil exists everywhere," Matthew says. "As does good. But you led us to believe all Baneem were evil. That they all had bad intentions towards humanity, when it simply wasn't true. If you'd explained..."

"I don't think you'd have listened," I say.

"I would have," he snaps, turning his dark stare to me.

"Really? You might say that now, four hundred years after you died. But in that moment, caught between life and death, burning with hatred for the Baneem that led to your death, would you really have accepted that any of them were good? Would you really have agreed to work for them?"

Matthew shakes his head. "No."

"I'm not saying Elizabeth should have lied to you all this time, but maybe, just maybe, she did what she thought was best. Through you, she's been trying to protect humans for two thousand years. She's been doing the right thing, but in the wrong way." I glance at Elizabeth, daring her to argue with my reasoning, but all she does is shrug and nod.

"An apology sounds empty at this point," she says. "Besides, didn't *you* have something you wanted to discuss with Matthew?"

I nod and stand, so I can face him as evenly as possible. "I can heal you."

"By sacrificing his magic," Elizabeth says.

It's impossible to guess what Matthew is thinking. He holds his expression utterly passive and the body of the golem completely relaxed, but I know he isn't. As time crawls by, all any of us can do is stand and wait for Matthew to make a decision.

"Give it some more thought," Elizabeth says, breaking the silent stalemate. "Take time to process what you've learned. Perhaps you and I should go somewhere more private and you can ask my anything you like."

"Or you can take his memories away," Sophie mutters.

The corner of Elizabeth's mouth jerks up a fraction, but she doesn't deny Sophie's accusation.

"No," Matthew says slowly. "I can think here."

"What's there to think about?" I ask. "Do you really want to stay trapped in the golem forever?"

Matthew shakes his head. "But I do not have the right to ask you to sacrifice your magic for me."

"You're not asking. I'm offering."

I'm surprised he's even contemplating my offer and that he's not shouting and screaming and demanding more explanations. It's impossible to know what's going on in his mind. Just because the golem looks passive and calm doesn't mean his thoughts aren't a raging inferno. But this is a decision he has to make, and he has to make it alone. No one, not even

Kim, can help him decide what to do, or how to come to terms with four hundred years of lies. He's barely had time to process everything and I'm asking him to allow the thing he has spent several lifetimes hating to help him.

A thousand reasons why he should accept my help run through my mind as I wait for him to say something, anything. Even a refusal would be good enough. Anything to ease the icy tension the room has been cursed with. Yes, he's reeling. We all are. He needs to get over it.

My unsympathetic emotions alarm me, but it was the same for me. I needed weeks to grieve Mum, probably a lot longer, but I couldn't, because there simply wasn't time. Kim made me realise that. Matthew made me see that with his threats. When all this is done, if we succeed, I'll grieve then. Matthew can process what he is and who the True Shamari are then. But now, he has to make a decision.

"Yes," Matthew says.

I blink, almost choking on his answer.

He lifts his chin, jutting it into the air. "Because I want to help you close the gateways. I haven't spent four hundred years trying to stop the Baneem, only to give up now." He stares at me. "Now isn't the time for me to give into anger or denial. I've done enough of that, even when you and Kim guessed I was using magic. I was a fool." His voice is bitter.

"No..." Kim begins.

"Yes. I should have seen it. You two did, but I chose to remain blinded by hate. This fight isn't over. I cannot help you trapped inside the golem, without access to any of my abilities." He smiles at me sadly. "But are you sure you wish to sacrifice your magic?"

I nod. I've never been surer of anything in my life, except the way I feel about Kim.

"It will never replenish," Tanith warns me. "And we don't know if there's an additional risk for you. Your human half might not cope with the strain. It is not a pleasant process, as I'm sure you can imagine."

I take a deep breath. "I want to do this. I need to do this." I smile at Kim, whose eyes are wide with worry. "I'll be fine. I promise."

"You don't know that," she whispers.

"I survived the things Saul did to me. I'll survive this."

Besides, they don't really need me to complete the plan. Kim can open gateways, even if she's reluctant to use magic. Hell, Matthew probably can too. Him being at full strength is far more important than me. He's trapped and decaying because of me. The only way I can make Mum's death mean something is if I give my magic to heal him, whatever it costs.

*

I'm not surprised that the Shamari have more than one amber vessel in which to store magic, but I can't help but gasp when we're led into a room with half a dozen of them.

Elizabeth removes the lid from the closest vessel, lifting it as easily as if it were made of polystyrene. I stare at the space hollowed out in the amber, roughly human shaped some like a natural sarcophagus, and shiver.

"You need to get inside," Tanith says, confirming my fears. "So your magic can be stored inside in order to heal Matthew."

"You don't have to do this," Kim says, touching my shoulder.

I swallow in an attempt to pull moisture into my throat, but it ends up feeling drier. "Yes, I do." I take a deep breath and then climb into the vessel.

The amber is warm but hard against my back. The limited space pins my arms against my sides. I can only look upwards, at the jade ceiling.

Elizabeth stands over me. "Are you ready?"

I nod, my mouth too dry to risk speaking.

"Once I have begun the ritual, I will seal the lid. When your magic has been fully removed, I'll let you out."

I frown. "Won't some of the magic seep out whilst you do that?"

"Probably."

"But we don't know how much magic it will take to heal Matthew. Surely we can't afford to lose any of it?" I prop myself up on my elbows and nod to Matthew. "Outside of the golem, you can be incorporeal, can't you? You don't need to maintain a physical manifestation."

Matthew's mouth turns down in a grimace. "I'm not sure I *can* physically manifest anymore."

"So you could be in here with me? As you heal, you're not going to suddenly become physical and crush me?"

I'm surprised when Matthew's deep laugh rumbles out of the golem; it's a sound I haven't heard in a long time. "No," he says, shaking his head and smiling. "I won't manifest and crush you." He takes a step forward and then hesitates. "Are you sure you want to do this? What you're giving up... don't do it because you feel guilty for what has happened to me."

"I'm not," I lie. "I'm doing it because we need you." I force a smile to my lips. "And no offence, but right now you're useless to us."

"You don't need me. Your plan to close the gateways will succeed with or without me. I don't need to be healed to remain here."

I scowl. "I thought you'd agreed to let me heal you."

"I have," Matthew assures me. "As long as you are sure."

"I am," I say in a defiant tone. "I want to do this." I look to Elizabeth. "Can you release Matthew from the golem, please?"

Elizabeth turns to Matthew and traces three sides of a rectangle on his chest. The fourth and final stroke goes upwards from the centre of the rectangle. In the instant she pulls his fingertip away, the golem crumbles to a pile of dry river clay, no trace of the facade that Sophie sculpted visible in the debris. Matthew's soul stands before us in his human visage, but he's incorporeal and monochrome, like a ghost. The edges of his form are wispy and he seems to be evaporating as I stare at him.

"How do you feel?" Elizabeth asks.

Matthew raises his hands and looks at them. "Weak. Incomplete."

"We'd better do this quickly," I say, laying back down. I'm terrified, but I can't lose my nerve. The golem is gone and, without my magic, Matthew will die.

Kim grabs my hand. "You'll be okay," she whispers.

"I know." I don't. Neither of us can be sure I will be okay after this, but it helps to say it and reassure myself as much as her.

She leans down and kisses me, her lips lingering against mine for a little longer than they should, given how many people are staring at us. She blushes as she pulls away from me, offering me a smile as Elizabeth stands over me in readiness.

"I'm ready," I tell her.

Her expression is blank as she traces a series of glyphs over my chest. At first, I try to see what she's doing, or at least to feel the way the pressure of her fingertip is moving, but it's impossible to keep up with her quick movements. She rests her whole palm on my chest. Instantly, I feel a shock of cold grip me and I gasp. Matthew's visage enters the vessel with me. It's the weirdest sensation. I can feel the strength of his soul, weakened though it is, encompassing me as we take up the same space. Elizabeth offers us a smile and then lifts the lid, slamming it in place.

I can still see the others, fuzzy and distorted through the amber. I watch as Elizabeth traces the square spiral glyph. Although nothing changes perceptibly, the space within the vessel feels smaller, more confining and suffocating, which isn't helped by the freezing grip the ritual has on me. I take a deep breath to stop myself from panicking. I have plenty of air. I'm not going to die in here. I hope.

I narrow my eyes, as the cold spreads through my whole body, focusing on a multitude of tiny bubbles of air, trapped within the sap as it dried and hardened, immortalised for all time within the orange fossil. My body tenses and I find it hard to breathe. It's a different sensation from when Adele lifted my soul from my body. That was painful and terrifying, but this is somehow worse. It's like something is being torn away from me. Something that's as much a part of me as my lungs, or my heart.

My entire life, I believed my magic was a curse, one that kept me running and afraid, never able to stay anywhere long enough to make friends. But the power to heal... how many people would covet that? What would others give to have my magic? Whilst I'm willing to throw it away. I shut my eyes. I'm not throwing it away. I'm using it to save an immortal. To save Matthew, who, despite his animosity towards me, has protected and helped Kim over and over again.

I grit my teeth as my magic burns with me, as though it's desperately trying to drive thousands of hooks into me to save itself from being torn from me. Every nerve in my body jangles with pain. In an almost instinctive reaction to the agony I'm enduring, I try to claw my way out of the vessel, even though I know there's no way out.

"Are you all right?" Matthew asks, his voice at once close and also distant.

I nod, even though I'm not. Tanith warned me having my magic taken from me wouldn't be pleasant, which now feels like a massive understatement.

My magic fills the space around me like smoke, first wisp like and fragile, but gradually becoming thicker until all I can see is a haze of pure white, strong enough to hide the dark hues of the amber from my vision.

My body shudders uncontrollably and then I'm left panting and sweating. The pain begins to ebb away, far more gradually than it took hold of me.

Matthew begins to glow brighter, his soul lapping up my magic as hungrily as ritual dragged it from me. In turn, the haze of my magic grows fainter. Matthew's soul radiates with power and heat, growing stronger and stronger with every passing second. I try to shrink away from the rapidly expanding energy, but there's nowhere for me to go. I need to shield my eyes from the light, burning my eyes, but I can't move my arms that freely. I snap my eyes shut, squeezing them tightly, but I can still see the light through my eyelids. Nothing else exists in this space except me and the brightness of Matthew's soul. The air feels like it's being squeezed out of my lungs. I begin to gasp, choking on oxygen that rejects me instead of sustaining me. I slam my hands up against the unyielding amber lid.

A voice filters to me. Kim's voice. It's quiet and muffled, but the urgency is clear and I guess she's screaming.

"Get him out! Get him out!"

A rush of air fills my lungs. Strong arms grab me and drag me from the vessel, dumping me on the floor, into Kim's waiting arms. I blink away the black spots that swim in my vision, to see Matthew rising from the sarcophagus. He is whole and brilliant. His mottled wings rise from his back, stretching out full span. His eyes are no longer dark, but pure white, an odd juxtaposition against his dark hair. He looks at me and nods. I try to speak, but I'm robbed of my voice. I've never seen anything so awe-inspiring. In an instant, he's kneeling in front of me, even though I didn't see him cover the distance.

"Thank you," he says, although I'm sure his lips haven't moved. "Sleep now. Rest." He traces a glyph on my forehead and his power drains the last remnants of energy from me, sending me into blissful sleep.

# CHAPTER NINETEEN

The pink light of dawn has started to filter through the window when AJ stirs and opens his eyes. I squeeze his hand, making sure the first thing he sees is my smile.

"Hey. How are you feeling?"

I don't want him to sense how terrified I've been that he wouldn't wake up, or how afraid I've been that losing his magic would be too big a price for his body to pay. Tension floods out of me when he returns my smile and raises his hand to stroke my cheek.

"Like I've fallen a thousand feet and somehow survived." His brow creases. "Everything hurts. Matthew?"

"He's fine. More than fine, actually. Your magic didn't just heal him, it supercharged him."

"I wasn't dreaming then."

I shake my head. "If you're referring to the white eyes and terrifying presence, no. He's dialled it down a bit, thankfully."

We were all left reeling when Matthew left the vessel and took on a corporeal form. The way I felt around him, when I first met him—unable to speak or think clearly—was nothing compared to the crippling awe that gripped my body when he unfurled his wings and pinned me in his stare. His dark stare, though hypnotic, had at least held a semblance of normality. But the white which now swallows his irises and pupils is like something out of a horror film. They pull me in even more so than before. They are captivating, filling my vision until it feels like I'm running through the endless fractals of a million snow-flakes swirling in a storm. In that moment, I changed my defini-tion of what a True Shamari is. It isn't Elizabeth, or the Baneem, like Tanith, in the splinter group. It's Matthew.

I roll my shoulders to wake myself from the vision of Matthew tattooed on my mind. "Everyone's waiting for you when you're ready. No rush."

He levers himself up on his shoulders. "Where are we?" He glances around at the simple room, brow furrowing.

There isn't much in here. A bed and a washstand which was filled with warm water when AJ was first brought in here. Now the water has gone cold. I assume the Baneem don't have indoor plumbing.

"The walls aren't jade," AJ says, slumping back down again.

"No. We're in the section Tanith and the other Ba... Shamari live in. This place is much bigger than I thought it was. A bit like a rabbit warren, though." I wouldn't be able to navigate back through the corridors. Although, to be fair, I was too worried about AJ to really pay attention.

"I feel like I could sleep for a month," he mutters drawing his hand over his face. He sighs and lets his arm fall onto his chest. "But I won't. I never asked... did the light spell work in the space between the worlds?"

I nod. "Yes. Although it was like standing in a vortex. If I'd let the metal go, it would have been pulled out of the gateway, so I had to push it out of the magic."

AJ grimaces. "Which is how you hurt your hand?"

"Yes." I run my hand around my wrist for a few seconds. There's no pain now, no indication that it was ever broken. Thanks to AJ. But he won't be able to heal me, or anyone else, again. I wonder if he feels the loss of his magic as acutely as I do. "But it worked," I say in a positive tone. "Which means our plan will too." I stare into his eyes. "We *can* stop the gateways being opened."

AJ smiles and seems to relax a little against the bed, before catching his lower lip between his teeth in thought. "Do they have the tools we need here to create the spell?"

I shake my head. "We have to go home to prepare."

"And then come back again, so we're going in the right direction when we release the spell into the space between the worlds." He peers at me. "Assuming the tunnel really did only allow one-way travel?" A look of regret crosses his face instantly and he looks away. "I'm sorry."

"It's okay," I assure him. "Sophie and I tried to turn around, but we couldn't. We were being pushed forward by the strength of the magic." I lean forward, resting my elbows on the bed, so I can stroke his cheek. "But right now, you need to rest more. Waiting a day or two for you to fully recover won't make a difference."

He shakes his head. I'm torn between hugging him for his bravery and berating him for his foolishness.

I frown. "I didn't think you'd be willing to rest." I sigh heavily. "When you're ready, then. It's your call."

Slowly, he pushes himself so he's fully upright. He sways slightly, prompting me to steady his back. When he nods, I move my hand away.

"I'll be fine," he says.

I couldn't be less convinced, but I smile anyway.

"Saul is still out there and he's still looking for me on earth. The sooner we shut down gateway travel, the better."

"You're useless to Saul now." I expect to see regret cross his face, but there's no trace of it.

"And what do you think he'll do when he finds out?" He puffs his cheeks out. "Saul is a cruel and vindictive man. I've ruined his plans by giving up my magic. When he finds out..." he clenches his fists.

"He'll want revenge."

AJ nods. "And we'll be lucky if he only decides to take it out on me." He breathes in deeply. "But, as far as we know, he's still in Uralahnd, whilst his goons are on earth doing his dirty work for him. When we close the gateways, he'll be trapped and we'll never have to worry about him again."

I'm not sure why, but I choke out a sob. "You make it sound so easy." Perhaps it's because finally, it feels like we've got the upper hand. Or because there's a potential end to the nightmare I've been trapped in since I found Charley, dead.

AJ pulls me to him, cradling me in his lap. I lean my head on his shoulder, nestling my cheek against the curve of his neck.

"I know I'm supposed to be the one holding it together, little miss positive. But I'm scared," I admit. "There's still so much that could go wrong. And you're right, Saul and his lackeys are still out there and they're still a threat."

He doesn't answer, he just holds me.

"I promised you we'd stop Saul, but what if I can't keep that promise? What if the spell doesn't work and we can't stop gateways being opened?"

"We could stay here," he says.

I pull away and stare at him, shaking my head. He rejected the idea when Tanith suggested it. Why would he change his mind now?

"We'd be safe and there are worse places to be. At least it's hot here," he jokes in a soft tone.

"What about everyone else? All the people the Baneem will hurt if we don't shut the gateways?"

AJ shrugs. "Are they really our problem? Would they risk their lives to protect us?"

I stare at him for a moment, horrified at the way he's talking. Did losing his magic somehow strip him of his compassion and bravery, too? I roll my eyes. His words have made me think about what we're doing and, far from changing my mind or weakening my resolve, they've only made me realise we *have* to follow through with our plan, however dangerous it might be.

"Very clever," I mutter, slapping him lightly across his chest. "Don't you turn into a master manipulator on me."

"I wouldn't dare," he says with a smirk. "I wouldn't want you coming to kick my ass."

We laugh. It feels good to let the tension out of my body. I hold his hands and bring them to my lips, kissing them.

"I should go and tell the others you're awake and that we'll be going soon."

"Right now?" He winds his arm behind my back, pulling me closer so our bodies are touching.

"I guess I could be persuaded to stay a little longer." I lift my hand, holding my thumb and forefinger a short distance apart.

AJ copies my gesture, only his thumb and forefinger are twice the distance apart as mine. He pulls me closer still, so I can feel his heartbeat thudding against my chest. Our lips are a hair's breadth away, his eyes searching mine, openly wondering. My breath quivers in my throat as we kiss. I run my hands over his back, applying pressure that forbids him from pulling away. Not that he's showing any sign that he wants to. His lips press against mine eagerly, one hand cradling my lower back, the other tangled in my hair, cupping the back of my neck.

I want more.

I slip my hands beneath his T-shirt, gently caressing his back. For a moment, he tenses. My heart lurches. Is he going to pull away? He melts into my touch, parting his lips from mine to kiss a pathway of desire across my cheek, over my jaw and down onto my neck. I tilt my head back, eyes flickering closed. His lips find my collar bone, nuzzling the circular neckline of my T-Shirt aside a fraction. Then his lips retrace their steps, coaxing mine towards his again until we're lost in a frenzy of kisses, his hands moving to cup my head, so he can trace gentle circles on my skull.

We rest our foreheads together, both taking breathless gasps in unison. I don't want the moment to end. I don't want him to pull away or stop. I try to kiss him again, but he tilts his head back a fraction, grinning in his endearingly playful lopsided way as I scowl at him.

"Are you sure?" he asks, concern echoing in his voice.

I nod. "Are you?"

He responds by kissing me and simultaneously pulling my T-Shirt up, over my head. I raise my arms, allowing him to free me of the garment and toss it onto the floor. He tries to kiss me again, but it's my turn to stop him by placing my fingertips against his lips.

"We can stop."

"Not this time."

He's right. Neither of us wants to. After everything that's happened, the awkward uncertainty has fled from us. I love him. I want his touch. I need his desire to match mine. I push myself closer to him, smiling as I stare into his hazelnut eyes and whisper, "I love you."

*

In contrast to the oppressive heat of the day, the nights in Uralahnd are cripplingly cold. I clap my hands together, blowing on them as AJ begins to draw a gateway on the wall. We've gathered in another garden, but this one isn't covered with any kind of dome. Elizabeth and Tanith are with us and, at the edge of the garden, several more of Tanith's allies stand, watching us. Their expressions are caught between curiosity and hope. I guess, for most—if not all of them—it's their first time seeing humans and a Changed other than Elizabeth.

"Good luck," Tanith says. "If your plan to stop gateway travel works, you will have brought an end to our struggle against the Baneem."

"It has to work," I say. I glance across at the self-named True Shamari. "What will you all do? Stay here or try to integrate back into Baneem society?"

Tanith shrugs. "We will see what happens. The Baneem may or may not be receptive to us. What I am sure of, is that many of them will need guidance to see beyond their hate for humanity and their lust for earth. Uralahnd is a beautiful world with infinite potential. We just have to find a way to make our brethren see that." She sighs wistfully. "We also have the Changed to think about."

"Have you called them home?" I ask.

"We have sent word to those on earth that they need to return. If they're going to be trapped here, it's time for the lies to stop."

I don't envy Tanith or Elizabeth the task of breaking the truth to the Changed. It could backfire on them badly. I'm not even sure they're making the right decision. I've been wrapped up in my own lies for a lot less time, but I'm not sure I could face telling my family the truth. It was hard enough telling Sophie about magic and not-angels.

Matthew snaps his head round to look at her, narrowing his eyes. "Even if there's a chance they'll turn against you?"

Tanith sighs. "The truth is better told than discovered," she says. "Besides, you took it remarkably well. I can at least hope the others will too."

"It was different," Matthew says. "Kim and AJ had already broached the possibility that my abilities were basically magic. I might not have wanted to listen to them, but their words did at least make me consider that everything I knew might not be the absolute truth. The other Changed haven't had that. They keep themselves far more distant from humanity than I ever have."

"Matthew's right," I say. "Don't do anything hasty. If we fail, nothing will change."

"I will try to move between this world and yours in a few days," Elizabeth says. "We will continue to keep our secrets until then, at least."

In theory, we'll have made preparations and enacted our plan within that timeframe. No one who might stop us knows of our plans. Of course, Saul doesn't need to know what we're planning to be a threat to us. He still wants AJ.

AJ turns around and gestures towards the gateway. It's complete and waiting for any one of us to press our hand against the final pictogram to activate the gateway. I puff my cheeks out. The memory of standing in the space between the worlds haunts me. Sophie loops her arm through mine and squeezes, either sensing or sharing my trepidation. Three more times, I remind myself. We'll only ever have to use a gateway three more times and then, hopefully, they'll be impossible to open.

"I wish you luck," Elizabeth says. "Your presence here has opened my eyes to how narrow-minded I had become. I trust you will succeed, but if you should fail, rest assured that I will seek to find a way to end the war. Humanity does not deserve to suffer any longer because of my mistakes and failings."

I smile at her. "I don't think you have anything to atone for anymore. I know the Changed have done a lot of good since you created them. They've saved a lot of humans from the Baneem."

"But not all those who have been targeted," she says in a regretful tone. "We are too few and those who wish to twist humanity are too many." She turns her attention to Matthew. "Will you come back to us?"

"Yes," he replies.

My chest tightens. He's been such a huge part of my life since Charley's death, that the thought of never seeing him again hurts me physically. But I know his place is ultimately here. He hasn't belonged on earth since the day he died.

"Let's do this," I say, huffing out a breath.

I raise my head high and, together with Sophie and Matthew, stride towards AJ. He strikes his palm against the final picto-gram, activating the gateway just as we reach it. I take hold of his hand, offering him a smile. Finally, after all of our struggles, loss and pain, I have genuine hope we will rid ourselves of the Baneem once and for all.

# CHAPTER TWENTY

After returning home through the gateway, we get a good night's sleep, before getting up early to start working on our plan. Together, we head towards the city's scrapyard, although, as we draw near, Matthew waits behind.

When we reach the end of the road that leads to the scrapyard, Sophie grabs my hand and tugs me to a halt. Her eyes are downcast and she's pinching her bottom lip with her teeth.

"What's wrong?" I ask.

"You two can find a decent piece of metal by yourselves, can't you?" she asks, waving towards me and AJ.

"Yes, but what's wrong?"

She sighs deeply. "I've been doing a lot of thinking since we discovered the truth about the Shamari."

Since her initial burst of anger, she has been quiet. She was there to support me whilst AJ recovered from having his magic stripped, but she has said very little. I didn't think anything of it at the time. After Charley died, whilst I was still in hospital, she spent hours with me, hugging me, offering me support without needing to say much. Now, anger towards myself wells up inside me. I should have known something was bothering her, but I was too wrapped up in my own problems to notice my best friend was suffering silently beside me.

She doesn't lift her gaze as she continues. "I thought I was okay with not knowing Dad's secrets, but I'm really not. I need to talk to him. I need to know how and when he found out magic was real."

"What if he tells you things you don't want to know?" I ask. "What if the truth is more painful than ignorance?"

She lets out a strangled noise as she forces a smile to her lips. "I'm pretty sure it *will* be more painful than not knowing. But right now, there's a huge rift between me and Dad. I really did think I was doing the right thing, Kim, promising I wouldn't ask him any questions in return for his help." She hunches her shoulders.

"But the truth could open up an even bigger gap between you. It could make things worse."

I feel terrible about trying to dissuade her, but I know about her father's involvement with magic. I know why her aunt and grandmother almost lost their minds, and I still dream about her father shooting me. I shudder. AJ lays his hand on my lower back, massaging gently. I know he understands.

Sophie finally looks up and stares at me for a few seconds. I don't know what's going through her mind, but her thoughts drive a series of emotions to her face. There's a flash of anger, which causes her eyebrows to pinch. Curiosity, which coaxes her lips apart but doesn't tease her unspoken question out of her mouth. Sadness, which makes her shake her head and dip her gaze again. It's an expression that tugs at my heart.

"Maybe it will make things worse, but at least, with things out in the open, we'll be able to build a bridge to cross the divide between us." She scuffs her shoe against the ground. "I don't expect you to understand, Kim, but I can't carry on, knowing everyone is lying to me."

I do understand, sort of. I know how much I hate lying to my parents and how much I despised lying to her, but I had no other choice. I *have* no other choice. All I've ever wanted to do is protect them all and I'm sure Sophie's father feels the same way. Except she does know about magic now and she's right in the centre of the storm at the moment.

"I think..." she begins, her voice cautious. "If you surround yourself with lies for long enough, they become a sort of twisted truth that you actually start to believe yourself. It's easy to convince yourself that you're doing the right thing and that it justifies making decisions for everyone else. But it doesn't." She stares at me. "I know you can't tell your family the truth. I know that, even if they did believe you, it would open up wounds that are best left closed. But I can't carry on knowing half-truths bundled up in lies. I can't." She inhales a deep breath, clenching and unclenching her fists as she does so. "So, I have to go and talk to Dad and I have to do it now, before I completely lose my nerve."

I pull her into a hug. "I get it," I promise her. "And when this is all over, I promise we'll sit down and talk too." I owe her that much.

She lets out a little sob and nods against my shoulder. "Thank you, Kim." She pulls away, wipes tears from her eyes and off of her cheeks, then she offers us both a little wave before hurrying away.

AJ and I trudge along the road to the scrapyard in silence. Sophie's words run through my head, forcing me to shine a spotlight on all the lies I've told since Charley died. Too many. I keep telling myself those lies protect everyone around me. But do they? By keeping silent, I allowed Gage to use his magic to control Mum's actions not once, but twice. Then there's Chris, who has to live with the knowledge that he stole from a shop, even though it was Gage who made him do it. The horrible things that happened to AJ and Matthew are down to my lies, too. Or at least, my inability to tell the truth. Who have I really been protecting? Like Sophie said, I've woven a web of twisted truths, which I'm completely entangled in.

"She wasn't getting at you," AJ says, as we begin to pick through the junk, looking for a good sized piece of metal.

"I know."

AJ wipes his hands on his jeans and gently clutches my shoulders. "Look at me."

Chin trembling, I tip my head back so I can meet his gaze.

"Everything you've done, everything you've withheld and every lie you've told, you've done for the right reasons."

"That doesn't mean I've been doing the right thing."

He presses his lips together, his gaze sad. "No, it doesn't. But dwelling on things you can't change won't help you either."

I laugh bitterly. "Like you've been doing?" I bite my lower lip, regretting my words.

He nods, no anger creeping into his expression. "*Exactly* like I've been doing. I blamed myself for what happened to Mum and Matthew." He tips his forehead against mine and breathes in deeply. "We can't change our actions, Kim. All we can do is move forward and try to learn from our mistakes." Easier said than done and we both knew it.

I step forward so I can wrap my arms around him. "You've come to terms with what happened, then?" I wish he'd let me help him more.

"I'm trying," he whispers. "I'm trying really hard." He lifts his head, tips my chin a little higher and kisses me. "I'll tell you everything," he promises. "When this is all over. When I've got time to let myself fall apart completely. I'll tell you everything and gladly let you help me put the pieces of my life back together."

He kisses me again and then we step apart and go back to our search.

Our search takes us past lunchtime, but eventually we find what looks to have been part of a car bonnet. The metal is a decent thickness and curved. It was originally flame red, but someone has badly spray-painted grey over the top. The edges are jagged where the metal has been cut and, as AJ tries to pick it up, he hisses and snatches his hand back, sucking at his finger.

"Let me see," I say, taking hold of his arm.

Blood drops from a fairly large cut on his middle finger. For a second, I expect the wound to start to heal.

"I guess we know that my magic has really gone," AJ says, as though he's reading my thoughts. There's a hint of sadness in his voice, which makes my chest ache.

I pull a tissue out of my pocket and wrap it round his finger. "Having regrets?"

"No." He gives me a lopsided smile. "I just need to learn to be more careful."

Together we pick up the sheet of metal carefully, making sure we avoid the jagged edges. It's not as heavy as I'd expected, but too unwieldy for one person to manage easily. Not that we have to take it more than a few streets.

Once we arrive at the cycle path, Matthew, who has been waiting for us, manifests and relieves us of our burden.

"Where's Sophie?" he asks, frowning.

"Gone to speak to her dad," I say. "They really need to talk."

He nods. "I'll take this back to the warehouse. Will you both be all right making your own way there?"

"We've got legs. We'll be fine, Matthew. Thank you."

We stand back as he unfurls his wings and ascends into the sky. It's weird being able to see him, knowing no one else can. Luckily, his aura will also extend to the piece of metal in his hands, otherwise there would probably be some panicked calls to the police station mumbling about UFOs. The thought makes me smile. I take hold of AJ's hand and we head back towards the warehouse.

It takes us a little over an hour to walk back, via a DIY store to buy an engraving tool and the supermarket to get some plasters and antiseptic wipes. I frown as I cast my gaze around the warehouse. The car bonnet is laying in the middle of the room.

"Where's Matthew?" I ask.

AJ follows my gaze and finally shrugs. "Enjoying being able to fly again?"

"Hmmm... maybe." I try to force down my concern. Matthew is powerful again, more so than he was before Stella attacked him. He can handle himself. "Let's get you sorted," I say, rustling the bag of supplies at him.

Once I've cleaned up AJ's finger, I unpack the handheld engraver. "We'll need power, which this place doesn't have." I grimace at AJ. "You *can't* go to mine or Sophie's houses, in case Saul's goons are watching."

"I'll sit the engraving out," AJ says with a shrug. "Matthew can get the metal where we need it without anyone seeing." He retrieves the piece of paper with the pictograms we need on and hands it to me. "You and Sophie can do this part."

"Sophie can do this part. I have the artistic skill of a brick."

AJ laughs. "I don't think being artistic has anything to do with it. The best I can draw are stickmen. A steady hand and the ability to copy is all it'll take."

I wrinkle my nose. "I'll still let Sophie handle it."

AJ's expression drops, causing me to turn around to look at the doorway. Matthew is helping Sophie through the half-removed boarding. She looks terrible. She wrenches her hand from Matthew and hugs herself. Her cheeks are damp with tears and there's a horrid gash down her right cheek, which is still dripping blood. Her left eye is black, her bottom lip swollen and cut. She's sobbing and shaking her head.

I get to my feet and hurry over to her, wrapping her in my arms.

"What happened?" I ask my voice calm and soothing even though anger is gripping me, making my insides churn. "Matthew?"

"I felt a gateway being opened close by, so I went to investigate," Matthew says.

"A gateway?" My mind is numb, unable to put connections together.

"I'm sorry," Sophie sobs. "I'm so, so sorry."

"Sorry for what?"

She pushes me away and dips her chin to her chest, guilt twisting her face. "Saul's men. I told them everything."

# CHAPTER TWENTY-ONE

Sophie begins to sob uncontrollably, so I stand behind her, put my hands on her shoulders and steer her to the camping mat. I push her gently down onto it and then hug her as AJ grabs the antiseptic wipes and, gently, begins to clean the cut on her face. From the grim set of his mouth and the way she winces, it must be bad.

"What happened?" I repeat.

"They were waiting at my house," she whispers. "They had Dad." She shakes her head and trembles in my arms. "They'd already hurt him, Kim. They'd wanted him to lure us to the house and he'd refused to. He'd kept his mouth shut and they hurt him."

I tighten my grip on her, offering her as much comfort as I can. "Go on."

"They told me they'd kill him if I didn't call AJ and get him to come to the house."

AJ pauses and lowers his gaze, his cheek muscles flexing as he grits his teeth.

"I begged them not to hurt him. I told them..." She shakes her head. "I told them AJ's magic was gone. I thought they'd let Dad and I go. How could I have been so stupid?"

"Because you thought they were reasonable people," AJ says quietly. "But they're not. The people Saul has working for him are cold and manipulative." He goes back to cleaning up her cheek.

"They kept hurting him," Sophie whispers. "Over and over until I answered their questions." She clenches her fists and then thumps them against her knees. "They know about our plan. I thought... I thought... I was stupid."

"No," I say. "You're not. You were scared and they were hurting your dad. You did what you thought you had to do to protect him."

I glance at AJ. He's still cleaning Sophie's cut, his dabs slow and gently. His expression is carefully guarded and I wonder what pain he's pushing down. It was the same for him. He did things he hates himself for to protect his mum.

"Where is your dad?" I ask.

"They took him," Sophie says, crumpling in my arms. "They said if we want him back, AJ has to go to Uralahnd. He has to go to Saul."

I draw in a sharp breath. "Why? AJ is useless to Saul now."

"Revenge," AJ says quietly.

"And to stop us from going through with closing the gateways," Matthew says. "They are assuming we won't trap AJ in Uralahnd."

"We won't," I mutter.

"I have to go," AJ says.

"No," Sophie sobs. "You can't. Saul will kill you. Like you said, he'll want revenge on you for ruining his plans."

AJ shakes his head. "He won't kill me. If me being in Uralahnd is the only thing stopping you guys from closing the gateways, he'll keep me alive and he'll keep sending proof to you all. But hopefully, he'll let your dad go."

"He won't," Matthew says. "We know he cannot be trusted. We know he is not a man of his word."

"Matthew's right," Sophie says, her words trembling from her tear-soaked lips. "They'll kill him as soon as you hand yourself over."

She breaks down again, almost retching as her sobs are so violent. I stroke her forehead and making shushing noises in my throat in an effort to calm her down, but I know it's useless.

I look to Matthew with wide eyes. He nods and crouches down beside AJ so he can trace a glyph on Sophie's head.

"Sleep," he says in a gentle tone.

Her head lolls forward and she sags in my arms. With Matthew's help, I lie her down on the camping mat and brush my own tears away.

"She needs stitches," AJ says, cleaning his hands with some bottled water. "A plaster or a dressing isn't going to fix up that cut. We need to take her to hospital."

"We can't," I say, staring at Sophie hopelessly.

"Kim..."

"Her dad is a judge, AJ. If we take her to hospital, they'll call the police. The police will try to contact her dad and, when they discover he's missing, they'll search for him. Her mum will be called, too. We can't have any of that happen."

He shakes his head as anger creeps into his expression. I place my hand over his.

"You couldn't have known this would happen. Don't be angry you can't heal her."

"That's not why I'm angry," he growls. "I'm angry anyone would do this to her and to her dad. The Baneem Saul has working for him are monsters. They're as bad as he is."

"That's probably why they follow him," Matthew says.

I stare down at Sophie. AJ's right, the cut almost certainly needs stitches. From its ugly nature, I guess she'll end up with a scar, which will be worse if it doesn't get treated properly. But taking her to a hospital will make everything more complicated. Guilt gnaws away at me. How can I even think about not getting Sophie the help she needs?

"I don't know what to do," I admit. "Everything's such a mess."

"Superglue," AJ sighs.

"What?"

"It's a cyanoacrylate. They tested their use in the Vietnam war for closing wounds. It was never approved, though, but it does work."

I frown. "Why wasn't it approved?"

"It can cause skin irritations," AJ admits. "They later developed a medical grade cyanoacrylate, which *is* used, but there's no way we can get hold of that, so superglue will have to do." He stares at me, eyebrows raised slightly. "We don't have many options, do we?"

"How did you know all that?" I ask AJ.

He shrugs. "I told you before, I read a lot whilst Mum and I were travelling. Plus, I wanted to be a doctor."

"Wanted?" I stare down at the floor. "You still can be."

He laughs bitterly. "I didn't take my G.C.S.E.s, Kim. I'd never get onto a medical degree. Besides, I was in trouble with school already, I'm sure they wouldn't take me back. Even if they did, I've got nowhere to live and no way to support myself. " He focuses his attention on Sophie again, gently checking over her other facial injuries.

I'm not sure what to say. It's not just the past AJ needs to come to terms with, but his uncertain future, too.

"I'll go get some superglue," I mumble, standing.

"I'll take you," Matthew says. "It'll be faster."

"No. Take Sophie, AJ and the metal to my house."

AJ turns his head sharply to stare at me. "A few minutes ago, you said I couldn't go back to your house."

"That was before I knew they'd taken Mr. Jenkins to Uralahnd. They know we're not going to leave Sophie's dad to rot there. There's no point in them looking here for you anymore. They want you to go to them, where they hold all the power." I crouch down and kiss his forehead, before giving him back the paper with the ritual on. "Go to my house, start work on the engraving while you wait for me to get there, okay?"

AJ nods.

I stand and turn to Matthew. "If I'm wrong, protect them both."

"Of course," he says.

Before leaving, I grab Professor West's book of pictograms from AJ's pile of things, stuffing it into my coat pocket. I hope I'm right and that all the Baneem really have gone back to Uralahnd and that I'm not sending AJ, Sophie and Matthew into danger.

*

I feel the bulky presence of someone walking right behind me as I turn onto my street.

"We need to talk," a voice says, before I have a chance to turn around to see who is invading my personal space.

My heartbeat quickens and goosebumps break out over my skin as I recognise Flame Guy's voice. I try to tell myself that if he wanted to hurt me, he would have already done so without announcing his presence.

"About what?" I hiss. "About how you and your associates beat my best friend and abducted her dad?"

"I wasn't involved in that," he replies in a gruff tone. "If I was, I wouldn't even be here. But it's why we need to talk."

"You knew about it though, didn't you?" I say. "You could have stopped it and you didn't."

He grabs my arm and pulls me to a halt. We're two doors away from my house and Matthew, who I know won't hesitate to act if he sees Flame Guy. He knows there's nothing stopping him from hurting a Baneem.

"And how would I do that?" Flame Guy asks me. His nostrils flare in anger as he stares down at me. "Look, Saul got bored of waiting for me to get results and sent Ike to take over from me. Anyway, I know Ike took your friend's father to Uralahnd and I know you'll go after him." He narrows his eyes. "I know Aran will."

"So you're here to stop us?"

He shakes his head. "The opposite. I'm here to help you."

I jerk my head back and wrench my arm from his grasp. "Why the hell should I believe you?"

He shrugs. "You've no reason to. But I helped Aran, didn't I? I didn't hurt your father and brother when I could have easily killed them. I've had time and opportunity to force you to hand Aran over, but I took a soft approach and landed myself in a pile of shit in the process." He leans closer to me. "I know you want to shut the gateways."

My eyes widen, but he carries on as if he hasn't noticed.

"Here's the deal. I help you and you let me stay on earth. That way, I'll be free of Saul forever."

I take a half step back, unsure if I can trust anything he's saying. "How could you help us?" I ask in a cautious voice.

"If you're going to get your friend's father back, you need to know the layout of Saul's compound. Aran's knowledge of it is sketchy at best, and limited. I know it intimately. I'll draw you a map. I'll tell you the weak points—where you can get in and out again without being seen. And I'll give you a key to the cells, where you friend's father is likely being kept." He holds his hands out in front of him, palms up. "That's it. That's my offer. Take it or leave it."

"And if I leave it?"

"Then I'll walk away," he says with a shrug. "I'll do my best to vanish and stay out of Saul's reach. One thing's for sure, I won't be going back to Uralahnd and I won't be using anymore magic. I don't want some bastard Shamari coming and hauling my ass to purgatory."

I glance towards my house. "It's not only my decision."

"I figured you'd say that. Go and talk to Aran. See what he says. I'll wait for half an hour, then my offer will be off the table and you'll never see me again."

"Come inside with me," I say. "It's better if it comes from you."

He purses his lips. "You've got a Changed in there," he says in an accusing tone.

"I promise Matthew won't touch you."

His brow furrows. "Matthew? Didn't Saul have him destroyed?"

I shrug. "He got better."

"Huh. That'll piss Saul off no end." He folds his arms. "Why should I trust *you*?"

"I could have called for Matthew already. He would have been out here to apprehend you before you could have turned and run."

He doesn't look convinced, but nods anyway. "Fine. But you'd better not be planning on double crossing me. I only have to get one spell out to kill you."

I shiver, even though there's no real weight behind his words. They're hollow, like he's lost his appetite for hurting anyone. I only hope it's true.

We find Matthew and AJ in the kitchen. The car bonnet is propped up in the corner, with a handful of the pictograms already engraved into the surface. AJ looks weary as he sits at the breakfast bar, eating some cereal. From the expression on his face, it tastes like cardboard. However, when he notices Flame Guy he stiffens and stares between us, slack-jawed. Matthew makes to move towards Flame Guy and then stops himself, looking at me questioningly. At least he didn't act first, ask questions later.

"Flame Guy is here to help," I say.

"Help?" AJ asks, his voice a pained squeak. "Help?"

"Wouldn't be the first time, would it?" Flame Guy asks. "And seriously, you guys need to stop calling me *Flame Guy*. My name's Leon." He holds his hand out to AJ, who doesn't move.

"You're one of Saul's men?" Matthew asks in a dangerous tone. He takes a step closer.

"No," I say, holding my hand up. "Leon is here to help." Somehow, his real name doesn't suit him anywhere near as well as Flame Guy does. "I promised you wouldn't hurt him and that we'd hear him out."

Matthew curls his upper lip. "You and your promises."

I ignore his curt words and turn my attention to AJ. "Will you listen to him?"

AJ blows a breath over his lower lip and nods. "Sure. Why not."

"Right," Leon says. "You need to get your friend's father back so you can close the gateways without trapping him. Right? I'll draw you a map of Saul's compound so you actually stand half a chance of accomplishing that. In return, you let me live here, on earth, in peace." He looks pointedly at Matthew. "I'm done messing with humans. I'm done hurting them. I just want to get on with my life, without fear of Saul stabbing me in the back. I won't be able to do that in Uralahnd."

"And a key," I remind him. "You said you'd give us the key to the cells."

"Oh yeah, sure." He pulls a large metal key out of his pocket and shows it to us. "You get this, too."

I move to AJ and rub his shoulder. "It's up to you," I say softly. "You've got to be okay with accepting his help."

He pushes the bowl of cereal away and hunches his shoulders. "How do we know we can trust you?" he asks. "How do we know this isn't part of Saul's plan and that you're not a Trojan horse?"

Leon snorts. "I don't even know what that means, kid. Look, I can't prove I'm on the level. But I did my best to help you. Remember? You'd never have escaped if it wasn't for the kindness I showed you." He rolls his eyes. "Ike was quick to shift all the blame for your disappearing act onto me. I was lucky Saul didn't end me there and then."

"Why didn't he?" AJ asks.

"Damned if I know. He turned his magic on me, left me in a right state, begging for bloody mercy and then ordered me to find you and drag you back. Told me it was my last chance to prove I was worth keeping around." He shivers. "Your father is the closest thing to evil I've ever seen."

As Leon talks, I feel the tension bunching up AJ's muscles. I long to ease it away, but I know I can't.

"He's insane," AJ says quietly. He tilts his head. "Who's Ike?"

Leon laughs. "Ice Man. That was the nickname you gave him, wasn't it?"

A flicker of a smile tugs at AJ's lips, but he banishes it quickly. He turns to me. "What do you think?"

"I think we need his help," I say. "We have to presume we're going to be outnumbered and outpowered. If Leon can help us even up the odds, even a fraction, we need to trust him."

AJ's pupils contract a little. I guess he's thinking over my words and deciding if we—if *he*—can truly trust Leon. "All right," he says eventually. "If you think he's trustworthy, that's good enough for me."

"Matthew?" I ask.

Matthew gazes upwards and shakes his head, the expression of his face one of tired resignation. "Fine." He narrows his eyes and stares at Leon. "But double-cross us and Saul will be the least of your worries."

I grab some paper and a pencil from one of the kitchen drawers and toss them onto the table. "Draw," I say. I pull the superglue out of my pocket, my fingers brushing against a small box containing the other thing I stopped off to buy. For a moment, I consider showing it to AJ and telling him my plan, but the less we say in front of Leon the better. "Go see to Sophie," I say, giving him the superglue. "Matthew and I will keep an eye on Leon."

*

It takes Leon about an hour to draw a detailed map, which he then explains to Matthew and I. When he's done, he leans back on his chair and clasps his hands behind his head.

"I think you're all insane to risk going into the Devil's den," he says.

"We have to," I reply.

"I know." He glances at the closed door.

AJ hasn't returned, not that I blame him. Even if Leon did show AJ kindness, he still stood by and let Saul and Adele hurt him. He stood by and let Saul kill Phailin. That won't be easy to forgive.

"How's the kid doing?" Leon asks.

"How do you think?" Matthew growls.

"That bad, huh?" Leon scrunches up his lips. "For what it's worth, I'm really sorry about what happened to him and his mother. But getting rid of his magic..." he whistles. "That was a sure fired way to piss Saul off." He leans onto the table and stares at both Matthew and I. "You might want to consider convincing him to sit this one out."

I shake my head, stand and cross over to the window. It's dark now and I'm feeling far too tired to play at being civil.

"What if Saul gets him?" Leon presses. "Or what if he freaks out? I guess he's told you what happened?"

"No." I wrap my arms around my waist. "Not really."

"It was bad," Leon says. "Really bad. Anyway, it's your choice, but I'm just saying, he might be unpredictable. He could fall apart, or he could flip out. Neither reaction is going to help you."

"He'll be fine," I say, though I'm painfully aware that my voice holds no trace of conviction.

Leon holds his hands up. "I've given you my advice, it's up to you what you do with it. But I saw, first hand, what Saul did to Aran, so you might want to listen." He stands. "Are we done? I get to walk out of here now?"

I nod. "Yes. Thank you."

"Good luck," he says. "Although I think you'll need more than that. I don't suppose I could convince you to leave your friend's father where he is and shut the gateways?"

"No." I turn to him, chin lifted high. "That isn't an option. We'll succeed. We'll rescue Mr. Johnson *and* close the gateways."

"I really hope you do," he says, heading to the door.

I see him out, breathing a sigh of relief as I shut and lock the door behind him. When I turn around, I see AJ waiting at the top of the stairs.

"Sophie's awake," he says in a dull tone.

"How much did you hear?"

"Most of it." He sits down on the top step and clasps his hands between his knees. "Maybe he's right. Maybe I should stay here."

"Do you want to?" I ask.

He looks up sharply. "No, of course not. I don't want you to face Saul without me. He's only a threat to you and Sophie and your families because of me. I should be there to help save Mr. Johnson and stop Saul." He breathes in deeply. "But I also don't want to be the reason we fail. I'm scared, Kim. I honestly can't guess how I'll react if I come face to face with Saul."

I walk up the steps and sit beside him. "You'll get through it," I say, gently prising his hands apart so I can take hold of one of them. I thread my fingers through his and squeeze.

"You'll hold it together, because you're stronger than Saul. I believe in you, AJ. I know you won't let us down."

He tips his head against mine. "Thank you," he whispers.

"What for?"

"For being my rock. I'm leaning on you so heavily at the moment. It's not fair."

"You aren't leaning heavily enough," I reply, coaxing him to turn his face so I can kiss his lips. "But when you're ready to open up, I'll be here. Okay?"

"Thank you." He kisses me and then glances towards my bedroom. "You'd better go and see Sophie. I'll get on with the engraving."

I squeeze his hand one last time, before standing and slipping into my room.

Sophie is sitting on the bed, her hands clenched together. Her face still looks a mess, but AJ has done a good job of sealing the cut on her cheek. The rest will heal in time.

"We're going to rescue your dad," I say, as I sit down beside her.

"I know," she whispers, her voice trembling. "I'm really sorry, Kim."

"Don't be." I hug her tightly. "You've nothing to be sorry for, understand? Nothing at all."

# CHAPTER TWENTY-TWO

Dawn makes the sky grey as I make myself a mug of hot chocolate. I've barely slept. I sent AJ to get some rest before he'd finished engraving the pictograms into the car bonnet. He was exhausted and I was worried he was going to make mistakes. Once he'd gone, I turned my attention to Professor West's book to figure out a spell of my own. By the time I was satisfied with the pictograms, I could barely keep my eyes open. I'd only managed a couple of hours sleep, before bad dreams woke me and drove me downstairs. Dreams of finding Charley. Dreams of losing AJ and Sophie.

"Morning," Sophie says as she trudges into the kitchen. She sinks down on one of the stools at the breakfast bars and stares at me wearily.

"You're looking better," I say, even though she's still pale and her face is still swollen.

She raises her eyebrows. "I look like shit." She glances over at the car bonnet. "Want me to finish the engraving?"

I shake my head. "No. I need you to engrave something else."

"Oh?"

I finish making my own hot chocolate and make one for her too. Then I hand her the paper I've been scribbling on and the small box from my pocket. She opens it up and stares down at the plain silver ring. It's the type with an open back, so you can adjust it to fit the wearer's finger.

"What will it do?" she asks.

"Hopefully, I'll be able to use it to deliver some poetic justice on Saul." I blow across the top of my mug, watching as the wisps of steam shy away from my breath, only to coil back into place a second later. "Don't tell AJ, okay? I don't want to get his hopes up in case it doesn't work."

"Okay. Do you have a magnifying glass?"

"Maybe. Give me a sec."

I run up the stairs to Chris's room and rummage through his things. He's got a bunch of stuff in drawers that he hasn't touched in years, mostly stuff he's grown out of. It doesn't take me long to find the science kit Charley and I got him several Christmases ago. We helped him do some of the experiments before he lost interest. As I thought, one of the tools was a magnifying glass.

When I get back to the kitchen, Sophie is sitting at the table, with the engraving tool set. She's practising on one of the metal baking trays.

"Hope you don't mind," she says with a grimace. "I think I've got to grips with this thing." She waves the engraving tool. "Do me a favour and hold the magnifying glass?"

I sit beside her and do as she's asked. I let her work in silence, the low buzz of the engraving tool filling the silence. I watch through the magnifying glass as she engraves each pictogram round the silver band. I'm amazed by her precision and neatness. By the time she's done, the ring looks beautiful, despite its purpose. She places it on my palm.

"I'll finish the car bonnet," she says, but doesn't move. "You're planning on going to Uralahnd?"

"We have to," I say. "To get your dad back."

"I'm not sure I can come with you." She stares at me through watery eyes. "Does that make me a terrible daughter?"

"No." I lay my hand over hers. "Of course it doesn't. We'll bring him home to you, I promise." In a way, I'm relieved. Sophie will be safe here. At the same time, I know I'll miss her presence, strength and support.

She pulls away from me as AJ wanders into the kitchen and gets to work on completing the pictograms on the car bonnet.

They are much larger than the ones she engraved on the ring, which is why they've taken AJ so long. I pocket the ring and smile at AJ.

"Do you want to get Matthew? I think he's in the sitting room. We'd better decide what we're going to do."

*

We gather around the kitchen table once Sophie has finished the engraving, Leon's map laid out on the table for us all to see.

"In theory, we should be able to sneak in and out without having to face Saul," I say.

AJ shakes his head. "If that's where Mr. Johnson is, he'll be under guard."

"If?" Matthew asks.

"The whole point of taking Mr. Johnson was to get me to Uralahnd. Saul is going to realise I'm unlikely to just hand myself over. He's got no reason to trust me. He'll be expecting us to try to break Mr. Johnson out. We have to assume we're walking into a trap."

"AJ's right," I say. "We have to plan for the worst." I put my finger on the map, outside of the compound. "We open a gateway far enough away that we're out of sight and we find somewhere to hide the car bonnet."

"We're taking it with us?" Matthew asks.

I nod. "Of course. We'll be travelling from Uralahnd to earth to release the spell into the space between the worlds *and* get home."

Matthew grimaces. "I thought we'd do that from my home."

"Ideally, yes," I agree. I reach out and squeeze Sophie's hand. "But Ike took that option away from us when he took Mr. Johnson. If we delay in setting the spell, Saul will send people after us. No, we have to do it together."

I wait for anyone to object, relieved when no one does. I press my lips together. It wasn't just the pictograms that kept me awake last night. My mind was also working over every possible plan. I'd already realised we were likely to be walking into a trap and, as much as I hate the idea, I know we have to spring one of our own.

I draw in a deep breath and meet AJ's gaze. "I need you to hand yourself over to Saul."

He jerks his head back a little, eyes widening and pupils shrinking. It's a better reaction than I'd hoped for.

I move to kneel in front of AJ, placing my hands on the sides of his face, forcing him to meet my steady gaze. "If we all go in together, we'll probably end up outnumbered. From what you've said, we could be facing at least six Baneem, including Saul." I glance at Matthew. "I'm pretty sure you can't stop six Baneem at the same time, can you?"

"No," Matthew says, his back stiffening.

"We need him to think you're alone, that you've fallen for his deal. He needs you alive," I say softly.

AJ nods, his lips clamped together.

"If he thinks he's won, he'll let his guard down. Then Matthew and I can sneak through the compound and deal with any Baneem we find, one by one."

"*Deal with*?" AJ asks.

"Neutralise their magic and knock them out," I say. "We don't need to kill anyone." I pause and search his face, but his expression is blank, his emotions closed off to me. He must be scared. I'm asking him to offer himself as bait. I'd be terrified and I've never been in Saul's clutches. "Then we'll come and get you and Mr. Johnson. I promise."

"Even if you've taken everyone else out *but* Saul, I'm not sure you and Matthew can stop him."

"We can," I assure him. "Matthew is stronger than before, thanks to you, and I'm not entirely useless."

AJ's lips briefly twitch into a lopsided smile, but it vanishes quickly. "Saul is different than Gage and Taylor. His god complex has made him insane, which makes him far more dangerous."

"I know it will be dangerous." I release AJ's face. "I know what I'm asking you to do will be dangerous, but I can't think of a better way. Can you?"

AJ inhales, his chest puffing out as though he's dragging courage into his lungs. "Okay."

"Okay?"

"I trust you," he says. "I trust Matthew. If you say you'll come get me, I know you will."

I take his hands, squeezing them as I grin at both him and Sophie. My heart is thundering in my chest and I know my palms are clammy with worry, but I keep my expression confident. I have to be strong for them both. I have to convince them both my plan will work and that within a matter of hours, we'll all be home safe, the gateways will be shut and this nightmare will finally be over.

# CHAPTER TWENTY-THREE

We step out of the gateway into an oasis of broad-leafed grass, beside a collection of half a dozen single-storey mud brick buildings. I curse myself under my breath for bringing us to somewhere inhabited, but there's nothing I can do about it now. At least it's night in Uralahnd. The blanket of stars above our heads offers enough illumination to reveal the dark form of Saul's ziggurat, squatting on the horizon across a lifeless and featureless desert. I'd guess it's a couple of miles away, but it could be more. Thankfully, the oasis is quiet.

"Are you sure Uralahnd can be beautiful?" Kim asks, gazing around.

"If the Baneem start to care about this world, yes," I reply. "Remember, they gave up on it and stopped working together to make it beautiful." I wave my hand in the direction of the desert. "I bet a lot of it is like that, inhospitable."

Having seen how lush the Shamari garden was, I can't help but imagine how beautiful this world was and could be again, if only the Baneem would stop focusing on hurting humans and concentrate on actually living. If we succeed, they'll have no choice but to do exactly that. I clench my fists and swallow down my doubt and fear. We will succeed.

"We should move," Matthew says. "The longer we linger the more chance there is that we disturb anyone who might be here."

We set out across the desert in the direction of the ziggurat. Matthew carries the car bonnet, which, despite his strength, is still a large and unwieldy object in his grasp. The ground is hard to walk over. The sand is soft, so Kim and I keep sinking into it, our feet slipping. A breeze blows grains of sand into our faces, making my eyes water and feel gritty. Sand finds its way into my trainers and, somehow, into my socks, irritating my skin with every step I take. I'd be happier if there was more cover, but there's none. Matthew can't extend his aura to Kim and I because of his burden. I keep glancing back over my shoulder, towards the oasis, expecting to see Baneem heading towards us. When I'm not glancing back, I'm looking ahead, scanning the wall that surrounds the ziggurat for any sign of people on guard.

"We should bury the car bonnet before we get any closer," Matthew says, once we've traipsed across the desert for twenty minutes.

"How will we find it again?" I ask.

The desert is featureless, the top layer of sand constantly shifting and forming peaks and troughs, like a sea moving in slow motion.

"We're directly north of the ziggurat," Matthew replies. "I'll count my steps until we reach it."

I gape at him. "You realise we've got at least another mile to go."

"I won't lose count," he says. "I won't forget."

I shrug. The three of us kneel down and try to shift the sand with our hands, but it falls back in on itself as fast as we can shovel it out.

"I swear it was easier to dig holes on the beach," Kim mutters.

"Damp sand," I say. "Much easier to work with."

"Stand back," Matthew says.

We obey and watch as he uses the curve of the car bonnet as a giant shovel, removing massive scoops of sand each time with ease. Once he's standing inside a large hole, he lays the bonnet down and then, together, we begin to push the sand back in, completely focused on our task By the time we're finished, my skin is glistening with sweat, despite the cold bite of the air. For a few seconds, it's possible to see where the sand was disturbed, but it doesn't take long for the wind to cover all traces of our work. I really hope Matthew can remember where we've buried the bonnet.

I stand and face the ziggurat. It still seems so far away, but part of me wishes it were further still. I hate Kim's plan, even though I can see the sense in it. I can't stand the thought of handing myself over to Saul. He might not want to kill me, but I'm pretty sure he does want to hurt me. I've ruined his plans to be a god on earth by ridding myself of my magic. I inhale deeply, knowing I can't put it off. We have to keep moving forward.

Too late, I register the smell of rotten compost wafting on the breeze. Kim lets out a muffled scream. I wheel round to see her being dragged away from me, a tendril of bright magic wrapped tightly around her ankle. I glance at Matthew, wondering if he sensed the Baneem any quicker than me, but I'm angrier with myself. I'd stopped looking over my shoulder and the sand would have masked the sound of the Baneem's footsteps.

I grab for Kim's arms, but the magic that holds her is faster, moving her out of my reach. She twists onto her back, coming face to face with a gaunt-faced woman.

"Who are you?" the woman hisses. "What are you doing here?"

I scan the area, but the woman is alone.

"Let me go," Kim says.

The woman closes her fist and draws it up to her chest. The invisible tendril around Kim's leg yanks her up, so she's suspended upside down. I look to Matthew, feeling helpless.

"Let her go," I say, my voice only just above a whisper.

The woman opens her palm, pushes it towards the ground, and then pulls it back to her chest in a quick movement. Like a puppet, Kim is slammed into the ground and hauled up again. Blood drips from a cut on her skull, making a tiny pool on the sand beneath her.

"We're not looking for trouble," I say. "But if you don't release her, you'll pay." I'm not sure why Matthew is hesitating in his reaction. Surely he could have saved Kim by now.

The woman snorts. "No one *passes through* here." She narrows her eyes and flicks her gaze up and down me. "You're the kid Saul's looking for, aren't you?"

I shake my head. "I don't know what you're talking about."

"Of course not," she says, her voice dripping with sarcasm. "Saul came through here yesterday, making us swear we'd hand you over if we saw you."

She flicks her other hand towards me, but Matthew steps between us and the tendril of magic meant for me snakes around his wrist instead. She makes a tugging motion with her arm, but Matthew doesn't move. Her eyes open wide.

"What are you?" she hisses.

She must have seen his eyes. They're too white to be anything but obvious, especially now he's standing closer to her.

"Let her go," Matthew says. "I won't give you another chance to comply."

She laughs in his face, which was probably the stupidest thing she could do. Matthew strides to her, deftly avoiding Kim as he does so. He raises his thumb to her forehead and drags it down in a trail of bright light to the end of her nose. He adds a horizontal line, cutting through the first, forming a blazing sign of the cross on the woman's head and then traces a circle around it.

The woman grunts as her magic dissipates along with the glowing pictogram and the scent of rotten compost. Kim plummets to the ground, slamming into the sand, leaving her gasping. I rush to her side as Matthew draws the pictogram for sleep on the woman's head. She slumps forward, unconscious.

"Her magic will be bound for several hours," Matthew says. "I doubt anyone will come looking for her before morning."

"We can't leave her here," I say, helping Kim to her feet and pulling her into a hug. "She must have seen us bury the car bonnet. What if she gets help and tries to retrieve it? She doesn't need to know what it is, to know it's important to us."

Matthew purses his lips. "What would you have me do with her?"

"Take her with us."

"AJ..." Kim says, returning my embrace. "We can't."

"We have to. There are obsidian cells in the ziggurat, which Leon gave us the key to. You should be able to lock her in one, whilst I distract Saul and his goons by handing myself over."

Kim looks doubtful, but nods anyway. I can guess what she's thinking—taking the woman with us will make an already dangerous plan even more risky.

Matthew scoops the woman up and slings her over his shoulder. "Now we can leave," he says. "And we should hurry."

Neither Kim nor I argue as Matthew strides out into the desert, forcing us both to jog to keep up with him.

*

The ziggurat is a lot further away than I'd anticipated. By the time we're standing in the shadow of the wall surrounding the compound, my feet are sore and my legs feel like lead. It would be easy to ask Matthew to reveal his wings and carry Kim and I over the wall, which towers several feet above our heads. But there's too much risk that we'd be seen and the alarm would be raised, taking away the slight chance of surprising Saul that we have. I press my hand against the wall. It's made of baked mud bricks, like the houses in the oasis. Although there are slight gaps where mud has been used to cement the bricks together, there's nothing to gain a purchase on that would allow us to climb the wall.

I glance back in the direction we came from. "Are you sure you remember where the bonnet is?" I ask Matthew.

He nods, following my gaze. "I do." He shifts the unconscious woman a little on his shoulders. She hasn't stirred once since he subdued her with his magic.

"Leon said climbing the wall at the back of the ziggurat would give us the most cover," Kim says, looking at the map Flame Guy drew. "Not that he offered any advice on *how* to scale the wall."

I puff my cheeks out. "Maybe I should go in through the front gate. It's got to be the best way of announcing my presence to Saul."

Kim stares at me hesitantly and I wonder if she's thinking about telling me not to go. It's a bit late to rethink our plan.

"I'll be fine," I say, pulling her into a hug. We're both trembling, which isn't comforting for either of us. "I'm the best distraction we've got and you and Matthew are going to save me. I won't be with Saul for long." I hold her a little further away from me, kiss her forehead and then release her. "Stick to the plan. In a few hours, we'll be back on earth and Saul won't be able to pursue us."

Kim nods, even though her chin is wobbling. "We'll be as fast as we can," she promises.

I smile at her. "I know." I pull the marker pen from my back pocket and hand it to her. "We can't risk losing this."

She curls her hand around mine, staring up at me until I manage to slip my hand free from her tight grip. I turn away from her, squaring my shoulders in a pretence at being brave, when really, I'm not. I'm quivering inside, terrified of what Saul might do to me. There are far worse things he can do to kill me and I know he'll relish hurting me. I tell myself I can survive whatever he does in the short time he has before Kim and Matthew reach me. I survived days in his clutches. I can survive a few minutes, an hour at most.

The gate is around the corner, in the centre of the wall on its longest side. Stella is standing there, inspecting her nails. She's so absorbed by boredom, that she doesn't notice me until I'm almost right up to her. Then she stares at me with wide eyes and quickly rights herself, her jaw becoming slack.

"I'm here to see Saul," I say, my voice as confident as I can make it. "Me for Mr. Johnson. That's the deal, right?"

Stella nods. "Yeah, sure." She grabs my arm. "I just never thought you'd be dumb enough to come after what happened to your mother."

I tug against her grip, not to pull away, but to put up a show of resistance. "How about you go and tell Saul I'm here. Tell him to let Mr. Johnson go and then I'll hand myself over."

She laughs in my face. "I don't think so. The way I heard it from your pretty friend, you have no magic left. Not that healing would have helped you against me. You're not in a position to bargain, Aran."

This time I do wrench my arm away from her and take several steps back. "Tell Saul I'm here. I'll wait."

She saunters towards me, exactly as I'd expected. She reaches out to my head, but I sidestep her. She tries again, I dodge again, content to play cat-and-mouse with her for a short time—long enough to convince her I'm not going to go inside with her without a fight, even though I am. I let myself stumble and fall onto the sand. Grinning, she advances on me. The sand is hard to move in, so it really does slow me down as I try to shuffle away from her. I turn and pretend to stand, purpose-fully losing my footing. I feel her hands close around my head. The smell of vinegar permeates the air. I can't move. My chest constricts as the most painful image possible floods my mind— Mum, dying.

# CHAPTER TWENTY-FOUR

Matthew and I watch from the shadows as two thugs, led by Stella, carry AJ into the ziggurat. I don't recognise either of the men, but AJ had told me there were at least two other men he'd never known the names of—or given names to. My hand is pressed over my mouth, stifling my desire to beg Matthew to stop them. We have to stick to the plan. But I know AJ will be gripped by terrible visions. When Stella attacked me, I saw Charley, so I'm pretty sure Stella will have triggered memories of Phailin's death in AJ's mind. I feel sick with guilt.

"We have to hurry," I whisper, once they've all vanished inside the ziggurat. "We can't leave AJ with them for long."

"We won't," Matthew says, touching my shoulder in a comforting gesture. "First, we take this Baneem to the cells and see if Mr. Johnson is there at the same time."

My mouth twists into a wry smile. "Somehow, I think it would be too easy if he were."

I consult the map. The entrance to the cells is via a walled garden, which lies at the front of the ziggurat, at the opposite end to where we are now. I lead Matthew along the back wall of the ziggurat. Leon promised us there were no windows at the back, which we discover to be true. Not that we let our guard down. We both stay watchful and alert, but my thoughts can't help straying to AJ and Mr. Johnson.

We creep round the side of the building. The start of the garden is obvious, as the side of the ziggurat gives way to wall, which is lower than the one surrounding the perimeter. Still, it wouldn't be the easiest to climb. To get over the last wall, Matthew used his strength to punch hand and footholds into the mudbricks for us both. He begins to do the same, climbing ahead of me to prepare the wall and make it easier for me to climb. He carries the woman in a fireman's lift as he goes. It doesn't take him long to reach the top of the wall and disappear over.

"Come on," he says a moment later, his voice barely loud enough for me to hear.

I hurry on up and over the wall, hanging from the top by my fingers and then letting go. I bend my knees as I drop to the ground, wincing as my feet and ankles hurt from the fall. I pull myself upright, standing on one leg then the other to rotate and test each ankle. Everything seems fine. I turn and survey the garden. It's teeming with greenery and flowers. There's a fountain in the centre, bubbling with water.

I point to the raised veranda. "Up there. That's where the cells should be."

I follow Matthew up the steps and along the veranda a little way until we come to a door. Matthew presses his ear to it, before daring to open it.

"This is too easy," he says. "I doubt Mr. Johnson is in here."

"We have to put her in a cell anyway," I remind him, patting the pocket with the key in.

Matthew nods and tests the door. It isn't locked. "Too easy," he repeats with a grimace, as he swings the door open.

He recoils instantly, hissing loudly.

"What's wrong?"

"My magic," Matthew gasps. "Even being close to the obsidian it feels like... like I'm suffocating." He staggers back away from the door and sets the woman down on the veranda. "I'm sorry Kim, I can't go in there." He stares down at the woman, his expression perplexed. "I'm not even sure it's fair to put her in there."

"I doubt it will be as bad for her," I tell him. "You're made of magic, but magic is only part of her."

"A big part." He dips his chin. "Do you think this is how the Baneem I captured were caged?"

I stare through the doorway. It's hard to see because there's no lighting inside and the obsidian seems to suck the moonlight away.

"Probably." I won't let myself feel sorry for any of the Baneem captured by the Changed. If they were half as terrible as Gage and Saul, they deserved to be locked inside of an obsidian cell.

I bend down and wrap my arms around the woman's chest, underneath her arms and start to drag her inside. "Stay here and keep watch."

Matthew nods and moves away, so he's standing in shadow. He might be able to make himself invisible to humans, but it doesn't seem to work on the Baneem. I guess it's because of their innate magic.

I drag the woman to the first cell, unlock it and haul her inside, laying her down on the floor. I lock her inside and then check each of the other cells but, unsurprisingly, they're all empty.

"Kim," Matthew hisses from outside.

My heart starts to pound as I edge back towards the door. Matthew has moved to stand in front of it, in a defensive posture.

"I didn't think Aran had come alone," a man says.

I don't recognise the voice, but the malice it holds sends a shiver down my spine. My mind instantly supplies a name—Ice Man. AJ told me that he'd never seen what magic Ice Man had, but that he'd given him the name because he was so cold.

"Get back," Matthew says as I enter the doorway, standing just behind him.

"Don't let him use his magic on you," I whisper.

Matthew raises his fists to defend his body. I know he'll have to get close enough to Ice Man to use any of his abilities. He'd have to get close enough, and gain enough of an upper hand, to be able to draw the pictogram that would nullify Ice Man's magic. Ice Man isn't going to be as easy to subdue as the woman, who is now lying in the cells.

"Oh, this will be fun," Ice Man says, smirking. "And easy." Despite his bragging words, he takes the time to crack the knuckles of his right hand and then his left, instead of moving any closer to Matthew. "You want to play rough? Trade blows? Sure, I can do that. Why spoil the fun and hit you with magic straight off?"

Matthew doesn't relax. He holds his stance so still he could be a statue fixed to the veranda. He doesn't speak, but his intentions are clear—Ice Man will have to come to him. The only movement Ice Man makes, is to push his pale blonde hair back from his forehead, out of his eyes. Then he lifts his fists, mirroring Matthew's position.

'What's the matter?" I say. "Scared?"

Ice Man bares his teeth. "Scared of a Changed and a kid? Never."

He charges forward, up the veranda stairs to throw a swing at Matthew. Matthew leans back a fraction, avoiding the blow with ease. The muscles in Ice Man's neck grow so tense, I can see his veins throbbing. He attacks again, aiming two quick jabs at Matthew's chest. Matthew blocks the first, knocking Ice Man's arm aside, but allows the second blow to hit. As Ice Man grins over his minor victory, Matthew's fist rams into his shoulder, knocking him off balance. Ice Man staggers back, his ankle slamming into the step behind. He almost falls, but manages to pitch himself forward, swinging towards Matthew's face. It turns out to be a feint. Matthew tries to block a blow that never lands. Ice Man's true attack hits home. An upper cut to Matthew's jaw. Matthew shakes his head, only to have to block a flurry of incoming blows. Most seem oddly half-hearted, as though Ice Man is toying with Matthew. In the middle of the flurry, he opens his hand, tapping Matthew's neck with his palm, causing black tendrils to blossom out from the contact site and coil upwards to his jawline and downwards towards his chest.

Matthew drops onto the veranda, curling up and wrapping his arms around his stomach. His white eyes are wide and staring, his nostrils flaring.

Ice Man laughs, jutting out his chest, before kneeling down beside Matthew. He leans in close, as though he's going to whisper, but he speaks loud enough for me to hear. "I told you it would be easy," he says. "You can watch the girl die, before I kill you." Grinning, he stands, and moves towards me.

I back away, into the room with the cells. He follows me, even though it'll dampen his magic. But then, he knows he can beat me without it.

"Now who's scared?" he asks, eyes gleaming as he advances on me.

I glance round him at Matthew. I can see the fear on Matthew's face, as he grips hold of his chest. He's not looking at me. He doesn't appear to be looking at anything. He's lost in whatever magic Ice Man cast on him. I have to get to him. I have to bring him back to me. I can't hope to defeat Ice Man alone. Unless... I thrust my hand into my pocket and curl it around the engraved ring. No. It's for Saul. I can't waste it on Ice Man. I have to find another way to beat him.

I grimace at the thought that we have several more Baneem to subdue in the complex. Ice Man, Stella, the two goons and Adele, not to mention Saul. There could be more, we have no way of knowing and nothing to help us except Leon's map.

I continue to back away until I reach the end of the corridor. The obsidian is cold against my back. I let Ice Man advance on me, waiting until he reaches out to grab me. Then I duck, step closer and bring my knee up hard, into his groin. He drops to the floor, gasping, wheezing and throwing curses at me. I jump over him and run to Matthew, dropping down to my knees so I'm facing the cells and Ice Man, who is still writhing on the floor. I know the groin-shot won't keep him down for long.

"Get up," I hiss at Matthew, grabbing the sides of his face. "Whatever he's done, you can't let him beat you. You have to get up. I need you."

Slowly, his empty gaze shifts to me, but he continues to shiver.

"Get up," I beg, as Ice Man stands and begins to limp towards me, his face contorted in pain. "Please get up, Matthew."

But he doesn't. I stand and try to run, but Ice Man bears down on me, knocking me down the veranda stairs and to the ground. Laughing, he twists his hands into my hair and pulls me to my feet. He drags me against him and wraps his arm around me, laying the flat of his palm against my chest.

"You're very spirited," he whispers. "But it's not enough. Not against me."

The stench comes first. Hydrogen Sulphide. Rotten eggs. The pain is next, starting in my chest. It's not physical, but as though a nightmare is forming there. My legs become weak, making me almost glad he's holding me upright. My lungs and throat start to burn, my mind becomes numb, incapable of any thought. Ice Man releases me and I drop to the ground in a heap. He stands, stepping back so he can stare down at me, a smirk crossing his lips.

"So easy. You're all pathetic, do you know that? Did you really think you could beat us?"

I can see his narrow-eyed stare, boring into me, but I can't do anything about it. I want to fight back, but I'm paralysed by the terror he has injected into me. Behind him, Matthew manages to stand.

"I promised I'd let the Changed see you die," Ice Man muses. "And yet... maybe I should keep you alive and take you to Saul, so you can watch him torture AJ. Maybe I should let *you* watch *me* kill the Changed."

I manage to shake my head and widen my eyes in a pleading gesture. He laughs again, his focus solely on me. Good. Let him think he's won.

"Please," I whisper through chattering teeth. "Please let us go."

"Let you go?" Ice Man asks, kneeling beside me. "Why would I do that?"

He wouldn't, but he's even more vulnerable now than he was a moment before. Matthew moves soundlessly towards him, face set in an expression of grim determination.

"I just want to go home," I whimper, making myself sound as pathetic as possible. It isn't hard. The pain in my chest is crippling and I keep gasping as I force each word out. "I'm sorry. I'm sorry that we tried to hurt you. You're right, you're stronger than us. I was stupid. Stupid."

He strokes my hair, making me shiver. "Yes," he agrees. "You were stupid, but I don't think you're nearly sorry enough. Once you've watched the Changed die, then you'll be truly sorry."

He starts to stand, which is the moment Matthew slams his forearm hard into the back of Ice Man's head. Ice Man's eyes bulge and then roll back into his skull. He begins to topple forward. I can't move, or shield myself. Matthew stops him falling by grabbing the back of his neck. He throws him to the floor and then stands over Ice Man, tracing the binding pictogram on his forehead.

I gasp as I realise the pain is lifting from my body and the smell of Hydrogen Sulphide is dissipating. Unconscious, Ice Man cannot maintain the spells he cast on Matthew and I.

"Are you all right?" I ask.

Matthew nods. As I watch, I see the tendrils of black begin to fade and vanish.

"How...?"

He stares down at himself. "Perhaps AJ's magic did more than just heal me." Frowning, he nods towards Ice Man. "We need to put him in the cells with the woman."

He drags Ice Man to the door, heaves him up and then tosses him as far into the room as he can. "You'll have to do the rest, I'm afraid."

I hurry inside and, with difficulty, drag Ice Man's unconscious body into the closest cell. He's far heavier than he thought he would be. The strain of lifting him causes the muscles in my neck, shoulders, arms and back to ache in fierce protest. I have to waddle backwards, making myself breathe deeply in through my nose and out through my mouth with each awkward step.

I drop him as soon as he's inside, kicking at his legs to get them through the door as well. Then I lock him inside and stare at him. It almost doesn't seem right, leaving him here, alive.

He'll be freed eventually and, even if he is trapped in Uralahnd, he'll still be cruel. He'll still relish the pain of others, even though they're his own kind. My fingers feel for the ring again. It would be so easy to go back into the cell, slip it on his finger and activate the spell. But Saul is worse. I have to save it for him. I lift my chin and then turn away from Ice Man, to join Matthew outside.

# CHAPTER TWENTY-FIVE

When my mind is finally released from the crippling memories of Mum's death, I realise I'm lying on cold stone. Slowly, I open my eyes and focus on the anxious, battered face of Mr. Johnson, staring down at me.

"Are you all right?" he asks.

I nod and sit up, wincing slightly as nausea rises up from the bottom of my stomach, making me gag. "Are you?"

His mouth quirks into an awkward smile, which doesn't come close to reaching his tired eyes. "I've had better days." His expression becomes more sombre. "Why did you hand yourself over to Saul? You must know he has no intention of letting me go."

I glance around the room, making sure we're alone. "We have a plan." I press my lips together, signalling I'm not going to say anymore.

Mr. Johnson's face floods with relief. His eyebrows lift and his eyes shine, for a moment detracting from his bruised and swollen features. I allow my gaze to wander over him, taking in the other obvious injuries he has. Both his hands are bruised and a couple of fingers on each hand are bent at awkward angles, likely broken. I swallow hard. I can fully understand why Sophie gave in and told the Baneem everything they wanted to know. I wouldn't have been able to keep my mouth shut, either, if it had been Mum they were beating.

"I'm sorry," I whisper. "I'm sorry this happened to you."

"I was involved with the Baneem long before I met you," he says in a grave tone.

It doesn't make me feel any better.

"Sophie told the Baneem that you gave up your magic. Is that true?"

I nod, suddenly unable to meet his gaze. I can't heal him. He must be in excruciating pain, even though he's doing his best to hide it. Is he putting on a show of being fine for my sake? I guess, as a father, he feels he must be the strong one, even if it's just a pretence.

I stand, pausing as I briefly feel dizzy, before wandering over to the door.

"It's locked," Mr. Johnson says. "It was the first thing I tried."

I try it anyway and then press my ear to it. I can vaguely hear dull footsteps heading closer. I stumble away from the door and press my back against the opposite wall, priming myself to act if at all possible. I'm not sure what I'll do, but if Saul's the one who's coming, I'm not going to let him hurt me or Mr. Johnson without putting up a fight.

When the door opens, it's Adele who walks in. The door is closed by someone just out of my view and I hear the lock clunking into place, trapping us all inside once more.

"Saul wants me to find out if your friend was lying," she says to me, speaking in a matter-of-fact tone. She must be talking about Sophie. She walks towards me.

I move away from her. "About what?"

"Your magic."

I grimace, knowing what she's going to do. I briefly wonder why she didn't bring at least one thug with her to pin me down. It would make it much easier for her to rip my soul out of my body. But then, if I was Saul, I'd be questioning why I handed myself over, knowing what a devious bastard he is. I'd have people searching for Kim and Matthew. A shiver snakes down my spine as my mind fills with fear for them. I try to push my concerns down so I can focus on the moment. Matthew can take care of them both. My magic didn't just heal him, it made him more powerful than he had been before. Kim is a lot safer than I am right now.

"You can't run," Adele says in a bored tone. "Why bother trying?"

I wonder how long I can avoid her in this small space. She's not exactly trying hard to grab me.

"Leave him alone," Mr. Johnson says, rising to his feet.

I notice he can't put much weight on his right leg, but he still hobbles forward, planting himself valiantly between me and Adele.

I put my hand on his shoulder. "Don't. You're already hurt. You don't know what she can do."

A cruel smile spreads across Adele's face. "Maybe I should show him? I don't think he can move anywhere near as quickly as you. How about, whilst you're being uncooperative, I examine his soul instead?"

I clench my fists. I know she will do it just to hurt him and make me feel guilty.

"Do it," Mr. Johnson snarls. "It can't be any worse than what's been done to me already."

"Oh, it can," Adele says, laughing. "Can't it Aran? Maybe you could explain to him what it feels like to have your soul ripped out of your body."

I grit my teeth and step in front of Mr. Johnson. "Don't touch him. You don't need to hurt him."

"Are you going to cooperate?"

"AJ—" Mr. Johnson begins, but I cut him off with a sharp glance over my shoulder. He stares at me for a second. I'm not sure what he sees in my face, but it seems to drain the fight out of him. He nods and limps back to the edge of the room where he slides down the wall into an awkward sitting position.

"Do what you have to do," I say to Adele. "But Sophie wasn't lying. My magic is gone."

"I'll be the judge of that." She nods to Mr. Johnson. "You might want to follow his example and sit."

I do as she says. I don't need her to remind me how terrible this experience will be.

She kneels down opposite me, placing her hands over my chest as she bows her head. The now familiar scent of rotting flesh fills the air as she begins to work her magic, making me wrinkle my nose. Behind me, Mr. Johnson wretches loudly, which makes my stomach heave. I breathe slowly and deeply, refusing to throw up. Adele begins to pull her hands away from me. The action causes pain to rip through me. I grit my teeth to stop myself from screaming. My entire body starts to tremble as she pulls my soul from my body. The light emanating from my soul is more subdued than I remember; still white but nowhere near as bright. The pain intensifies and my whole body begs me to release it in a scream, which I trap inside my body, behind my still gritted teeth. My jaw aches with the effort of keeping my agony internalised. And then, for a moment, I feel weightless. I am consumed by the light of my soul, wrenched free of my body. In that second, the pain drifts away from me and fades into nothingness. A part of me longs for the sensation to remain, even though I know it would eventually mean my death. Then Adele pushes her hands back towards my chest, forcing my soul back into my body. The pain returns from nothingness, more overwhelming than before. I drop to the ground, curled up in a ball, gasping and trembling.

Adele stands. "You really don't have any magic left. Your soul is as dull as a human's."

"I am human."

She raises her eyebrows. "And that pleases you?"

I nod.

"Pathetic." She purses her lips. "How did you remove your magic?"

I grin up at her. "Probably in the same way Saul was planning on taking my magic from me. And yours." I know it's not true. Saul, like all the Baneem, believes he can't use the pictograms.

Her eyes narrow. "What are you talking about?"

Her confusion throws me. "Didn't Saul let you in on that part of his plan? How do you think he was going to create his hidden army? Do you really think you and I would have enough strength to transfer the souls of numerous humans into Baneem?" When she doesn't reply, I force my grin to widen. "Didn't you realise that was his plan? Gage bragged about it to Kim, before she killed him."

Anger flashes across Adele's face. "You're lying."

I push myself up onto my hands, continuing to stare up at her. "Am I?"

"He was going to kill the Changed one by one," she says, though her voice is wavering.

"Really? Don't you think the Changed would figure out what was happening?" I shake my head. "No. Saul *knew* he'd have to strike as many Changed as possible in one go. But to do that, he'd need far more power than you or I could give. But outside of our bodies, our magic would be an immense pool that he could use for his plan." I roll my eyes and give her a massive shrug. "I understand why he wouldn't want to tell you. Would you really have stayed and played along, knowing you were going to end up losing your magic? Knowing your soul would end up as dull as a human's?"

She hisses in a breath. "You're lying," she repeats.

"Ask him," I say. "Watch his reaction closely before he lies to your face."

She begins to back away from me, shaking her head. "You're lying," she says again. She twists round as the lock clicks and the door opens, breathing heavily as Saul saunters into the room.

"What's taking so long?" he demands. "Is Aran's magic gone or not?" He's completely focused on Adele, ignoring both me and Mr. Johnson.

It should hurt, that my own father won't even acknowledge my presence, but I realise I couldn't care less.

"Yes," Adele says, stumbling over her reply. "His soul is completely dull." She glances back down at me. "I was trying to get him to tell me *how* he got rid of his magic." Her eyes narrow as she looks back to Saul. "Would you happen to know how it was done?"

His cheek muscles twitch before he gets around to shaking his head. "No."

"Just how many Baneem souls were you planning on hiding in humans at a time?" she asks. "One? Two? A dozen?"

"I... hadn't got that far," Saul says, straightening his back. He twists his face into a snarl. "And now the plan is worthless anyway. I should kill you for that alone, Aran."

"Go ahead," I taunt. "I'm not afraid of you, not anymore."

"Oh, you should be," he says, stepping round Adele to crouch in front of me. "Even without your magic, I can extend your suffering. I can cause you unimaginable pain."

"Worse than having my soul ripped out of my body? Worse than having my magic removed?"

He hooks his upper lip up. "Far worse."

"Don't change the subject," Adele says, standing behind him. "How many souls were you going to have me move between bodies?"

Saul stands and rounds on her. "I told you, I hadn't got that far."

"Liar," she hisses.

Saul glances back down at me. "What have you been saying? Why would you listen to this snivelling wretch, Adele?"

"Were you trying to create an army?" she asks. "I know I wouldn't have the strength for that." Disgust floods her face. "Were the Baneem going to be as expendable as the human vessels? Was I going to be expendable? Were you going to take *my* magic, as well as the boy's?"

Saul's eyes narrow a fraction and his lips flatten, before he puts on an expression of wide-eyed innocence. "He's trying to get into your head, Adele. He's trying to turn you against me. Why would you listen to him?"

His words sound utterly false to my ears and, by the look of fury eclipsing Adele's face, I know she can tell he's lying as well.

"Without me, you'd have nothing," Adele hisses. "*I* figured out that his pathetic human body was shrouding his powerful soul. *I* figured out we could put Baneem souls in human bodies to trick the Changed." She prods her fingertip against his chest. "*I* am your plan."

Saul's mouth twists into a cruel smile. "Exactly." He steps forward, grabbing her wrist before she can react. The smell of burning rubber fills the air. "And I'm ever so grateful for everything you've done for me, Adele. But, yes, Aran is quite correct. I was going to take his magic and yours."

She starts rasping for breath as the skin on her arm becomes shrivelled and dry. "If you kill me, my magic will be gone forever."

"Does it matter?" he asks. "My plan is already in ruins, thanks to Aran." He pulls her close, brushing his lips against her forehead. "Besides, I don't have to kill you to render you powerless against me." He grabs the back of her head and pulls her lips against his. She tries to scream, but his mouth covers the sound.

I drag myself from the floor and leap at Saul's back, wrapping my arms around his chest in an attempt to pull him away from her. He's been responsible for enough death and suffering, without adding Adele to the long list. We both have. A chill creeps into my body where it touches him. My teeth clatter together. I let go, as though he's a burning object and thud to the ground, pain stabbing at my chest.

"Don't," I croak. "Stop. Please."

The words have barely left my lips when Saul lets Adele go. She drops to the ground, her skin withered, her hair white. She's still breathing, barely. She glares up at him, her thin lips pinched, her fingertips clawing against the flagstones. She moves her twisted lips, but only a hoarse whisper escapes, not powerful enough to form into words that could match the venom in her eyes.

Saul turns and glares down at me. "See? I can do far worse things than kill you, you pathetic wretch."

I realise then that I'm crying. Tears are coursing down my cheeks and my chest is heaving in a series of loud sobs.

"What happened to her was your fault," Saul carries on. "If you hadn't twisted her against me, I wouldn't have had to hurt her."

"No," I hiss. "You hurt people because you want to. You could have placated her with words, but you barely even tried. You were going to take her magic from her, which would have destroyed her anyway. I won't let you force your guilt upon me. Not again. Never again."

Saul laughs. "You bear as much guilt as I do, Aran. The only difference is, you care."

He walks out. I listen as the lock clunks into place again and then curl up, unable to look at Mr. Johnson, or Adele's withered form. I survived Saul once. I will survive him again.

# CHAPTER TWENTY-SIX

I rub my left eye, as though I can erase the bruise that's blossoming there. Beside me, Matthew crouches down on the floor, tracing pictograms on each of the foreheads of the two Baneem we've just overpowered. They're the first people we've seen since leaving Ice Man in the cells.

It turns out that the ziggurat is almost entirely empty. Matthew and I have been following Leon's map, sneaking through the corridors of the ziggurat for fear of turning a corner and finding ourselves face to face with an army. Gradually, my pulse rate decreased to a lazy rhythm, so I was no longer on edge, no longer worried I might have to fight or flee with a moment's notice. Until we *did* walk around a corner, right into Baneem. But two men hardly make an army. Luckily, they were as surprised as we were. Matthew managed to draw the pictogram of sleep on one without a fight, whilst I barrelled into the other and knocked him to the ground, tussling with him until Matthew stepped in and sent him to sleep.

Matthew drags the two men into one of the side rooms, closing the door on their unconscious bodies. We don't have time to carry them down to the cells.

"Let's get going," I say, giving up on nursing my eye. My vision is a little blurred, which is more annoying than painful.

I consult the map once more as we walk through the corridors. This place is like a rabbit warren. Every corridor looks the same and there's so many twists, turns and side passages it's disorientating. Without the map, we'd be hopelessly lost. We're nearly at the point Leon had marked as Saul's rooms. There's no guarantee AJ or Mr. Johnson will be there, but they haven't been anywhere else, either.

"I'm starting to think Gage was bluffing," I say. "Saul doesn't have an army. He never did."

"From what AJ said, Saul could've only formed his plan *after* he found out about the nature of AJ's soul. Just because he didn't have an army of Baneem ready to leap into action, doesn't mean he doesn't have the means to gather one together."

A shiver runs down my spine at Matthew's words. He's right, of course. Gage was eager enough to do Saul's dirty work for him after being released from purgatory. I wonder what Saul promised him. He might not have needed to say much of anything to add fuel to Gage's need for vengeance.

Matthew puts his arm in my way. I bump into him, cursing as the breath is knocked from my lungs.

"Listen," Matthew says, pointing down the corridor.

At first, I hear nothing, then gradually the rhythmic thud of footsteps reaches my ears.

"One person," Matthew whispers. "Possibly a woman." He points back the way we've come from. There's a corner a few dozen feet away. "Hide. I'll deal with whoever it is."

I open my mouth to protest, but Matthew shakes his head sharply. I shrink slightly away from him, unnerved by how stern his gaze is. I still haven't gotten used to his pure white eyes, they're even more unsettling than the golem was.

I put my hands on my hips, trying to make myself look braver than I feel beneath his stare. "I can take care of myself, you know."

"If it's Stella, she'll use your memories of Charley against you." Matthew's brow furrows. "You don't deserve to see those memories again."

"What about you? She nearly killed you the last time you encountered her, or have you forgotten that?"

He flashes me a confident grin, yet I notice a shred of concern in the way his cheeks flex. "Go. I can't be worrying about you as well as myself."

We don't have time for a discussion, or an argument, even if Matthew's protective big brother routine got boring a long time ago.

I wait out of sight as the footsteps move closer and closer.

"What the—" Stella's voice exclaims. "You're alive?" There's a pause. When Stella speaks again, her voice is quavering slightly. "You're here? I thought you bastards couldn't survive in Uralahnd."

"You thought wrong," Matthew says, his voice low and dangerous.

"Whatever," Stella says, disgust filling her voice. "This time, I'll make sure you're dead."

Her footsteps rush closer. She must be attacking Matthew. I hold my breath, waiting for the fight to be over. All Matthew has to do is get close enough to draw a pictogram, either to make her sleep or to temporarily block her magic. Heck, he could punch her out first. He must be physically stronger than Stella. But the fight drags on. Stella grunts occasionally, but otherwise there's nothing but a chorus of feet shuffling over stone. Curiosity tugs at my gut. I shuffle to the corner and peer round, not sure what to expect.

It's worse than I thought. Matthew is losing. He's trying not to let Stella touch him, but I can see she's managed it more than once, as black tendrils are snaking over his cheeks and arms. Worse, his brow is furrowed and he keeps swiping at his eyes and shaking his head, as though trying to rid himself of phantom images. The fact that he's not consumed by the visions Stella is making him see is a testimony to the strength AJ's magic has given him. It looks like Stella is playing with him. A smirk curves her lips. She's a cat, toying with an injured mouse, biding her time before she destroys him. Matthew is entirely on the defensive. Every so often, he tries to duck in close enough to press his thumb against her forehead, but he never quite manages it. I almost call out to him to demand why he doesn't just plant his fist into her smug face, but I bite my tongue instead. Matthew needs help, but making myself a target is only going to make things worse.

I slip into the closest room. We'd already searched it and found it empty of Baneem or anything else useful. It was a simple bedroom, with only the barest of furniture. I'm not even sure it's currently being slept in as there are no personal effects in sight. But then, the ziggurat can probably hold hundreds of people and we've only encountered four so far. Knowing Saul and Adele are rattling around in here somewhere doesn't make the ziggurat seem any less empty and desolate.

I take another look at the room, searching for anything I could use for a weapon. I wish I still had the metal rod that Sophie and I cast into the space between the worlds. The best likely candidate is a wooden chair. I grab it, but realise straight away it's too big and unwieldy. I turn it onto its side, throw the blanket from the bed over it and hold it in place as I kick at one of the legs. The thick woollen blanket muffles the dull thud of my sole striking against the wood. The leg splinters away from the crooked nail holding it in place. I test the weight of the wood in my hand and swish it through the air. It'll do. As quietly as possible, I carry it back to the corner so I can see what's happening.

Matthew and Stella are still trapped in a stalemate. Matthew is good enough at evading, but the visions are too big a distraction for him to fully focus. His movements are becoming more erratic, his eyes wider and wilder. More black tendrils snake across his skin. He's being worn down. Soon, Stella will be able to overpower him.

Luckily, Stella has her back to me. I grit my teeth. The painful memory she made me relive of Charley, dead, fuels my anger. Without hesitation, I run around the corner with the chair leg held high above my head. I slam it across the back of her head. She slumps to the floor like a sack of potatoes, splinters of wood showering down around her. For a second, I stare at Stella, my breath coming in harsh rasps. I can't deny it felt good. I can't deny I wanted to hurt her for what she made me see and what she did to Matthew. But the satisfaction quickly gives way to fear. What if I've killed her? I drop down to my knees and check her over. She's bleeding but still breathing. Relief prickles at my skin and I shake myself back into the moment.

I turn my attention back to Matthew. He's standing, staring straight ahead.

I scrabble to my feet, grab his arm and shake him hard. "What the hell were you doing?"

He jerks his head back and blinks at me, mouth opening without sound. Thankfully, the black tendrils are beginning to fade from his face and arms.

"Do you think we have time for you to dance with Stella?" I carry on. "Why didn't you just punch her?"

A squeak comes out of Matthew's throat. "I..."

"You're not bound by those stupid restrictions. You *can* hurt Baneem. You knew what she'd do to you. You should have struck first."

Matthew hangs his head. "I forgot."

My breath catches in my throat. "You *forgot*?" I throw my hands up in the air. "AJ and Mr. Johnson are at Saul's mercy and you *forgot*?" I shake my head and stare at Stella, feeling a sense of gratification that I was able to deal with her without magic or superhuman strength.

"I'm sorry," Matthew mutters. "I've lived by those rules for hundreds of years."

I glare at him. "You didn't have a problem hitting Ice Man over the back of the head."

"That was different."

"How?"

He avoids my angry gaze, looking everywhere but at me. "You were in danger. I didn't think, I just acted."

"Save the big brother act," I snap. "Block her magic and then let's go. We have to find AJ and Mr. Johnson. We can't leave them with Saul any longer."

# CHAPTER TWENTY-SEVEN

Adele doesn't have a key. Not that she was willing to tell me that. No, she made me search her, a grin splitting her withered face. I don't blame her for hating me, it's my fault Saul used his magic on her. I turned her against him. I wonder which of us she hates the most.

"What's Saul going to do with us?" I ask.

Adele turns her watery gaze towards Mr. Johnson. "He'll kill him," she rasps. "Why he didn't do it earlier, I'm not sure. You..." she curls her upper lip into a snarl. "He'll make you suffer."

"Yeah, well, I'm not sure what else he can do to me." I doubt my feigned nonchalance is fooling her or Mr. Johnson. I only hope Kim and Matthew make their way to us quickly.

"Kill your girlfriend?" Adele says. "Saul knows she's here. He's not stupid enough to think you'd hand yourself over without some kind of plan." She chuckles, though the sound is crackly and splinters into a pained fit of coughing. "She'll be found, Aran. And when she is, she'll be delivered to Saul."

I shudder and turn away. "She's not here."

"Liar."

I stand and pace to the door, slamming my fists against it.

"Don't waste your breath talking to her," Mr. Johnson says. "She's trying to get to you. I've seen plenty of police officers employ the same tactics with suspects. She's nowhere near as skilled as they are."

Adele hisses at him.

"She's a pathetic husk of a woman," Mr. Johnson continues. "Trying to scare you, so she can feel better about her own situation."

Adele shrieks and tries to lunge towards him, but her weakened body collapses to the ground, leaving her sobbing and clawing at the flagstones. I actually pity her, despite what she's done and what she's capable of.

"We have to get out of here," I say to Mr. Johnson. "If Saul was never planning on letting you go, he's got no reason to keep you alive."

He rolls his shoulders back and slowly gets to his feet, wobbling slightly. His ashen face only goes a small way to revealing how much pain he must be in. He grits his teeth in grim resignation as he slumps back down to the floor. "I'm not sure I'm in any fit state to escape this place. It's huge."

I regret giving Kim the marker pen, although I'm fairly sure Stella would have taken it off me if I'd kept hold of it. I stare down at my wrists, wondering if I can use my blood to create a gateway again. I grimace. Although I wouldn't be fighting against my magic, I would be fighting against blood loss. Staying here is dangerous, but risking my own life would be stupid.

I test the strength of the door with my shoulder. It feels too solid for me to batter down alone. Instead, I return to Adele and crouch down beside her.

"What would I have to do to get Saul in here?"

She stares at me, pursing her lips.

"There's someone outside the door, right? Someone let you in here and locked the door behind you. Who is it?"

"Stella," she says. "She won't let you out."

I return to the door and press my ear against it, listening. If Stella is still out there, she's being silent. I drop down to the floor and peer underneath the door. There's only a tiny air gap between the wood and the stone floor, but I'm able to see an empty corridor. I can't decide if Stella's absence is good or bad.

"She's gone," I say, pushing back up to my feet. "Why would that be?"

Adele shrugs. "Maybe Saul sent her after your girlfriend."

"Too lazy to find her himself?" I ask. "Or too scared?"

Adele croaks a laugh. "Scared? Of a human?"

Of course they think she's alone. Everyone believes the Shamari can't travel to Uralahnd. For once, the lies are giving us an advantage.

"Too lazy then," I say. "Why do you all jump to his every whim? What did he promise you?"

Adele clamps her lips together and turns her face away.

"See, I don't get it," I carry on. "You *know* he was planning on double-crossing you all along. Yet even now, when he's left you so weak, you're still acting like you owe Saul loyalty. Why?"

She smiles weakly. "Your father can be very persuasive. Why don't you ask your mother just how persuasive he can be?"

I curl my hands into tight fists as I glower at her. "At least Mum had the sense to turn her back on him," I whisper.

"He still destroyed her," Adele points out. "He destroys everything he touches."

"Then why help him?" I demand.

"It's better to work with men like your father, than to work against them. He came to me, I wasn't stupid enough to say no." She sighs and stares at her withered hands. "I didn't expect him to cross me when I was doing everything he asked me to."

"But he did. So what are you going to do about it?"

Adele's lips twist into a smile. "There is one thing I could do to help you, but you won't like it."

I narrow my eyes. "Go on."

"As your friend said, the ziggurat is large and it's hard to find your way around. Even if your girlfriend can evade the other Baneem in the building, how will she ever find you?"

I keep silent, not wanting to let her know Kim has a map. Not that I'm sure we can trust Flame Guy any more than I can trust Adele.

"You can't get out of this room," Adele says, her smile widening. "Not physically anyway."

I raise my eyebrows. "What are you suggesting?" I ask, as if I can't guess.

"I can release your soul from your body, allowing you to leave this room and find your girlfriend, then you can lead her back here."

Mr. Johnson coughs loudly. "It sounds like a one-way trip to me."

"Not at all," Adele replies indignantly. "Aran, you know the soul can survive out of the body. For a short while, at least." She stares at me expectantly.

For a crazy moment, I consider saying yes. Tumultuous thoughts run through my head: what if Flame Guy's map was all lies? What if Kim and Matthew have already been caught, or worse, killed? I know my consciousness will go with my soul. I could find Kim.

I shake my head. "You must think I'm stupid."

Adele's mouth drops open in mock horror. "Of course not."

"Mr. Johnson is right. It would be a one-way trip. The only way I'd get back into my body, is if you put me there. Why would you do that? By letting me die, you'd get revenge on Saul for what he did to you."

She shakes her head. "I know I've wronged you in the past, Aran, but I swear, I want to help you."

"No. I'm done with clutching at lies. You're right, Kim is on her way here. She will find me. That's all the hope I need."

Adele rolls her eyes, sighs and leans back against the wall. "Such romantic notions are for fools." She closes her eyes, as if falling asleep.

I don't care what she thinks.

A rattling sound draws my attention to the door. I stare at it, waiting for the lock to click open and for Saul and Stella to come inside. Instead, someone knocks against the door.

"AJ? Are you in there?" Kim's voice is quiet and cautious, but it's unmistakably her.

I hurry to the door, pressing my ear against it. "Yes. Stella might be close by, though, be careful."

"Stella is unconscious. Don't worry. Hang on, we'll get the door open."

"What about Saul?"

There's a pause. "There's no sign of him at the moment. Stand back."

I do as I'm told, knowing full well it'll be Matthew, not Kim, who opens the door. There's a loud crack as the wooden door buckles inwards and the frame splinters. Dirt flakes down from the disturbed mud bricks. Kim picks her way over the debris and throws her arms around my neck.

"Are you okay?" she asks.

I nod and run my fingertips around her bruised eye. "Are you?"

"Yes," she says through a brave smile. "Nothing that won't heal."

I wrap Kim in my arms, savouring the precious seconds we can spare together. My chest swells with a mixture of relief and pride. She made it to me, with nothing more than a few bruises.

She glances around the room, her eyes widening as she sees Mr. Johnson. She untangles herself from my embrace. "I'm so sorry," she gasps, touching her fingertips to her lips.

Mr. Johnson pushes himself to his feet. "It's not your fault," he assures her.

"We should go," Matthew says from the doorway.

"Who's that?" Kim asks, nodding towards Adele. "What happened to her?"

"Adele," I say. "Saul attacked her with his magic."

Adele, who I had thought was asleep, lets out a thready laugh. "You should tell her why, Aran."

Kim glances between us, but doesn't ask the question. She goes to Mr. Johnson and ducks under his left arm, supporting his weight. I follow her lead, supporting him from the opposite side.

"Let's go," Kim says, glancing round Mr. Johnson to give me a smile.

"I don't think so."

Saul's voice makes me freeze. Slowly, I force myself to look towards the doorway. Matthew is standing inside the room now, with Saul behind him. Saul's hand is pressed against his back and I can see blackness starting to coil around Matthew's body. His face is a portrait of anguish. I'm not sure how Saul crept up on him, not that the how matters much now.

Saul moves his hand to Matthew's shoulder and pushes him to his knees. "That should hold the Changed for now." He smiles at Kim and I. "The question is, which one of you do I kill first?"

# CHAPTER TWENTY-EIGHT

Together, AJ and I help Mr. Johnson back down to the floor. Then we stand in front of him, side by side. I slip my hand into my pocket so I can ball my fist around the engraved ring.

"You could let us all go," I say.

Saul laughs. "Why would I do that?"

"Because if you attack us, you won't win." I raise my chin into the air.

Saul's eyebrows raise a fraction. "Your pet Changed was easy to overpower," he waves his hand in our direction. "Which leaves a Baneem with no magic and two humans. What threat are any of you to me?"

It's my turn to laugh. "Seriously? You have to ask? We've gotten rid of every one of your lackeys." I tilt my head to the side. "Well, all of them except Adele, but you did that for us." I take a step closer, despite AJ's wide-eyed stare begging me not to. "You're all alone, Saul and you're outnumbered."

"Numbers don't matter when I have magic and you have none."

I shrug. "Suit yourself. Don't say I didn't give you a chance to let us all go. Whatever happens next, you've brought it on yourself. Remember that."

For a moment, Saul stares at me, his face full of contemplation. I'm not sure what he's thinking. Perhaps he's actually considering my words, or maybe he's convincing himself that I am bluffing. Except I'm not. In my hand, I hold the power to stop him. I just have to slip the ring on his finger.

Saul runs his hand through his hair. "I think I'll start with you," he says, smiling at me. "You're either brave or stupid, I'm really not sure which. Either way, I'll squeeze the life out of you."

"No," AJ says, pushing in front of me. "I won't let you touch her."

Saul advances on him. "And how are you going to stop me, Aran? You are weak and pathetic, just like your mother."

AJ snarls and makes to lunge forward. I drop the ring back into my pocket. I grab his arm and tug him to me, wrapping my arms around his back so I can hold him fast. He struggles against me, but somehow, I maintain my grip, stopping him from attacking Saul.

"Trust me," I whisper, as I push myself up onto my toes and kiss his lips. "I know what I'm doing."

He stares at me, his eyes full of pain but also hope. "I can't lose you."

"You won't, I promise."

His brow crumples.

"See, weak and pathetic," Saul spits. "Even a girl can push you around."

AJ clenches his teeth, but keeps his gaze fixed on me. "I trust you."

I release him, breathing out my relief as he stands alongside me again. His hands are balled into tight fists and I can feel tension radiating from him, but for now he's holding fast and not doing anything rash.

"Go ahead," I say, slipping my hand back into my pocket to reach for the ring again. "Start with me. I know you want to make AJ suffer. Hurting me is the best way of doing that. You've taken everyone else from him."

Saul eyes me suspiciously. My words and actions must seem like madness to him. He wasn't wrong when he said I was either brave or stupid. I hope I'm the former, but I can't be sure. Either way, I'm terrified. I can feel myself shaking even as I tell myself the ring *will* work. Doubt gnaws away at my outward show of bravado. I haven't tested the spell engraved into it, there was no way I could. But the spell *will* work, it *has* to.

I take a couple of steps forward. "What's wrong? Having second thoughts about destroying the last person you could call family?"

"I don't need family," Saul snarls.

"Or friends," I say in agreement, glancing down at Adele. "Or lackeys. You were going to double cross them all anyway, weren't you?"

"What do you care?" he asks.

"I don't," I say, taking another step forward. "You want power." I look over my shoulder at AJ. "You said he had a god complex, right?"

AJ nods, his whole body trembling with barely contained anger.

"Compared to you, I am a god," Saul hisses.

"You're not even close to being a god," I say. "As a human, I have access to magic that you never can. You can't open gateways. You can't contact the Shamari. Even AJ, your own son can do those things, with or without his natural magic. But you can't. And you think AJ is weak and pathetic." I'm standing directly in front of Saul now. I'm so close I can feel his warm breath on my face as I glare up at him. "You're the pathetic one. Your power is limited."

"Limited?" He places his hand on my shoulder. "Do you want to see how limited my magic is?"

"I know you can kill me," I say, my voice almost daring him to try, even though I'm quivering like a frightened rabbit. "But that's all you can do. It's why you're so jealous of humans. Despite our *lack* of magic, we have so much more than you. We're capable of not only reaching for our dreams, but surpassing them too. Whereas you can't even make the world you live in beautiful. You're trapped in an eternal dark age because of your magic. It's a noose around your neck. Your magic is the shackles that keep you trapped in a world you loathe, surrounded by people you've taught yourself to hate, because every one of them reminds you how limited *you are*."

He leans down to whisper in my ear. "I'm going to enjoy killing you."

I grit my teeth, bracing myself for the pain I know I'm about to feel. He tightens his grip on my shoulder and twists me round, so my back is pressed against his chest and his arm is pressing against my neck.

Then it starts. Pain so intense it steals my breath and replaces all my thoughts with agony. The hand holding the ring shakes and my fingers threaten to spring open and drop it to the floor. I manage to twist my neck so I'm staring at his hand as it rests on my shoulder. I try to lift my arm, but it won't respond.

"Leave her alone," AJ gasps, stumbling forward.

He tries to tear Saul's grip away from me, but his father is too strong.

"Don't," I manage to say through my gritted teeth. "Trust me."

AJ falters back, staring hopelessly between Saul and I. His shifting expression tells me he's fighting an internal war, where one side is desperate to believe in me and the other can't stand to see me in pain.

"I need you to trust me," I gasp. "Please."

The last thing I need is for Saul to shift his attention to AJ. Whilst he's focused on me, AJ, Matthew and Mr. Johnson are relatively safe.

AJ presses his hands against his eyes and turns away, his shoulders shuddering. Then he wheels back round, making me hold my breath. But instead of attacking Saul again, he slips round his father, to Matthew, and starts to pull him away. I'm glad he's got a focus for his fear.

My knees buckle, but Saul holds me upright. Black spots are forming before my eyes and every nerve in my body is jangling in agony. With my empty hand, I grab at Saul's hair and pull myself round to face him in his grip. His eyes widen a fraction, but then his snarl deepens and a fresh wave of pain courses through me, causing me to cry out. I press my forehead against his shoulder, panting heavily as I try to push through the pain. When I look up again, Saul is grinning at me, his cold gaze boring into me.

"Not so brave now, are you?"

I wonder why he hasn't already killed me, or turned me into a shrivelled husk like Adele. I grab his hand and start to prise one of his fingers up. His cheeks flex, which makes me think I'm causing him pain, though it's probably only a fraction of the agony I'm feeling. Even so, it spurs me on. I pry his finger back as far as I can and then slip the ring onto his finger and swipe my thumb around the pictograms. They flare brightly for a second.

"What the—" he begins.

His face contorts in agony and he releases me. I drop to the floor, gasping, as he staggers backwards, clutching at his body as though a thousand needles are being driven into his flesh.

"What have you done?" He gasps, dropping to his knees.

I push myself into a sitting position as AJ hurries over to me. "It's called poetic justice," I say between gasps. I feel sick, but the pain is slowly ebbing away from my body. "On earth, some people believe in sympathetic magic. I'm not entirely sure about all the ins and outs, but as I understand it, the basic gist is that whatever you do unto others, will come back onto you. Threefold." I let AJ help me to my feet and, even though I'm trembling, I manage to take two wobbly steps towards Saul. "So do what you want to me, or to any of us. But you'll feel the pain much, much more than we will."

Saul shrinks away from me, shaking his head as he claws at his finger trying to remove the ring. He can't move it. He scrambles to his knees and shuffles towards me, hands clasped in a pleading manner.

"Take it off," he pleads. "I'll give you anything you want."

I shake my head. "There's nothing I could possibly want from you. Now get out of my sight, before I decide to kill you instead of making you suffer in a hell of your own creation."

He stands and swings his fist at me. AJ intercepts and takes the brunt of the punch on his chest. Saul doubles up on pain.

"I warned you," I breathe. "*Anything* you do will come back onto you, times three."

Saul glares at me, his gaze murderous. For a terrible moment, I worry he'll attack me anyway, destroying himself in an effort to kill me, rather than live with what I've done to him. Instead, he turns and stumbles out of the room. I listen until his faltering footsteps fade into nothingness and then I turn and sag into AJ's arms. I wrap my arms tightly around his neck, breathing in his scent. He holds me just as tightly, his presence grounding me and making me feel safe.

"Thank you," I whisper against his ear. "Thank you for trusting me."

# CHAPTER TWENTY-NINE

Together, we make it back to where we buried the car bonnet, without any sign of Saul. The damage done to Matthew's manifestation began to heal as soon as Saul disappeared, allowing him to break free from his stupor. He carried Mr. Johnson on his back, whilst AJ and I trudged through the sand in the blazing heat of day.

"I wish I could help," Mr. Johnson says, as he watches us struggle to shift the sand to free the car bonnet. "What are you going to do with that?"

"Stop gateways being opened," I say. "Saul was dangerous, but there are hundreds more Baneem like him. We can't stop them all. The Shamari have tried for thousands of years and failed. This way, they'll be trapped here, in their own world."

I dust the sand off the car bonnet and glance around. Without a long walk, either back to the ziggurat or to the village, there's nothing solid to create a gateway on.

"We'll need two gateways," AJ says, as though sensing my thoughts. He stares down at the sand. "We send Mr. Johnson back first and then open a second one to cast the spell into the space between the worlds."

I grimace. "Do you think there will be time?"

He shakes his head. "I can't use marker pen on sand, Kim. The best I can do is trace the pictograms in the sand. We'll have seconds at most."

I stand I place my hands on either side of his cheeks. "Then you have to go through with Mr. Johnson."

"No." Tears fill his eyes. "I'm not leaving you to do this alone."

"You have to."

He shakes his head. "No. If there's a sacrifice to be made, I should make it. You have a family and a future. I have no one, except you. If..." He grits his teeth and glares at the ground.

I tilt his face upwards, forcing him to look at me. "That's exactly why it should be me who takes the risk. Don't you see? I have too much to lose to let myself get trapped in the space between the worlds. I have to get out, because I can't let my family grieve for me like they did for Charley. I can't let Sophie or you deal with everything that's happened alone." I move my face towards his lips, pausing a hairsbreadth from actually kissing him. "I have to help you rebuild your life, so you can have the future you deserve, Doctor Jao."

He tries to force a smile to his lips, but I smother the weak action with a kiss. Afterwards, I lean my head against his chest, listening to the hurried flutter of his heart. I drop my hands to his so I can gather them up and squeeze them tightly.

"I'm fulfilling my promises," I say. "It was my decision to try to stop all the Baneem. You've already been through far too much for me to ask any more of you. I have to do this. Okay?"

"It's not okay."

I realise I'm crying as I kiss him, our tears intermingling on our lips. "I know," I whisper. "But you have to let me do this, AJ. I need to know you're safe. I need another reason for making it through. Please understand."

He pulls me close and rests his chin on my head.

"There won't be time for us both to get through," I say. "It has to be me."

"We could all go back to earth," he says. "We could go to the Shamari compound and create a longer lasting gateway. We don't have to shut the gateways here and now."

"Yes, we do. AJ, every second we delay, a human could be opening a gateway for a Baneem. That's one more Baneem trapped on earth, hurting humans. We have the means to stop gateways opening now. We have to do it." I kiss him again. "I love you. I'm not going to leave you, I promise. Trust me."

His chest shudders as he forces out a laugh. "I do trust you. That's the problem." He lets go of me and steps backwards, nodding. "You remember how to open a gateway?"

I smile and nod. "I've seen you do it enough times."

"We'll be waiting at your house, with Sophie."

"Thank you."

He shakes his head. "Don't thank me. I'm being a coward, letting you take this risk. I don't understand why you have to do this, but I do trust you. I trust you'll make it back to me."

"Like you made it back to me," I whisper. "Open a gateway for you and Mr. Johnson. Now."

He starts to trace the pictograms in the sand using his fingertip.

I turn to Matthew. "You're not going with them, are you?"

He smiles solemnly and shakes his head. "The Changed are going to be trapped here forever, Kim. The truth of what we are is going to come out and they're going to need help. I have to stay. Besides, what would I do on earth. My soul was magically enhanced so I could live beyond death in order to stop the Baneem. I'll be redundant. And, as someone who is immortal, I can't think of a worse fate. At least here I might be able to find a purpose." He sweeps his head in a gesture at the desert. "It's not just the Changed who will need help, but the Baneem, too. Uralahnd was beautiful once, it can be like that again."

My mouth goes dry. "There will still be Baneem on earth, Matthew. They haven't been recalled. Who will stop them? We can't. We'd never find them. We're not drawn to magic. You are. You can't stay."

I ball my hands into tight fists, unable to accept I'll never see him again, even though I know he's right. In a way, my fear isn't for him, but for myself and AJ. What will happen to him if I'm trapped between the worlds? I start to sob as Matthew steps up to me and places his firm hands on my shoulders. "You can't."

"I have to, Kim." He tucks his finger under my chin, forcing my face up so I have to meet his eerie white stare. "I'm not asking for your permission, but I would like your understanding."

Understanding. It's exactly what I asked for from AJ. He couldn't give it to me. I press my lips together and twist my face away from Matthew's touch. I do understand, no matter how much I don't want to. The Shamari are his family, despite the lies. I squeeze my eyes shut and flop forward against his chest, hugging him so hard I'd be afraid of crushing his ribs if he were human.

He strokes my hair. "It has to be this way."

"I know."

He pushes me back onto my feet, using the edge of one finger to brush the tears away from my face. "You don't need me to protect you anymore, Kim. You haven't in a long time. I doubt there's anything you couldn't overcome. You've grown into a strong and courageous young woman. I'm proud to have had you in my life, even if I did meet you through tragedy."

I can feel myself starting to break down again, though I try to push back the tide of tears threatening to overwhelm me. I don't feel strong or courageous right now. I feel alone and frightened.

"It's ready," AJ says from behind me, his voice gruff.

As I turn to him, I see his eyes are red and puffy from crying. I want to hold him and tell him it will be okay, but I know my words will sound empty to him right now.

"Thank you," Matthew says to AJ. "For what you gave up for me."

AJ nods. He helps Mr. Johnson to his feet, supporting him. As he is unable to do it himself, I conjure up the image of my house in my mind and press my palm against the central pictogram. The gateway flares into life and AJ and Mr. Johnson step down into it, vanishing from our sight. Seconds later, there's a rush of energy, as the gateway snaps shut.

I stare at it, breathless. It was too fast.

"I'm not going to make it, am I?"

"Yes," Matthew says. "You will."

I stare at him. "How?"

"I'll open the gateway."

As I watch, he unfurls his magnificent wings and begins to pluck thirteen feathers. He traces the wheel in the sand and then lays a feather where each pictogram should be. He holds his hand out to me, his expression expectant. It takes me a moment to figure out he wants the marker pen. I hand it to him and watch as he draws each pictogram with care. My heart swells to breaking point that he's willing to use magic, to help me.

"My feathers will sustain the spell for longer," he says. "You remember when you drew a pictogram on my feather to contact me?"

I nod.

"It won't give you much time, but it'll be more than you would have had." He smiles at me. "Thank you for everything, Kim. Thank you for opening my eyes to the truth."

I haul the car bonnet up and stand ready, as he presses his hand against the central feather. The gateway flares to life, brighter and more powerful than any we've opened so far. I start to lug the car bonnet through, relieved when Matthew helps by lifting the weight. He helps me until he's at the edge of the gateway and then releases it, leaving me to finish my task alone.

# CHAPTER THIRTY

I'm standing in darkness, light and wind battering me, begging me to move toward the exit point. But I can't, not yet, no matter how much I long to. I suck in a breath and then press my hand against the car bonnet, activating the spell. The opening ahead of me begins to close faster. I grimace, but I haven't finished my task yet. I can feel the wind threatening to rip the bonnet from my grasp and send it flying through the exit. I can't allow that to happen. Somehow, I have to push it out of the vortex, into the void. I set it on the pathway of light and kick at it with all my strength, screaming into nothingness in the hope externalising my efforts will lend me strength. Inch by inch, the bonnet moves through the torrent of light. I kick again and again, finally allowing myself to drop down onto the pathway, so I don't have to concentrate on standing.

Then the bonnet is through, rotating off into the darkness. I scramble onto my hands and feet and propel myself towards the rapidly contracting exit as quickly as I can.

# CHAPTER THIRTY-ONE

I yelp as my shoulder hits a hard surface. Energy laps at my trainers, crackling around my toes as the gateway snaps shut. I lay in a tight ball on the ground, not daring to open my eyes, or breathe.

"Kim?"

AJ's voice forces me to look up.

"Are you okay?"

I nod and let him help me up, then I fling myself at him, holding him and kissing every inch of his face until I realise we're not alone. My cheeks blaze with heat as I catch sight of Sophie and her dad.

"Your trainers are a little worse for wear," Sophie says, her eyes gleaming.

I pull away from AJ as rapidly as I clung to him and stare at my feet. Sophie's right. The tips of my trainers and socks are missing and my toes are singed. I wiggle them, almost choking with laughter as they respond to my command. Sophie wraps her arms around me. I return her embrace, waggling my fingers towards AJ, asking him to join us. He does and I hold them both. Laughing, crying and coughing until I'm finally able to control myself. Still I don't let go of them.

"Did it work?" Sophie asks, once we're all a little calmer.

I shrug. "There's only one way to find out. AJ?" I think I'm shaking too much to be able to draw neat pictograms. "Will you try to open a gateway?"

Sophie fetches him a pencil. As AJ drawers a gateway on the wall, I hold my breath, whilst Sophie squeezes my hand. AJ presses his palm against the gateway, there's a burst of light, but it gutters and dies a second later. The wall remains the same, solid, with the pictograms and the wheel still intact.

"You did it," Sophie says, resting her head against my shoulder. "You actually did it."

"*We* did it," I say, knocking my head against hers. "You helped too." Exhaustion washes over me. I wipe my hand over my face. "I want to see my family."

Sophie nods. "Me too. And we can go to them soon." She glances at her dad. "But I think a trip to the hospital is in order first."

Mr. Johnson gives her a pained nod. "I think so too." He sighs and shifts his attention to AJ. "What are you going to do now?"

AJ looks down at the ground and shrugs.

"Do you have somewhere to stay?" Mr. Johnson asks.

"No."

"Would you consider staying at my house, despite everything that's happened?"

AJ stares at him, eyes widening. "Why would you do that for me?"

Mr. Johnson looks down at his twisted fingers. "You risked your life to come and save me. It's the least I can do." He smiles at Sophie. "Besides, I think my daughter would never forgive me if I turned you away."

"What about school?" AJ says. "I'm pretty sure I'll be kicked out for vanishing the way I did."

"I'll sort it out," Mr. Johnson says. "Don't worry. As Kim said, you deserve a future."

"Thank you," AJ mumbles, rubbing the back of his neck.

"Hospital," Sophie says. "Now. I'll call a cab."

AJ and I wait with Sophie for the taxi to arrive, but after she's seen her dad into it, I linger on the curb.

"What's wrong?" she asks.

"There's something I need to do," I say. "And I'd like you to come with me."

Sophie glances into the taxi, at her dad.

"I'll go with him," AJ offers.

Sophie smiles at him gratefully. "Make sure he doesn't give the nurses and doctors a hard time, okay?"

AJ laughs. It's so good to see a genuine smile on his face as he slips into the back of the taxi, beside Mr. Johnson.

"Will you meet us there?" he asks.

I nod. "In about an hour. Okay?"

"Okay."

*

Sophie and I walk into the memorial garden, our arms looped. She strokes my hand as we walk, in silence. I know where Charley's rosebush is. It's bare and has been cut back heavily, leaving only short stumps. The whole garden is absent of flowers, a sad testimonial to the lives represented here.

"I was so angry at her when I first found out about magic and Gage and everything else," I mutter.

Sophie rests her head against my shoulder.

I stare at my curled fingers, imagining her peach prom dress laying torn and tattered there. "Why didn't she tell me?"

"Probably for the same reasons you didn't tell me to start with. She wanted to protect you."

"But if I'd known... maybe I could have protected her."

Sophie wraps her arm around my back. "If you had been in her position, what would you have done?"

I shrug.

"Have you told Chris?"

"No... but that's different. He's just a kid." I squeeze my eyes shut and bow my head. It takes several deep breaths before I'm composed enough to speak again. "I wish she was still here."

"I know."

"When she died... I couldn't imagine life without her. I still can't. I need her, Sophie."

Sophie lets me go and steps in front of me, smiling. "You are the bravest, most capable person I know. Charley would be proud of you. You know that, don't you?"

I press my lips together, struggling to hold back tears. I press my hands against my chest, trying to rub away the constant, dull ache that resides there. "It still hurts. Will it ever stop hurting?"

"I don't think so."

I grimace, knowing AJ's pain must be as great as my own, if not greater. "Aren't you supposed to try to make me feel better?"

"It's a good thing," Sophie says. "The hurt reminds you how much you loved her. How important she was to you. It reminds you of everything you've overcome, because you refused to believe she'd take her own life. Charley's spirit lives on in you, Kim. Do you understand what we've done? What you've done? You've made sure no one will ever be hurt in the same way Charley was. So believe me when I tell you Charley would be proud of you. Because I know, if she could have, she'd have stood by you and fought with you to end this."

I brush the tears from my face, trying to ignore my chattering teeth. "What do we do now?"

Sophie shrugs. "We go to our parents, let them know we're okay. Hug them like we're never going to let them go."

"And then what? What do we tell them?" I look upwards at the pale grey sky. "It's easier for you. Your dad can smooth things over with your mum. But me... I have to tell them something."

"The truth?"

I almost choke as I burst out laughing. "They'd think I was insane, Sophie. I'd end up in the room next to Tia, or maybe sharing one with her. You only believed because I showed you Matthew. With AJ's magic gone and the gateways no longer working, we have no proof magic even exits."

Sophie pinches her lips together. Her eyes widen into solemn discs. "Kim... It's time for the lies to stop, you must know that.

If we're going to move forward, we can't be held back by deception. Besides, your parents deserve to know why certain things have happened." She places her hands on my shoulders. "They deserve to know how Charley died."

My chin quivers. "They'll hate me. They'll blame me for everything. What Gage did to Mum and Chris... Dad's house getting set on fire... They'll hate me."

She squeezes my shoulders. "No, they won't, because they love you. I'll be with you when you talk to them. So will AJ. Your parents need to know the truth, Kim. They already lost Charley. If you continue to lie to them, they'll lose you too, because you'll get so eaten up by guilt it'll destroy your relationship. Like it almost destroyed ours."

I stare down at the frosty ground, peering at the tiny fractals that trace across the paving stones. "Okay." I breathe in deeply. "I'll tell them the truth. All of it."

# CHAPTER THIRTY-TWO

I tap my pen against my chemistry revision book, mouth scrunched up tightly as I ponder the example question. The Sixth Form common room is busy with people eating lunch, cramming for exams and chatting. Sophie sits opposite me, doodling in her art sketch pad. She still has a slight scar down her cheek, but there's no other trace of the beating the Baneem subjected her to.

"Are you coming over this evening?" she asks without looking up. "You visit a lot more regularly these days." Her lips curl into a cheeky grin.

I stick my tongue out at her.

"Oh, very mature." She drops her sketch pad onto the table, placing the pencil on top of it.

I glance over the top of my revision book to peek at what she's been drawing. It's a girl, vaguely similar to her, surrounded by faceless entities. "Are you still having nightmares?"

She nods.

I drop my gaze back to the question I've been studying. "Is AJ?"

"Yes, but we don't talk about it. I don't think he's quite settled in yet. But it's fun having AJ around. He does more chores than me!" She drums her fingertips on the table. "It's been a month. How long will it take to put everything that happened behind us and get back to normal?"

I shrug. "What's normal?"

"Good point."

"I'm sorry I got you involved."

She blows air through her pursed lips. "Stop apologising. You've said you're sorry every single day." She leans across the table, plucking my book out of my hands. "It's over. There's been no trace of any Baneem since we shut the gateways down. We need to try to put everything that's happened behind us and live our lives. Starting with our English mock exam tomorrow."

I roll my eyes. "Yay, exams."

Despite my sarcasm, I know she's right. We're free of the Baneem now, and free of lies. Sophie spoke to her father first and then cried on me. But once she'd recovered from the truth, we drove to the hotel her mum and my parents were staying in. Sophie, Mr. Johnson and AJ helped me talk to my parents. Despite my fears that they'd have me committed, they listened, silently, to the whole story. And then they hugged me so tightly I thought they'd crack my ribs.

"Come around to my house to *revise*," Sophie says, breaking into my thoughts.

I laugh and bat my hand in her direction, but she jerks back so I fall short of slapping her lightly. I lean back in my chair, sighing as my laughter ebbs away. Laughing feels good. Even thinking about exams feels good. It feels normal.

"Speaking of *revising*," Sophie says, nodding her head to the doorway. "I'm going to grab some lunch." She scoops up her sketch book and pencil and slips away towards the food hatch, as AJ wanders across the room.

He looks out of place in his school uniform, but over the last month everyone has got used to him wearing it. He leans down and kisses my cheek, before dropping down into the chair beside me. His face has fleshed out again over the last few weeks and colour has returned to his cheeks. His eyes sparkle constantly with genuine hope. I twist round on my chair so my knees are touching his.

"How's catch up going?" I ask.

Although I have been visiting Sophie's house a lot more, it's her I've been spending most of my time with. I only get precious snatches of time to spend with AJ, whilst he fever-ishly tries to catch up on coursework and exam prep so he can take his G.C.S.E.s this summer.

"Okay. I just got another round of marks back."

"I hope they're great."

"They're good enough." He takes my hands, moving his thumbs in tiny circles over them.

A shiver of delight slips up my back, teasing a smile out of me.

"Maybe, tomorrow night, after your exam, I can take some time off." He leans towards me.

I lean forward as well, closing the distance between us. "I'd like that." I kiss him slowly, eliciting a couple of whistles and whoops from the room around us. When our lips drift apart, my cheeks are blazing fiercely. I focus on his chestnut eyes, blocking out everyone else in the room. "I'd like that a lot."

## THE END

# ABOUT THE AUTHOR

Clare Davidson is a self-motivated, character driven fantasy writer, mother, teacher and all-round creative whizz, from the UK. Clare was born in Northampton, but spent her early years living in Malaysia, before coming home and settling with her family in Leeds. After spending time at Lancaster University where she met her husband, Clare has now returned to Leeds with husband, daughter, new baby son, crazy dog Rukia and Pirate the white cat in tow. In between being a full-time mother, wife and domestic goddess (in theory) and being plagued by various animals, Clare is the author of the fantasy book Trinity and more recently, the urban fantasy series Hidden. Her aim is to drag you into her fantasy worlds and never let you go. She's evil that way!

# CONNECT WITH CLARE DAVIDSON

Website: http://www.claredavidson.com
Facebook: https://www.facebook.com/ClareMDavidson
Twitter: https://twitter.com/ClareMDavidson
Goodreads: http://www.goodreads.com/ClareDavidson
Mailing List: http://eepurl.com/zpjGf

# ALSO BY CLARE DAVIDSON

## TRINITY

Kiana longs to walk through a forest and feel grass between her toes. But she is the living embodiment of a goddess and has enemies who wish to murder her. Her death will curse the whole of Gettryne. Locked away for protection, she dreams of freedom.

Her wish comes true in the worst possible way, when her home and defenders are destroyed.

Along with an inexperienced guard and a hunted outcast, Kiana flees the ravages of battle to search for a solution to the madness that has gripped Gettryne for a thousand years. Pursued by the vicious and unrelenting Wolves, their journey will take them far beyond their limits, to a secret that will shake the world.

Available now in paperback and for Kindle.